Rivers
Flow

A Follow
the Rivers
Book

Jim H. Ainsworth

SUNSTONE
PRESS

SANTA FE

Sunstone books may be purchased for educational, business, or sales promotional use.
For information please write: Special Markets Department, Sunstone Press,
P.O. Box 2321, Santa Fe, New Mexico 87504-2321.

Cover design • Vicki Ahl
Printed on acid free paper

Library of Congress Cataloging-in-Publication Data

Ainsworth, Jim H.
 [In the Rivers' flow.]
 Rivers' flow : a follow the Rivers book / by Jim H. Ainsworth.
   p. cm.
 Originally published as: In the Rivers' flow: Thomaston, Me. : Dan River Press, 2004.
 ISBN 978-0-86534-757-1 (pbk. : alk. paper)
 1. Boys--Texas--Fiction. 2. Farm life--Texas--Fiction. 3. Droughts--Texas--Fiction. 4.
Texas--Fiction. 5. Domestic fiction. 6. Mysticism--Fiction. I. Title.
 PS3601.I57I5 2010
 813'.54--dc22

                              2010008271

WWW.SUNSTONEPRESS.COM
SUNSTONE PRESS / POST OFFICE BOX 2321 / SANTA FE, NM 87504-2321 /USA
(505) 988-4418 / ORDERS ONLY (800) 243-5644 / FAX (505) 988-1025

In memory of
little Richard, the brother I never knew

For

Caden, Peyton, Bailey, Taylor, Landon, Hannah,
and Gray Boy
read, read, read,

Acknowledgments:

Dr. Fred Tarpley and Jan Epton-Seale....

Your names and influence have graced the pages of many books.
Thanks for adding this one to the list.

Chapter 1

Rivers blood coursed through ten-year-old Jake Rivers' body, but the flow had never captured his heart and mind. For generations, every Rivers descendant has told stories of lives saved, extraordinary athletic feats, and uncommon happenings associated with an ultimate plane of experience they called the Rivers' flow. That is, everyone up until Jake. He buried his face in the feather mattress and covered his head with a pillow, trying to get the flow stories to go away. It seemed to work until older sister Trish walked down the dog trot and into her bedroom. He heard her humming through the cracks in the pine board wall as she prepared for bed.

The flow seemed easy for Trish. She had been grade school valedictorian and was so smart the teachers had let her skip a whole year of school. Called the best shooting and dribbling guard in the state, she made all-district in basketball her sophomore and junior years in high school and could play baseball or softball with the best boys in school. A big poster in her room boldly predicted her next accomplishment.

Texas State Champions Class B —1954-55
Klondike High School

It was her last year for basketball, and Jake felt certain she would make good on her prediction. They called her a tomboy, but she was not just good in sports. She was pretty, too. She had already been Mayday Queen and Prom Queen, and she still had a year left of high school.

Jake's older brother Gray Boy, a year younger than Trish, first found the flow in Blue Bottom Creek. He and Shep, a Rivers cousin, and Arliss Lee, a cousin from the other side of the family, were drifting down the creek toward the Sulphur River in a flat-bottom boat when they decided to take a swim. They chose the wrong spot to slip out of the boat. A school of water moccasins resented their intrusion and bit all three. Arliss Lee and Shep were bitten once, Gray Boy twice. The flow saved Gray Boy and Shep from drowning and helped them to get Arliss Lee to the creek bank. The Rivers cousins never even got sick from the poison, but Arliss Lee was in the hospital for three weeks and nearly died. Even Dr. Olen was amazed that any of them survived.

Gray Boy attracted everything and everyone, especially girls, by his very presence. The flow seemed to cast his whole being in an almost visible glow. He was athletic and made reasonable grades, but took neither sports nor school seriously. He simply flowed through them, seeking to squeeze both for every ounce of pleasure they offered, but unwilling to give them the hard work they demanded. In looks, he was everything Jake wanted to be.

Jake had seen the dark side of his brother's personality, but he envied the bright side. Friends followed Gray Boy around, craving the spotlight that was always on him. His mere arrival usually prompted the uninhibited and intense pursuit of a good time. Gray Boy....he wore the name like a mantle of honor, as if a king had given it to him. His real name was Gray Griffin, but Dr. Olen Bartlett had called him Gray Boy when he gave him that first spank, and the name had stuck. It sat on Gray like meringue on a chocolate pie. It was a term of endearment when his parents used it, and when his friends spoke the name, Gray Boy always came out a little louder, as if by shouting it, they could somehow share in all it symbolized. To Jake, the name sounded like the name of a song on the hit parade, or the name of a winning race horse. He wanted one like it, but could not earn it. He was just Jake Ridge Rivers. Jake, after a friend of his father's who had been killed in World War II, and Ridge, after a movie star that his mother thought was handsome. Jake had never seen either.

Jake's little brother Tuck was only two, but...well, he was the flow. He was not even supposed to be in this world. Dr. Olen had told Mattie, Jake's mother, that Jake would be her last child. When Tuck was born, the doctor pronounced him a miracle, but the family just said he was a gift from the flow. Tuck seemed to be in the flow all the time.

Jake used to love the stories about the flow and how it had affected his family and saved or changed their lives. Now, those stories just made him ashamed. It was time for him to experience it himself, and he was afraid he never would. He hated school, was quiet and shy, and was too small to be a powerful player in any sport. He did not understand the way machinery and equipment on the farm worked, and worse, he was not interested. He could not even fix a flat on his bicycle and expect it to hold air long enough to pedal down the driveway. Compared to his siblings and his father, he just did not measure up.

It made him feel better to pretend that the flow was not real. Griffin Rivers, his grandfather, explained it by saying, "Flow is the difference between the way things are and the way they ought to be." Jake did not know what that meant, but Papa Griff could not be pressed for more details. "Don't worry about it boy; you look a lot like your daddy did on that baseball diamond. He was the best shortstop in this part of the country. If he hadn't married your mama and started having kids, he might have played in the big leagues."

Jake doubted his own baseball abilities. "They say I'll never be big enough or strong enough for the majors."

Griffin laughed. "Who's they? I'll take hustle and speed anytime over bulk. Anyhow, if you can't play baseball, I know you'll be big enough to rope calves."

Jake pulled the pillow from his head and tried to imagine himself being as good as his father, but could not. Baseball did seem to offer a slim chance for Jake to find the flow, and the chance would come soon. Delta County was organizing a Little League. Four teams of fifteen boys would be selected from all over the county. Jake just had to be one of the sixty boys chosen. If he was not, maybe Papa Griff would teach him to rope calves. If that did not work, he would not be fit to bear the Rivers name.

Gray Boy was due home any minute, and Jake wanted to be asleep before his brother crawled into their shared bed. He needed to pee, but hated to get up. A slop jar sat under his bed, but using

3

it somehow seemed feminine and the splashing was loud enough for his parents to hear. Besides, emptying a pot full of stale urine in the morning disgusted him. He used the slop jar only in absolute emergencies. Slowly sneaking out of bed and across the floor to the corner of the bedroom, he found the round hole in the hardwood floor. With only one thin wall separating him from his parents and baby brother and no door on his bedroom, he had to be quiet. On his knees, he aimed and fired away. Perfect. Not a drop on the floor and not a sound.

Since he was already up and unable to sleep, he sneaked out the bedroom door and started down the dog trot hall past Trish's bedroom. The linoleum that had covered the wood floor years ago had almost worn away, so Jake had to be careful to avoid splinters. The spring on the screen door squeaked as he gently pushed it and stepped out onto the porch that ran across the front of the Rivers tall farmhouse. He sat down, let his legs dangle off the high porch, and listened to the sounds of crickets rubbing their legs together and bullfrogs croaking, the sounds of late spring. Hoots from the owl who liked to roost in the hay barn were like a greeting from an old friend. Blue Bottom Creek was less than a mile south, and he listened for the familiar lonesome howls and yips from the packs of coyotes that regularly traveled its banks. The coyotes were quiet to-night. He had used a push mower to mow the lawn that afternoon, and the smell of fresh-cut Bermuda grass and bitterweeds wafted across the yard.

Dressed only in his underwear, he felt exposed sitting in the moonlight, so he moved to his favorite spot under the porch. He sat on an old piece of cardboard and swirled his toes in the cool dirt. His father's words echoed in his ears. "A boy your age has got nothing to worry about. You'll find out later what real worries are." But Jake was worried. It seemed more like scared than worried. Scared was worse. At least, school was out of the way for awhile. He had made it through the fourth grade, but was sure that the real test would come in the fifth. Gray and Trish had warned him about Mrs. Thrasher. "Give her any trouble and she will thrash you." Summer stood between him and those days of reckoning.

Summertime provided an escape from his worries about

school, but not from Sunday school and church. He had vowed not to return, but his conscience was already working on him. Again, he was afraid. The hellfire he heard about from the preacher seemed to be in his future. He was clearly not one of God's chosen ones. In fact, the entire Rivers family was in danger. Only his mother had been baptized, and she did not attend church regularly. If the preacher knew about the flow, their fate would surely be sealed. Jake's doubts about the flow always crept into his mind when he thought about church. Did God know about the flow? Would He punish the Rivers for believing in it?

He watched each set of headlights coming down Texas state highway 24, trying to identify the family's '39 Ford. With headlights in the protruding fenders like two bullfrogs on lilly pads, it would be easy to spot. The car was almost as old as his brother, but Gray Boy drove it like it was new. Jake didn't know what time it was, but it seemed to be time for his brother to be home. If he was late again, that meant a clash between his father and his brother, and the Rivers' home seemed cold for a long time after a serious argument between them. He was remembering their last clash when he heard the Ford's familiar rattle.

Jake moved across the porch in time to avoid the car lights as the olive green Ford approached the Rivers' dirt driveway. As he made his way back to the bedroom, the Ford's tires squealed as Gray made the turn too fast. The transmission made a grinding noise as Gray shifted gears. The sound of tires spinning and gravel slinging from 24's shoulder made Jake cringe. Jake heard his father shift in the bed and mumble something to his mother about the Ford being fifteen years old.

With the bedroom windows open and little noise from the wind, Jake heard the car door slam and his brother's approaching footsteps. Rance and Mattie's porch bedroom or the kitchen was the closest way for Gray Boy to reach the room he shared with Jake, but Gray chose to go around to the front and come through the dog trot. Jake was sure he did not want to wake their parents and start a discussion about his driving, where he had been, or what he had been doing. The old house had only two bedrooms, but both were big. Trish's bedroom even had a fireplace. Bricks from the chimney

5

had fallen and closed it years ago, but on the rare occasions when it rained, the smell of damp soot from long ago fires still filled the house. A dog trot down the middle of the house separated the bedrooms on the west from the kitchen and living room on the east. Rance had built a sleeping porch for himself, Mattie, and the new baby when they found out she was expecting.

Gray started coming out of his clothes as soon as he entered the bedroom. Tossing them on an old chair, he walked over to the hole in the floor and peed. Gray did not bother getting on his knees, but prided himself on being able to hit the hole while standing up. Jake had heard him joke to his buddies that he could almost stick it through the hole without bending his knees. He was glad he had not left any dribble on the floor for his brother's bare toes to touch. Jake pretended to be asleep as Gray Boy crawled in beside him. They hated having to sleep together, especially on hot nights, and carefully avoided touching.

Chapter 2

An hour after daylight, Jake's eyes opened when he heard Rance make his daily walk down the dog trot. The spring on the screen door squeaked as his father stepped out on the front porch of the tall farmhouse to watch the sun rise. Jake glanced over at his brother's side of the bed. Gray Boy lay on his side, sound asleep. Jake dropped his bare feet to the wood floor, picked up a shirt and a pair of jeans, and followed his father through the dog trot. He pulled on his pants and buttoned his shirt before going through the screen door. Rance appeared deep in thought and did not acknowledge Jake when he stepped out. Jake picked up the small practice rope that Papa Griff had made him from clothesline and sat on the edge of the porch a few feet away from Rance. He wanted to watch his father without bothering him.

The front porch ran the length of the house and was deep enough to offer protection from the weather. From a distance, the house looked like a two-story, but the roof height was only to accommodate the tall ceilings.

Rance had made cowboy coffee in a pan and held his full cup on a saucer. He was dressed in overalls with one gallus unhooked, a khaki long-sleeved shirt, and brogan shoes. Jake's mother said that Rance used to wear colored shirts, but Jake had never seen him wear anything but khaki or gray, always long-sleeved. When he dressed up, he wore khaki pants or jeans and his dress boots instead of overalls and brogans. Jake considered his father a handsome man, but secretly wished that he dressed more like Papa Griff, more like a cowboy. Rance Rivers had straight, coarse black hair and eyes so dark brown they looked black. Jake had the black eyes, but his hair was fine and blond. He ran his hand across his burr haircut and wished for hair like his father's.

Early morning was his father's time for thinking, so Jake busied himself throwing loops at the stakes his mother had driven in the hard ground to hold up shrubs she had planted next to the porch. The shrubs were gone, dead from thirst and heat, but the stakes remained. Jake tried to watch without Rance noticing. His father's movements were captivating and had a soothing effect on Jake. As he sat with his feet dangling off the porch, Jake alternated catching each foot with a loop and pulling the slack, pretending his feet were running calves. With each pull of the slack, he turned his head slightly to study his father. The skin on the back of Rance's hands always captivated Jake. He looked at his own hands and wondered if his would be the same when he grew older. Jake's hands were brown from the sun, but Rance's face and hands seemed to resemble a well-worn penny. The skin most exposed to the sun had started to take on the texture of the smooth leather of his father's only pair of good boots. Jake liked to clean and polish those old boots, but no matter how well he and Rance took care of them, the soft lines grew deeper each year.

Rance straddled the porch rail, leaned against a post, and poured part of his coffee into the saucer. Steam rose off the coffee as he blew it and sipped. When he had "saucered-and-blowed" the whole cup, he set saucer and cup on the porch rail and reached into his overalls pocket for his Prince Albert tobacco. With the other hand, he withdrew OCB papers from the smaller pocket in the bib. Almost unaware of his own movements, Jake put a finger to his own tongue just as Rance wet his finger and peeled off a single, thin paper, using his index finger to cup it into an open roll. Shreds of tobacco fell into the paper as Rance shook the tin can. He licked one side of the paper, folded it over, and gave the end a twist. One roll-your-own cigarette ready to light. With dexterity born of thousands of repetitions, Rance flipped the Zippo lid, rolled the spark wheel against the flint and ignited the fluid, sending a small flame to the twisted end of his cigarette. Jake cupped his hands to shelter his own imaginary cigarette from the wind as he lighted it.

Not in the mood for teasing or cuffing, Jake looked away when Gray Boy stepped out on the porch. He and Rance had milked their small dairy herd before daylight. Gray wore only a pair of faded Levis; no shirt or shoes had replaced his morning milk clothes yet. A small tuft of black hair was starting to spout in the middle of his chest. His stomach was flat and hard, his arms lean and muscled. Gray Boy stared as Rance took the first pull from the cigarette. "Don't see how you keep from burning your nose off with that flame thrower."

Rance spoke without looking at his oldest son. "Men know how to use lighters. Only boys burn their noses. That's why boys shouldn't play with fire . . . or tobacco." Jake smiled at his father's rebuke. All of them recalled when Gray had burned his eyelashes off after sneaking the lighter and "makins" from his father's pockets.

Two small whirlwinds blew up on the dirt road that led to highway 24 as Gray went back inside. The whirlwinds reminded Jake of the drought. He understood why they called those miniature vortexes of wind dust devils. They seemed to be reminders of the presence of the devil. He imagined the dust they created entering his nostrils and traveling down his throat, making him wish that the air had a good washing.

The dirt driveway that led from the Rivers' house to highway 24 was less than half-a-mile long. The once proud oak trees that had lined the short road had shriveled and died from thirst. They had long since been used for firewood. Two chinaberry trees had survived on the east side of the yard, and a clump of crepe myrtles kept lonely vigil on the west side. They seemed out of place in the otherwise austere landscape. Neighbors owned the land on both sides of it, but the Rivers family owned the driveway. The road stuck out like a handle to a frying pan from the rest of their eighty acres that lay south behind the house and barns. The land gradually sloped until it became murky bottomland at the banks of Blue Bottom Creek.

The cotton crop Rance had planted in the back pasture never came up. The pool where the cattle drank was well below its banks and in danger of becoming completely dry. Jake followed his father's look into the glaring Northeast Texas sky, both seeing nothing but a sky that looked more white-hot than blue. Rance stripped the cigarette butt and sprinkled it over the porch rail. He glanced toward Jake but seemed to be talking to himself. "The place ain't had a decent rain in more than two years." The remark did not require a reply. Jake could not remember a time when they had enough rain.

Mattie came through the screen door carrying the last of the pan-boiled coffee. "Want the rest of this awful stuff? I sure can't drink it." Rance extended his coffee cup toward her, and she poured the rest of the liquid into his cup, using a tea sifter to hold back most of the grounds. She set the pan down on the porch rail and took the cup from his hands. She grimaced as she took a sip. "Did you get hot last night?"

Rance nodded. "A little. Guess summer nights are coming early again this year. Sure miss having the dog trot open to catch the breeze."

Mattie put her hands on the porch rail and stretched her back. "Maybe, but I sure like sleeping on the screened-in porch. "

Rance glanced toward Jake and lowered his voice as he spoke to Mattie. "Guess Seth was only part right. I've still got a place at the table, but I may have enjoyed myself right out of a place to sleep."

Jake felt his face grow warm. He had heard his Uncle Seth tease Rance about losing his place at the table. He hadn't understood the teasing completely, but knew it implied some secret between his mother and father. Calmness washed over Jake and he turned away, grinning, when he saw Mattie lean her back against Rance. "Small price to pay, don't you think?" She looked over her shoulder to get his response.

Rance winked. "You mean Tuck or the other thing?"

She laughed and poked him with her elbow. "Both, of course." She ran one hand through his hair. "You going to get your hair all butchered up again this summer?" Rance nodded and smiled as she grabbed a handful of his coarse, straight, black hair and pulled gently. "Well, you tell Fitzhugh Meador that I said to leave enough to part, at least." Mattie's expression changed from playful to serious as her eyes traveled the length of the porch where Jake was sitting. "This old house is about to fall down. When are you going to fix that hole in the porch? It's big enough for one of the kids to break a leg. Tuck could fall completely through it." Mattie looked to Jake for confirmation. "Right, Jake?"

Jake smiled but knew better than to answer. Rance looked at the hole as he tossed the grounds from his coffee into the yard. "The first day it rains and I can't work around here or make money working for somebody else, I'll fix that hole. I need to fix that old lightning rod, too." They all looked at the twisted metal rod that dangled against the side of the house. The old house had expelled the brackets and screws that held the rod against it like splinters from an infected finger.

Mattie shrugged her shoulders. "Might as well take down all those silly things. All they do is make noise when the wind blows. I doubt they protect much from lightning. Besides, a good bolt of lightning might improve the looks of this place." Jake's mother made no secret of her dislike for the big house.

Rance appealed to Jake. "Don't you think those old rods are pretty?" Jake nodded. He did like them. They ran the perimeter of the house, across the roof and down each corner to the ground. Same for the old hay barn. The rods were ornate, with round marble-looking balls supported on twisted metal legs with spear points looking skyward. They made him think that their home had really been something in its day, something much more than it was now.

Mattie moved away from Rance, stretched again, and yawned. "Guess I better get back to cooking another coal oil breakfast." It was Mattie's usual criticism of the kerosene stove she fought every day. Rance smiled as he watched her walk through the screen door and all the way down the dog trot.

Chapter 3

The next Saturday night, Jake was not welcome in the car and knew it, but that only slightly dulled his enthusiasm for the trip to the picture show. Gray had complained about bringing him, but their father's instructions were clear. "Take Jake or stay at home." Gray cut the engine in front of Seth and Tillie Rivers' house and turned toward Jake. "Get in the backseat, Jake." Jake knew the drill and was already reaching for the door handle. He pushed the back of the front seat forward and climbed into the back as Shep Rivers, their cousin, entered the car. The seats in the back were not as threadbare as the ones in the front. Jake watched and listened, keeping silent, while his brother and cousin bantered with small talk and wild laughter.

Each was dressed in a white tee-shirt and starched button-fly Levis without belts. The similarities ended there, however. Gray Boy had his thick, black hair cut into a flattop, with the sides left just long enough to succumb to a comb. The sides were neatly combed back, not quite long enough for a ducktail. Shep also had a flattop, but his hair was brown and full of unruly curls that had already started to disengage from where Shep had combed them. Gray's shirt lay tight against his body as if it had been made to fit him, though Jake knew Mattie had bought it on sale at J C Penney's. The white shirt contrasted sharply with Gray's dark skin and emphasized his taut chest muscles and flat stomach. The sleeves embraced his biceps. Shep's shirt had already started to come out of his jeans, and his smaller arms did not fill the sleeves.

Jake mentally compared himself to his brother and cousin. His jeans looked rumpled when compared to their starched Levis. He was wearing his best shirt, bought last fall with his cotton patch money. It was bright green and had diamond shaped snaps instead of buttons. He had thought it the prettiest shirt he had ever seen last fall, but his habit of wearing it every time it was not in the wash had taken its toll. It looked tired compared to their dazzling white tee-shirts. . Rance had always cut Jake's hair in the yard under the chinaberry tree or on the porch. A burr was simple. When Jake asked for a flattop, Rance obliged, but left the sides short. When Jake went in the house to look in the mirror, he almost cried. The top was not flat, and the cut seemed to emphasize his cotton-top. Mattie had told him that blond hair looked good against dark skin, but Jake was not convinced. Jake and Shep accepted that Gray Boy was the brightest star in their small galaxy and were satisfied to bask in his reflected light.

Jake was disappointed when Gray turned the car toward Cooper as they reached highway 24. He had distinctly heard him tell their father that they were going to Commerce. Jake liked the Palace and Bloody Bucket theaters in Commerce better than the Sparks theater in Cooper, but knew better than to express his opinion. Commerce was eight miles west of their home, and Cooper was eight miles east. At a safe distance from his house, Shep pulled out a crumpled pack of Lucky Strikes from his jeans pocket. Gray Boy whistled. "Where'd you come by those?"

"Found 'em on the side of the road."

Gray Boy nodded his head and turned a skeptical stare toward Shep. "Sure you did."

"No, I really did. You know I don't steal cigarettes. If I was a thief, you think I would keep smoking somebody else's butts all the time?"

Gray gave him another skeptical look.

"All right. Maybe I did see 'em drop out of Daddy's pocket when he was gettin' in the car. I didn't tell him they had dropped, but that ain't the same as stealin'."

"Well, since you put it that way, hand one over. I wouldn't want to smoke a stolen cigarette or somebody's leftovers, but I would smoke one of Uncle Seth's ready-rolls."

When both boys had cigarettes lighted, Shep folded the Luck-

14

ies into his shirt sleeve and looked back at Jake. "You ain't gonna tell, are you Jake?"

Jake continued looking out the small side window as he shook his head. "Nope." He was disappointed that Shep would have to ask. Jake watched for signs of Tuck playing in the yard as they passed their house again on the way to Cooper. Tuck was out of sight, probably playing in their usual place under the porch. Only a mile from home, they passed Klondike school, built out in the country, a couple of miles away from town, to be closer to the center of the school district. Looking at the empty schoolyard, Jake heaved a sigh of relief. Summer school was at least two months away. As they neared Klondike, Jake stared out the window at the bleak landscape. It was late spring, but looked like late summer. It was hard to ignore the large oak trees that were dying. Was the only home he had ever known really going to turn into a desert? That morning, Mattie had reminisced about spring rainfalls, the greening of grass and planting of spring flowers. Although he knew better, Jake felt as if she were talking about another place as well as another time. He could not remember a spring in Northeast Texas when the grass had been green. To take his mind off the drought, he watched for any rare new '54 Fords or Chevys they might pass on 24.

Toward the south, he could barely see the tips of trees that lined Blue Bottom creek. Fed from the runoff of water when rare rain fell upstream, they were still green. The giant dead oaks and the Blue Bottom reminded him of his grandfather. Griffin Rivers had left West Texas to come to Northeast Texas, chasing rainfall, but dry weather followed him. He liked to reminisce about the way this part of Texas had been before the drought. Jake only knew that it was not like the Texas he saw portrayed in picture shows, even schoolbooks.

His part of Texas seemed to have a little of everything that the rest of the state had, but not enough. This corner of the state that touched Arkansas, Louisiana, and Oklahoma was flat in places, hilly in others. There was an occasional valley, a few hills, but no mountains. It was not desert, though people were predicting it would be soon. Jake had seen big pine trees in Deep East Texas once, but Delta County was home to big oaks, elms, hickories, and

15

bois d'arcs.

The air here was often heavy with humidity in spring and fall, even with drought conditions. This area of Texas was also known for its heavy black soil. Black gumbo, they called it. Good for cotton, the big cash crop. Cattle and cowboys were here, but there were more overalls and brogans than hats and boots. Jake wished it was like the Texas he saw portrayed in picture shows, with lots of big ranches, cattle, and cowboys. If his grandfather had not left West Texas, Jake might be a real ranch hand by now.

Jake's daydreaming was rudely interrupted when the Ford lurched suddenly to the right. His nose was rudely pressed against the window as Gray Boy made a sharp right turn at high speed. It felt as if the old car was on two wheels. Jake looked through the rear window and saw Cardwell's store on 24.

Gray grinned at Shep. "Let's take a quick loop through Klondike to see if the Clayton girls are out in the yard." Cardwell's store formed the top of a T that connected Klondike to 24. Downtown Klondike, population 85, was at the bottom of the T. Not finding the Clayton sisters in their front yard or on the porch, Gray eased across the railroad tracks and passed the deserted depot and post office before making a circle in the middle of the street. Jake stared at the familiar bois d'arc stumps that had served as foundation supports for a bank, livery stable, and large general store that had been part of Klondike before The Great Depression. Gray stopped the Ford in front of Dad Flannigan's, cut the engine, and jumped out. "Going to get us some Doublemint. I plan on needin' fresh breath."

Shep put his arm out the window and slapped his hand on the door to get Gray's attention before he went into Dad's. "I brought along something else we might need."

Shep tried to conceal what was in his hand, but Jake strained to see the two small, round packages that were wrapped in gold foil.

Gray Boy laughed. Are those the same ones you've been carrying around since school started last year? Hell, they're probably rotten as dirt."

Jake wondered what was in the gold foil, but knew that asking

16

would be a reminder of his unwelcome presence. As they left Klondike and headed toward Cooper, the heavy woods along Blue Bottom creek snaked closer to Highway 24. Delta County was named because it formed a delta at the three forks of the Sulphur River. A system of creeks ran through primitive bottomland on their way to the river. Before the bottoms were drained and levees built to control flooding during The Great Depression, the untamed wilderness inspired stories of wild men and beasts. Lee Pelt, Mattie's father, was known for his bottomland stories. Jake loved to hear about the smelly, sulphur fog that rolled along the creek banks, wrapping itself around visitors' legs like an affectionate cat before swallowing them forever. There were stories of water moccasins, babies being devoured by feral hogs, and panther sightings. Jake's grandmother called them "painters". There were even stories of people who had stayed in the bottomland so long that they had become part animal.

Jake was jerked back to the present as Gray made a loop around Cooper's downtown square, shouting out the window at friends. He parked the Ford on the square and gave Jake a warning look as they left the car. Jake kept a respectable distance between himself and his brother as they walked toward Sparks Theater. He took his place at the end of the line in front of Sparks and watched dried weeds, expelled from the cracks in the brick streets, blow across the downtown square of Cooper. Dust devils picked at the dry leaves and candy wrappings that had piled up against the tall sidewalk. Two years with almost no rain and five years without significant rain left trash in the gutters, and the square in need of a good washing. The weeds and trash seemed to harmonize with the glut of cars and people. It was Saturday night, and downtown Cooper was awash with people who came to town to buy their groceries, go to the picture show, or just sit and watch their neighbors. There was a kinship of shared misery on the square that somehow eased the worry about the drought that was slowly draining the life from Northeast Texas.

The hot spring wind reminded Jake of the drought, but the picture show marquees in front and behind him flashed with promises of refrigerated air and escape. He slowly advanced to the front of the line of white moviegoers, a dime and two pennies - the price of admission - clinched tightly in his fist. The Sparks theater marquee read "On the Waterfront---Marlon Brando." It sounded terrible to Jake. He turned and stared longingly at the brighter marquee of the Grand theater behind him with flashing lights surrounding "Last of the Pony Riders--Gene Autry." The line of colored people wait-ing for entrance into the Grand snaked all the way to the end of the street and around the corner to City Hall.

Jake's eyes grazed his brother as they traveled down the line. Gray Boy gave him a stare that said to turn around and look the other way. Jake did not recognize the pretty girl standing beside his brother, but their meeting at the picture show had obviously been planned. She was probably from Cooper and the reason they had gone to the Sparks instead of the Palace in Commerce. Gray had his arm casually draped across the girl's shoulder as he made small talk with Shep. He occasionally let his arm or hand press against the girl's breast as he leaned forward to speak to his cousin. She did not seem to mind. Shep laughed and made animated conversation with Gray, but seemed a little awkward and shy when he spoke to the girl beside him.

Jake counted the people in front of him. Only nine left. He could smell popcorn, feel the cool air, and taste the Milk Duds. He shoved his twelve cents into the slot in the glass booth and the pretty, young attendant pulled his ticket off a large perforated roll. Inside, he handed his ticket to Mr. Sparks and stared at the popcorn machine. With money for only one snack, he settled on Milk Duds and entered the cool, dark sanctuary of the theater. Adjusting his eyes to the dark, he searched for a friend from Klondike in the dark rows. At the Palace in Commerce, there would have probably been at least one. Disappointed, he sat on the opposite side, as far away from his brother and cousin and their girlfriends as possible.

As Movietone news played, he watched young couples kiss in the dark, a regular occurrence at the Sparks, but seldom seen at the Palace. The Three Stooges drew his eyes to the screen. As Marlon Brando's image appeared, Jake immersed himself in the story, im-pervious to everything except what was happening on the screen. Too soon, the movie was over, and Jake felt the warm evening air as he jumped down from the tall sidewalk and started for the car. Gray and Shep came out later, strolling with their girlfriends. Jake jumped into the back seat, and the two couples squeezed into the front. The pretty girl beside Gray turned to face Jake. "How did you like that picture show, Jake?"

"Aw, it was pretty good, I guess, but that guy talks like he's got both sides of his mouth full of chewin' tobacco. I couldn't understand much of what he said." When everyone laughed, Jake felt his face flush and wondered if he had said the wrong thing. He groaned inwardly as they left Cooper and headed toward Klondike. Jake recognized the dirt roads that led to Piss-Elm Crossing, his brother's favorite parking place. Shep whispered "Going to the woods" to the girl beside him.

Only one car could cross the rickety old bridge at a time. Gray always stopped the Ford in the middle to enhance the sense of danger that he craved. Gray Boy joked that he liked to park on Piss-Elm bridge because girls couldn't escape without falling off into Blue Bottom Creek, but Jake thought it was because of the huge elm trees that stood sentry on both sides, keeping the area in perpetual, almost total darkness.

Gray cut the engine and turned in his seat to stare at his little brother. Jake knew the drill. Shep and his date leaned forward to allow Jake to squeeze between the front seat back and the door. The timbers creaked and groaned as he stepped out, still coming to a rest after Gray's sudden stop. Feeling the Ford moving gently with the boards, he closed the door and cautiously stuck his head back inside. He wanted one more whiff of the pretty girls sitting beside his brother and cousin. "When can I come back?"

"Thirty minutes." Gray Boy kept his eyes on his date.

"How will I know?"

"I'll honk the horn when I'm ready. Quit asking questions and go on." As he moved away, Jake saw the dark outlines of Shep and his date as they crawled over the front seat to the back.

Jake longed for the scents and safety inside the car as the stagnant smell of the Blue Bottom drifted across his nose. The girls had smelled a mixture of perfume, fingernail polish, and shampoo, an <u>intoxicating, comforting smell to Jake. Trish usually smelled like</u>

that, minus the fingernail polish. He was afraid in the dark, but knew exactly where he was. Trying to keep his mind off of panther stories, he recalled killing his first squirrel here last year with a single shot .22. Only a few yards down the creek, a sharp bend in the creek bed collected silt. The silt made a nice place for him to sit and wait for an unsuspecting squirrel, rabbit, or dove when he hunted. When it used to rain, he made it his own private beach, but it was too dark to go there tonight.

He walked along the dirt road toward the family's leased bottomland cotton patch, seeking out the minimal moonlight that filtered through the trees along the lane. When he reached the field, he looked out across the rows his father had just planted and smelled the earthy scent of freshly turned soil. Rance had carved the small forty-acre patch of cotton out of the heavily wooded bottomland by removing trees and stumps. The patch was bordered on three sides by the trees that lined the banks of the winding Blue Bottom Creek and a huge levy designed to keep the area from flooding. Few two-legged creatures had stepped on the dark ground under the trees that grew on the other side of that levy.

Jake knelt down, let the moist dirt filter through his fingers, and thought of his little brother. Was what he had overheard from his parents true? Had Tuck really brought enough rain to the patch to allow his father to plant a crop? Would they be rich if the crop came in? A horn honked twice and Jake ran back down the lane. He was not ready for Saturday night to be over. As he tried to listen to Gray and Shep's whispering on the way home, he started to dread Sunday school.

***

At Sunday school the next morning in Klondike, Jake kept his hands under his legs just above the knees. He felt the cold metal of the folding chair against his hands as he focused on a dead cricket between his feet. Blood rushed to his face, warming it, then to his ears, tingling them. His eyes were burning a little, and he wondered if they were red like his face must be. He wanted to disappear. After nine weeks of perfect attendance at Sunday school and church in Klondike, Jake heard the teacher ask the question he had been dreading. "Please raise your hands if you have been saved by accepting Jesus Christ as your personal savior."

All of his Sunday school classmates raised their hands. Jake continued to sit on his. If he wasn't saved, what was he? Lost? Jake did not know why he had not been called to walk down that aisle, did not understand why God had not whispered into his ear when the preacher kept telling him that He wanted him. Most of his classmates had heard the call only six weeks into the Sunday school program. One thing was for certain—Jake would not be getting his Bible. You had to attend twelve straight weeks of Sunday school to get that, and Jake was not going to make it to ten. Either he was not ready for God, or God was not ready for him.

Chapter 4

Jake made another foray into the woods while two-year-old Tuck sat between the rows of cotton shoots, both fists pushed tightly against his eyelids. They were playing hide-and-seek in the bottomland cotton patch by Piss-Elm Crossing while their parents enjoyed a Sunday afternoon picnic. When Jake had been banished here only a few weeks before so that Gray and his girl could neck on Piss-Elm bridge, the patch had looked wild and untamed in the dark. With the green cotton shoots now appearing in neat rows, the patch now looked civilized. It had been conquered by his father. Rance had pronounced it a good stand of cotton.

The bottoms were different in daylight. Humidity, copperhead snakes, and mosquitoes were more of a threat than panthers. It was still dark in the deepest part of the woods, but Blue Bottom creek was dry enough for Jake to hide in. Today, he was big brother, and he liked that role better than being little brother. As he looked over the creek bank, Jake saw a small cottontail rabbit hop up and sit between Tuck's legs. When he opened his eyes to look for Jake, Tuck saw the rabbit and smiled. Jake looked toward his parents to see if they were watching. They were not, so he began easing his way around the cotton field to tell them without disturbing the rabbit. As Jake approached, Rance downed the last of his iced tea and leaned back on one elbow. Mattie straightened the ragged quilt they were using for their picnic, then lay her head against Rance's thigh. Jake held one finger to his lips and pointed toward Tuck.

Mattie sat up to get a better look. "Just look at that." She pointed toward her son. A small squirrel had moved to the other side of Tuck, sat back on its haunches, and intently watched the small boy. Tuck paid little heed to the squirrel or the rabbit, but seemed to welcome their presence. As he started toward the woods to find Jake, the rabbit and squirrel followed. Jake looked at his parents and shrugged his shoulders.

Rance stood and put his hands on his hips. "I don't know why that kind of thing keeps surprising us. It happens every time Tuck goes outside. Animals love him. I'm surprised that a bird isn't sitting on his head or shoulder. A mockingbird usually does."

Mattie drew both knees close to her chest and rocked back and forth. "What amazes me is that he doesn't try to grab them or shoo them away. He just sits there like he's talking to them without saying anything."

Rance rose to his feet. "I think he is communicating with them in some way we don't understand."

Jake watched as the squirrel and rabbit continued to follow Tuck, even when he walked in circles. Jake had tried to coax rabbits and squirrels to come close to him, but they never did. Mattie stepped off the quilt and picked up one end. Rance picked up the other, and they shook the dirt and crumbs away. As they moved the ends of the quilt together for the first fold, Mattie turned to Jake. "Go get your little brother. It's time to go home. Y'all have to milk."

Mattie stretched to reach the back floorboard of the Ford with the folded quilt. Through the back car window, she saw a shadow cross the sun. As Jake and Tuck emerged from the rows of tiny shoots of cotton, clouds covered the sky, and they heard the first clap of thunder a second after seeing the first streak of lightning. As the boys walked up to the Ford, drops of rain were already spotting the dust on its hood and windows. Jake grinned and looked at his father.

Rance was not sure yet, but forced a tentative smile. "We better get out of this bottom. We're liable to get stuck."

Mattie laughed as she held Tuck and pressed his cheek tightly against hers. She put him down on the seat between them and pulled the seat back forward to make room for Jake to get in the back of the coupe. The rain in the middle of drought was exhilarating, but it slowed, then stopped just after they crossed the railroad tracks that separated the bottomland black soil from sandy land. Rance stopped the car on Dogtown Road and stepped out to look toward the cotton patch. Jake looked through the rear window, then at his little brother. The rare smell of fresh rain touching dry soil drifted through the car. His sense of elation changed to one of foreboding.

Tuck seemed not to notice the isolated thundershower, giving his attention to a small top he had found in the floorboard. A solid gray line of rain continued to fall on the cotton. The isolated thunderstorm was so small and close that it seemed to touch only the cotton field. Back in his seat, Rance gently put his hand on Tuck's soft curls. "He did it again."

At bedtime that night, Jake made his usual stop to kiss his mother goodnight and tousle Tuck's hair as he lay in his small bed beside his parents. Mattie lay on her side, her black hair spread across the pillow like a moonlight shadow. Rance lay beside her, his face to her back. Jake spoke to his little brother, but studied his father's face, illuminated into tiny squares by moonlight filtering through the screen that surrounded their porch bedroom. Rance was smiling as he glanced over Mattie's shoulder. She was staring at Tuck, now asleep in the small bed, moonlight casting a glow across his small body.

As Jake moved through the bedroom door toward the bed he shared with Gray, he heard his father whispering. He moved back toward the door and peeked in. Rance raised to one elbow and put his chin on Mattie's shoulder. Mattie snuggled against her husband and put both hands under her cheek. "I know he's ours, but he does look like a little angel. He is just the sweetest thing. I feel guilty for saying it because I know all babies are sweet, but he seems so special."

Rance put his free hand on her arm and squeezed. "He makes rain, too."

Mattie lay quietly for a few seconds. "If he does, how come it doesn't rain here? Have you forgotten this dairy and the cotton you planted in the back pasture that didn't even come up?"

"Both times he has visited the bottomland patch, it has rained. And it didn't rain anywhere else. That's more than coincidence."

"He's played plenty of times in the home patch, and it didn't rain there."

Jake moved away from the door toward his bed as Rance rolled on his back, put his hands under his head, and stared at the ceiling. "Maybe you haven't noticed that we still have water in both pools. Neighbors on both sides have dry pools. The one in the pasture is not very deep. It should have been dry weeks ago."

"That may be true, and if it is, I'm grateful for it. But it doesn't pay the bills. With feed as high as it is, we're losing money on the dairy. I'm ashamed to buy groceries anymore; we owe Cardwell's and Camp Lake so much. We don't just need rain; we need for it to rain money."

When his father did not answer, Jake eased into bed, pulled the sheet up to his neck, and wondered if they were going to starve. A few feet away, a noise close to the back yard storm cellar startled him. He looked out the large window by his bed and saw a piece of tin hanging loose from the storm cellar door, banging in the breeze. Another repair job for his father. The screen on his bedroom window was ripped in several places. Gray used to tease him that the holes were from people trying to get in. Jake had tried to close the window on a cold spring night, but it was stuck. His father would close it next winter.

He had stood on a chair and tried pulling down the roll-up shade, but it hung after coming down less than an inch. The yellowed and cracked shade still hung in the crooked position where he had left it. Jake rolled on his back and stared at the tall, pineboard walls and ceiling. Cheese cloth and canvas that had been used for wallpaper backing and bits of wallpaper always seemed to be trying to free themselves, but tacks refused to let them drift to the floor. He imagined that he could feel the dust drifting down as rats, encouraged by silence, began to move across the ceiling, causing the bits of wallpaper to move.

Just after daylight, Jake felt his father shake him. "Get up and get your breakfast, son. Eat something that will stick to your ribs. I'm going to drop Gray in the hayfield, then go to Cooper for parts for the baler. I want you to finish the raking. Think you can ride your horse cross country after you finish cleaning up the milk parlor?"

Jake nodded. He was not very hungry, but picked up a sausage and biscuit on the way to the dairy barn. He scooped the cow patties from both lots and pitched them in the honey wagon, then cleaned the milk parlor. By nine o'clock, he had dusted the lime dust from his clothes and pulled himself aboard Scar, the family's five-year-old gelding, for the trip across Blue Bottom Creek to the hay meadow. He carried his rope to practice roping fence posts on the way.

In less than half an hour, he was pushing back limbs and peeking through the dense woods into the hay meadow. Gray Boy was pulling the baler with the Case tractor. Gray saw Jake and Scar emerge from the woods and pointed to the B-Farmall and the hay rake. Jake tied his horse and climbed aboard the small tractor.

Just after noon, all the hay had been raked into rows for Gray Boy to pick up with the baler. Jake roped the steering wheel and muffler of the B-Farmall as Gray Boy pulled the baler down the rows with the Case. The cranky baler picked up the grass and spat out completed bales in its wake. Both brothers recognized the slowing of the familiar "kerchunk, kerchunk" sounds as the grass was compacted into bound square bales. They knew it was about to stop. With a bale halfway out the chute, it quit.

Hack Gentry's baler seldom lasted more than a dozen bales without breaking down. Their father was due back, but Gray wanted the chance to fix it himself. He walked to one side and then the other, adjusting things with wrenches and hitting others with a hammer. He started the engine again, seemed satisfied with what he heard, then rolled under it with a crowbar to pry or pull loose whatever was causing the final problem. Confidence washed his face and movements.

Jake watched with feigned interest, but he had no idea what the problem was or how to fix it. In his pretense and for lack of anything else to do, he absently put his hands in various working parts of the baler, as if touching it somehow had a healing effect on the contrary machine. Just as he stuck his hand in the part where the baler compacts the grass into hay, Gray dislodged the last offending batch of grass and the parts started to move again.

"Kerchunk." The sound of the movement surprised Jake. He had not expected Gray Boy to actually fix it. He drew back to avoid becoming part of a bale of hay. Jake was quick enough to avoid being pulled in, but not quick enough to keep his right thumb from being caught. The old machine slammed it into a bale of hay. He had to laugh a little as he held up his right hand, thumb tingling, but still attached.

Gray rolled out from under the baler. "You dumb little bastard!" He held up Jake's arm to inspect it. "Hell, the damn thing has got to be crushed. What's wrong with you? Don't you know better than to stick your hand in the moving parts of a hay baler?"

Jake's relief turned to fright as he sat down and leaned against the baler's tire. He examined his thumb and fervently wished that he could have that second back. The tingling was giving way to throbbing and stinging. It was starting to turn a little blue. His head spun as he thought of his predicament and how stupid he had been. He and Gray had no way to get him out of the hay meadow and home except aboard Scar. Gray's stare made things worse. "What are you looking at?" Jake asked.

"Just wondering when you were gonna start bawling."

"I ain't gonna bawl." Jake's eyes started to fill, and his nose began to run as the words escaped his mouth. He snuffed it back up, wiped his nose and eyes on his shirt sleeve, and started for his horse. The welcome rattle of the Ford coming across the hay meadow stopped him. He knew without looking that his father was driving. He was the only one who could shift gears in the old car without grinding. Rance stepped out of the car and saw Jake sitting against the baler wheel, holding his thumb. Hack Gentry, Rance's best friend, closed the passenger door on the pea-green coupe.

Jake silently gave thanks. Other than his mother, these were the two people he most wanted to see at a time like this. His father would make things right with the thumb, and Hack would not tease him for doing something stupid.

Rance glanced at Jake, then turned toward Gray. "What happened?"

"He stuck his hand in the baler when it was broke. I fixed it and it crushed his thumb."

Rance dropped to one knee to examine it. "How bad is it, Jake?"

"Don't know."

Hack squatted for a closer look. "Can't believe he ain't crying. I would be. Damned old baler is more trouble than it's worth." The baler and the hay meadow belonged to Hack. Rance was leasing the land and borrowing the dilapidated equipment.

Rance held the thumb gently in his palm. "Does it hurt much?"

Jake shook his head. It was pulsing and starting to swell already, but it really didn't hurt too much. The more the men talked, though, the more scared he became.

Rance stood, frowned, shaded his eyes, swept the meadow with a glance, then turned back to Jake. "Better get you to Dr. Olen's. Gray, you keep baling as long as she'll hold up. Hack, you mind getting him started?"

"Not at all. Good luck, Jaker Ridge. You'll be okay." Jake liked it when Hack called him Jaker. Hack was a man to be admired.

Dr. Olen Bartlett and the Bartlett Hospital were twelve miles away in Cooper. Rance and Jake pulled up behind the doctor's car in less than ten minutes. On the way, increasing pain told Jake that his thumb was really damaged. When Dr. Olen showed them the X-rays, it seemed to Jake that all the bones were turned to gravel. He looked at his father's ashen face.

Dr. Olen laughed out loud at their expressions. An olive-skinned, handsome man about the same size as Rance, he had a slight curl in his thin, dark hair. Jake saw gentleness and confidence in his expression. Dr. Olen could fix anything. "It's not as bad as it looks, but it is going to swell and look pretty nasty. He'll lose the thumbnail, of course." The doctor laughed again when he saw Jake's face. "No long term damage, though. A boy your age recovers quickly from broken bones. You'll be good as new in a few weeks." Dr. Olen tousled Jake's hair and handed him a small metal guard, some gauze and a roll of adhesive tape. "Have your mother put this on when you're ready to use the thumb a little."

Jake was relieved, but a few weeks? He needed to be well by tomorrow for Little League tryouts. On the way home, the tears finally came.

Rance looked across the car seat at his son. "The worst part is over, Jake. Why are you crying now?"

"I won't make a team because I won't be able to hit or throw. This is my right thumb."

"I'll go with you to explain your situation to the men picking the teams. Other men and boys will be there who have seen you play before and can tell the coaches."

Jake looked down into the floorboard of the old Ford. It was covered with shop rags and wrenches. "You have to finish baling and hauling hay."

Rance bit his lip and kept his eyes on the road. "The hay can wait. I'll take you to the tryouts."

Chapter 5

Jake lay restless in his bed that night. The calendar said it wasn't summer yet, but it was hot and the sheets were clammy. Every time he turned, they clung and turned with him. His thumb seemed to double in size every ten seconds. He examined it in the sparse light to see if the nail was tearing itself away from the rest of his thumb. He was sure it had to be. Stretching both arms across the bed, he lay spread-eagled on his back, propping the thumb on Gray's pillow. He wanted to enjoy the whole bed before his brother arrived to take most of it. Moonlight filtering through the open windows allowed him to stare at the pine board ceiling fourteen feet above him. Remnants of wallpaper and cheesecloth backing hung from the ceiling and along the walls. Rats running in the attic sounded more like small cats or squirrels.

Since the family had only one vehicle, Jake had expected to stand out on highway 24 the next day and hitchhike to the tryouts. Now his father was to take him. He wasn't sure if that pleased him. He didn't want to be embarrassed in front of his father if he didn't make a team. He had bummed rides to sandlot and pasture ball games before, but this was different. This was big time. A branch of the official Little League had been formed in Delta County, and tryouts were to be held only once. Just when school was out and things started to go his way, something always happened—like the thumb. He lifted it toward the moonlight and gingerly touched it with his left hand. No way he could make a team with that.

The next morning, Jake sat shirtless at the breakfast table, staring at his thumb and nursing a glass of blue-john milk. Most days, Mattie would have sent him back to his room for a shirt, but she decided to relax the rules because of the thumb. "You're up early. How's the thumb?" Mattie picked up Jake's hand gently and examined the angry digit. "Looks like it's getting better already," she lied. Jake felt better, even if his thumb didn't.

"I've got to get your daddy's breakfast started." After several tries, Mattie succeeded in lighting the kerosene stove. Jake liked watching his mother make biscuits. Doing it every day had made her as proficient at the procedure as his father was at making a roll-your-own cigarette. Mattie cut the biscuits with the round tin cup, then dropped them in the shortening-lined pan for baking. It was hot in the kitchen and the worn-out stove made it hotter. Mattie had one skillet frying eggs and bacon that Jake figured was for him. Rance had brought in a few slices of salt-pork from the smokehouse, and she threw them into another skillet to fry while the biscuits baked in the oven. The smell made Jake a little sick at his stomach.

"Where's Trish?" Jake asked.

Mattie dropped a fried egg and two strips of bacon, still crackling, onto his plate. "I'm letting her sleep in." Jake stared at the well-done egg, splattered with dark bacon grease. The white was crusty and turned up on the edges. He was glad he didn't have to eat it.

Mattie loaded Rance's plate with white, doughy biscuits as he came in to sit at his usual place, then put the remaining biscuits back into the oven. Rance liked his biscuits barely browned, even a little doughy. He liked salt pork and wanted the fat left on meat. For breakfast, he usually had cowboy coffee, biscuits with salt pork followed by biscuits with ribbon cane or sugar syrup stirred well with lots of home-churned butter.

Mattie stood at the sink, washing pots and pans while the biscuits baked. She looked over her shoulder at Rance as she reached for the teakettle of hot water that sat on the stove. "Wish this house had hot running water like the barn does. You know, some families actually have houses that are nicer than their barns."

Jake had heard it all before. He knew what his father was thinking. Hot water was required to pass inspection in a dairy barn, but it was still a luxury in a house. Rance sopped a biscuit in the ribbon cane and looked out the kitchen window. "I know lots of people who don't have any kind of running water in their houses. Take Roy Hocutt, for example. That's where I'm heading after breakfast."

"What for?"

"He's got a couple of boar hogs that need cuttin' and a horse with the strangles."

Jake swelled a little with pride for his father. People who had known Rance for a long time called him Doc because he had been the substitute veterinarian for the community since he was a boy. He could measure land, figure board feet in lumber, read as well as draw construction plans, and build or repair most anything. He could guess the weight of a cow or hog within a few pounds, and his pocket knife was kept razor-sharp for the times when a boar hog needed to be turned into a barrow or a stud into a gelding. Jake could do none of those things and wondered why none of his father's best traits had passed to him.

Tuck walked into the kitchen in his underwear, rubbing his eyes. He shuffled bare feet over to where his mother stood by the sink and leaned his back against her legs. She leaned down and pointed her finger to her lips and said, "Shusha." Tuck took her face into his hands and planted a kiss on her puckered lips. She picked him up and said, "Hug." He put both arms around her neck and patted her back with both hands. Staring over Mattie's shoulder at Jake, Tuck closed one eye in response to his brother's wink. When Mattie set him down, he walked over to Jake's chair, stood on his tiptoes, and stared into Jake's plate. Jake smiled and led him around to his left side, away from the thumb.

Tuck sat on Jake's knee, never taking his eyes off the egg and bacon. Using his left hand, Jake tried to cut the egg with only a fork. Clumsy because of the thumb, he dropped his fork on the floor. Mattie picked it up, cut the egg, and handed the fork to Tuck. Jake watched his little brother eat while he waited for the biscuits to come out of the oven again. He would have butter and homemade jelly with the biscuits for his breakfast, letting Tuck have the bacon and egg.

Jake loved the morning ritual with his little brother. Tuck had

33

inherited the best physical features of each member of the family. He had the men's skin coloring and eyes the color of his father's cowboy coffee, but his hair was like the women's ...soft and thick. It was a light brown, almost blond color, and, unlike Jake's straight, unruly hair, had a soft curl to it. Jake patted Tuck's leg with his good hand and Tuck squeezed his shoulders together, smiling at Jake as he took his last bite. A smidgen of plum preserves painted the corners of his mouth.

Jake never ceased to be surprised at the warm, calming effect of Tuck's direct gaze. He knew there was something special, even magical, about Tuck but never spoke about it. With those soft, round eyes, Tuck seemed to convey something meaningful to everyone who met him. Jake envied those qualities, but not his brother. He yearned for Tuck to transfer some of those qualities to himself. He wanted Tuck to help him find the flow.

"Morning." Trish walked through the kitchen to the porch, stopping only to tousle Jake's short hair and kiss Tuck on the forehead. She walked with purposeful, athletic strides, swinging her arms like the athlete she was. Jake's sister did not priss. She strutted. Her hair was pulled back into a ponytail, and a bobby pin held a curl on each side of her forehead. The pins seemed out of place, a reluctant concession to femininity. Trish drew water from the cistern and poured it into a pan. Jake watched as his tomboy sister washed her hands and face.

Gray, still dressed only in Levis, walked into the kitchen and sat at the table without speaking. Jake was used to his brother's silent moodiness at breakfast. Bad mood or good, Gray Boy still controlled most rooms he entered. Today, he changed the mood to somber. Jake resented it and left the breakfast table.

On the back porch, Jake drew water from the cistern and poured some into a wash pan and some into an empty Garrett's snuff glass. Rance had built a crude shelf that held the wash pan, Lava and Ivory soap dishes, a saucer for toothpaste, and snuff glasses for toothbrushes and rinsing. A cotton rope had been strung above the shelf between two posts. Wash rags and towels, fastened with clothes-pins, hung from the rope. Jake removed his toothbrush from the snuff glass and mixed some baking soda and salt for toothpaste. As he brushed, Griffin Rivers and Buddy came through the pasture gate. Griffin rode Buddy all the way to the back porch and relaxed in the saddle while his grandson rinsed and spat over the shelf into the yard.

Griffin had been a widower for more than ten years and lived alone in a three-room shotgun house against the east fence line, less than a half mile from the back porch where Buddy stood now. "Mornin' Bolivar," he offered his usual greeting to his grandson.

Jake had no idea where Bolivar as a nickname had come from, but he liked it. Jake dropped his tooth brush into the snuff glass. "Hey, Papa Griff."

"Rode that horse today?" came the daily question from his grandfather.

"Not yet, but I intend to if I can with this thumb."

"I heard about that. You're lucky to still have a thumb. Just the same, a horse that ain't worth using ain't worth havin'. Guess your ropin' practice is on hold for awhile, too."

"Yes sir."

"Your mama make any coffee?" That one did not require an answer. Griffin dismounted and wrapped the reins loosely around the corner post on the porch. In his early seventies, Griffin Rivers looked like an older version of Rance, just a little taller, gray-turning-white hair, and flowing white mustache. Still lean and erect, he dressed like the cowboy he was. Buddy was his only means of travel. Jake stared and admired his grandfather's cowboy clothes. Griffin always wore long-sleeved shirts buttoned all the way to the neck.

"You must be feelin' dancey today, Papa." Jake nodded toward the red wildrag around his grandfather's neck. Jake had never seen him without one. In the summer, he wore it loose and used it to wipe away sweat and keep the nose clear of blowing dust. In winter, he wrapped it tight around his neck and used it for warmth. Griffin smiled and nodded as he stepped onto the porch.

As Griffin reached for the screen door handle, Jake noticed that the cuffs and collar on his faded blue shirt were a little frayed, but it was clean, starched, and ironed. Griffin wore a felt hat like the one Rance wore, but the brim was a quarter inch wider. He wore his regular jeans and boots with riding heels that slanted forward, a little taller than Rance's dress boots. If he was going to town and feeling good, he sometimes tucked the jeans into his boot tops. That was what Jake really liked. Stitched in blue and red, those boot tops were the prettiest yellow-soft leather Jake had ever seen.

Griffin carried a pocket watch in his jeans that he had used in his earlier days with the Texas and Pacific railroad. From the braided leather lanyard and the fob made from the rowel of an old spur, Jake knew the watch was in its usual spot today. Griffin wore a well-used Ranger belt with silver buckle, two keepers, and a tip.

From inside, Jake heard his mother's whisper. "Can't you stop him from tying his horse to the corner of the porch? He's going to pull the house down one of these days."

Jake smiled at his mother's complaint. Griffin Rivers wouldn't own a horse that pulled back when tied. It was a horse sin. Jake had been told that Buddy had never pulled back but once in his life, and that was because a cat crawled up his leg. Griffin had made him regret that sin. Jake pushed himself to a sitting position on the cistern so that he could hear what Papa Griff had to say through the kitchen window.

"Morning, Mattie girl," Griffin stepped into the kitchen and offered his usual greetings to his daughter-in-law as he hung his hat on the back of the door next to Rance's.

"Missie, . . . Gray Boy," he nodded his greetings to Trish and Gray Boy.

"Mornin', Papa Griffin," they answered.

He took a seat at the end of the gray Formica and chrome table. The house had settled enough to make the table lower on the side against the porch window. Jake smiled as he watched Griffin frown and drum the Formica table top with his fingers. Griffin had made no secret of his preference for the old pine table with the shaky legs when Mattie received the new gray table and chairs last Christmas. Griffin reached over and set Tuck on his knee, nuzzling his cheek with his mustache, "How're you, Tuck?"

Tuck giggled at the nuzzling and said, "Hey, Papa."

"Morning, Mr. Griffin." Mattie spoke to her father-in-law. "Care for some of Rance's cowboy coffee? He just made a second pan." Jake wondered, but never asked, why people called his grandfather Mr. Griffin instead of Mr. Rivers.

"Rather have yours, but if that's what's offered, I'll have some."

Mattie poured the coffee into his cup. "Rance ate the last of the ribbon cane, but I can offer you sugar syrup with warm biscuits and some fresh butter."

"No, thanks. I already had breakfast," he replied.

Mattie ignored the reply and set the biscuits, sugar syrup, butter, and coffee in front of him. He picked up the fork, gave a few syrup-soaked bites to Tuck and went to work on the rest. Griffin looked to the head of the table and nodded at his son."How're you, Rance?"

"I'd be a lot better with a two-inch rain."

"Hell, two inches wouldn't even begin to fill in the cracks Buddy stepped over gettin' here this morning."

"That's for damn sure, but it might get me a second cuttin' on the hay meadow. The first one ain't gonna be worth much," Rance replied.

"You gonna finish baling it today?"

"If we can hold Hack's old baler together with haywire and a prayer."

Griffin turned his attention to Trish. "Missie, looks like you got your mind on something besides hay. Found yourself a feller?"

Trish's face colored a little as she used her fork to push around the food on her plate. "No, I was just thinking about work. I've got a summer job waiting tables at the City Café in Commerce. Won't be pulling bolls this year."

"Well, watch your p's and q's. I've seen a few rough customers in there."

Breakfast finished, Griffin rode off toward highway 24. Rance and Gray left for the hay field. Jake and Tuck watched their grandfather and Buddy until they were out of sight, then crawled through the fence into the horse lot beside the dairy barn. Scar had been named for Dr. Sixgun's horse on the radio show that the Rivers listened to most Saturday nights. The gelding ran to Jake, expecting to be fed, but quickly turned his attention to Tuck. A few of the recently-milked dairy cows returned to the lot when Tuck came outside. They strained over the fence to reach Tuck with their tongues, licking him as if he were a block of salt.

Jake fed Scar some dairy feed and a block of hay and brushed his coat, mane, and tail while the horse ate. Tuck sat on the horse's back while Scar ate his feed. Rance's admonition played in Jake's mind, but he ignored it. "Would you like for somebody to comb your hair or sit on your back while you're eating?" Rance had said. Jake was sure that Scar liked him too much to kick him, and he knew he wouldn't hurt Tuck. He left Scar to finish his feed and began scooping up cow patties from both lots. Tuck went under the front porch of the house to play. An hour later, Jake was dragging a tow sack full of lime across the dairy parlor floor. When he stepped outside the barn, he was white all over. Clear lines showed when he pulled the bandanna from his face to his neck. In the washroom of the barn, he stripped down and washed himself off over the drain.

When he finished dressing, Jake put his ball inside his glove and wrapped a shoestring around it, keeping the ball snug in the glove's pocket. He hung the glove on the bat and leaned both against a fence post while he bridled Scar. Grabbing a handful of mane, he swung aboard the horse and rode him bareback around the lot to get him untracked. Rance seldom allowed use of the saddle, so Jake just imagined he was an Indian when he rode bareback. He waved goodbye to Tuck, then leaned down to pick up the baseball glove and bat on his way to meet his father. Traveling as the crow flies, they were through the bottoms, across Blue Bottom Creek and in the meadow in short order. The baler had stopped again when Jake arrived. By the time Rance had it running again, it was time to leave for the tryouts.

Chapter 6

At the ballpark in Cooper, kids were already gathered in groups. Jake sat on the Ford's fender and scanned the unfamiliar field while Rance put the metal guard on his thumb. He knew he had friends who were going to tryout, but he didn't see a single boy he knew. He winced when his father squeezed the thumb. "I need a cast or something so I can bat and throw a little, at least."

"Dr. Olen said a cast wouldn't work. It will just have to run its course, Jake. Go over there with that group of boys while I try to find out what's going on."

A few minutes later, Jake found himself standing under a pop fly. His left hand functioned well, so he caught it with his glove. However, his return of the ball with the right hand was awkward and weak. He felt the Cooper boys' eyes on him. It probably looked like a girl's throw to them. Naturally bashful, Jake avoided meeting the other boys' eyes and wished for a familiar face. The boy next to him leaned into him with his shoulder, pretending to use Jake as a prop for a little snooze. Not used to such familiarity from strangers, Jake stepped back and braced himself, recalling his father's words. "If you have to fight, get in the first lick and don't let up, especially if the boy is bigger than you." This boy, like all of the others, was bigger, but not by much. The boy smiled at Jake's combative stance. "Name's Bo Randall."

Relieved, Jake responded, "Jake Rivers." He might actually be friends with these boys from Cooper.

A group of men with clipboards lined them up and rotated them around the field for fielding and batting practice. Jake caught all of his ground balls and managed to get all but one to first base in the air. They were weak throws and the pain made his eyes water, but they made it. He hit two of the three balls thrown to him, but neither hit made it farther than the pitcher's mound. He caught all of the long fly balls, but his throws fell short of the infield. He knew he wasn't going to be chosen for a team. Another year without the flow. Each time Jake made an error or a weak hit or throw because of the thumb, he looked at the men with clipboards. He did not see his father until the tryouts were over. Rance was talking to the important men. He called Jake over and asked him to show the men his thumb. Jake displayed it. It was now an angry purplish-red, the thumbnail had started to twist, and the skin had started to crack. It looked like the whole thing could burst and spew blood and torn flesh any minute.

The youngest note-taker whistled. "You made these tryouts with that?"

"Yes sir," Jake replied.

The elder of the four men smiled. "I 'magine you'll make a team, boy. Don't you worry."

Rance and Jake laughed and talked about baseball season as they started home. Jake might actually get to play real Little League baseball, uniform, cap, cleats, and all. To celebrate, they stopped at the Dairy Queen on the outskirts of town and picked up a couple of hamburgers and Cokes to go. Back home, Jake put on his lime-dust clothes and rode back to the hay field with his father. Hack had arrived late to help, and he and Gray had managed to get everything baled. Jake saw Rance's expression turn grim when he looked at the number of bales on the ground.

"Hardly worth the effort." Rance posed both a question and statement to Hack.

"Better than nothin', I guess," Hack replied.

"I can't afford to start buying hay, Hack. Dairy feed takes everything as it is." Rance pulled a piece of straw from one of the bales and chewed on it. Jake and Gray mimicked his motions. He spit out the stem and turned to the boys. "Let's go milk; then we can load 'em up and take 'em to the barn."

It was well past dark before the hay was in the barn. In spite of the thumb, Jake managed to make himself helpful with the use of a hay hook. He dragged the bales to Gray Boy for stacking in the loft. Mattie and Trish brought red beans, cornbread, fried potatoes, and iced tea outside to eat under the moonlight. Old boards across a pair of sawhorses were set up to serve as a table for their picnic under the chinaberry tree in the side yard. As the last bales were being stacked, they heard Tuck's small voice drifting across the cow lots to the barn. "Supper's ready." Tuck took his duty seriously and kept repeating his call until Rance, Gray, and Jake emerged from the hall of the barn. They were sweaty and stinging from the hay, but hungry. Rance laughed at Tuck's persistence. "All right, boy. We're coming. Are we having a picnic?" Getting the hay in was always cause for a little celebration, even if the hay crop was short.

The next morning, Jake pulled up the three-legged milk stool, washed Jessie's teats and udder, put his head against her stomach, and tested the thumb with the first pull on a teat. As the first small stream hit the bottom of the bucket, he knew he could milk without putting too much pressure on the thumb. Milking Jessie for milk and butter to use in the house was his job most mornings. Jake neither understood nor questioned why Rance and Mattie thought that the Jersey cow's milk was superior to the Holsteins' being milked in the dairy parlor or why Mattie didn't like the idea of mixing milk from several cows for the family's own use.

The cadence of the streams hitting the foaming milk was different because of the thumb, but the bucket was filling. The faint hum of the dairy starting its twice daily routine was usually dreaded, but was soothing today. It was otherwise quiet in the old lean-to off the side of the hay barn. Time to think. Jake enjoyed the smell of fresh-cut hay that filled the barn. A couple of barn cats begged for a spray of milk. Careful to put his arm against Jessie's back legs to keep her from stepping in the half-full bucket, Jake pointed one teat at the cats and squirted a few streams of milk at their faces. He hadn't seen a rat in the barn for several weeks, so they deserved a reward.

Jake knew that Little League team rosters were to be posted in Cooper today, and the first game was Saturday night. Only two more days before the first real game, and he did not even know if he had made a team. Not making a team would mean another summer without a chance to experience the flow. At breakfast, he would ask- - no, plead with his parents to take him to Cooper to look at the team rosters. He took the milk into his mother and watched her run it through a piece of cheesecloth into two gallon jars to drain off cow hair and other things that might have made their way into the bucket.

"Aren't you needed in the barn?" she asked.

"Not yet. Do you know if anybody is going into town today?" Jake asked.

"No, I don't."

"Do you think you or Daddy might take me to town today?"

She knew why he was asking. "Go finish your chores, and we'll talk about it after breakfast."

When Jake emerged from the dairy barn covered with lime, the car was gone. It wasn't unusual for him to take his breakfast later than the others, but today, he needed to go to town and check that roster. He ran to the back porch where Trish was working the churn. She was letting Tuck work the paddle. Mattie was at the kitchen sink.

"Where's Daddy?" Jake asked.

Trish and Tuck kept moving the churn's paddle. "He and Gray have gone to Dallas. He has a cousin over there that has a truck for sale and he thinks he might buy it."

Jake's disappointment over being left behind was tempered with the excitement of possibly getting a truck. He wondered if they had come into some type of new good fortune that allowed them to buy one. Jake sat on the porch and watched Trish pour the butter into molds. When Mattie stepped out to pick up the molds for the ice box, he asked the question that was bothering him. "Why was I left behind?"

"Because the word is that you may have ball practice this afternoon or tomorrow afternoon, and Daddy didn't want you to miss it." Mattie answered with a wink and smile.

Jake's eyes brightened. "How do you know that I made a team? Do you know what team I'm on? How'll we find out about practice?" Jake fired the questions as fast as they came into his mind. He had many more, but Mattie held up a warning finger to stop him.

"The team rosters, if that's what they're called, are supposed to be posted at Welch's store this afternoon along with the first practice times. Hack is going into Cooper today and has promised to bring back everything you need to know."

"What time?"

"Before milking. Now stop with the questions and go take this jar of milk to Mr. Griffin. Tell him I'll have butter tomorrow if he drops by."

Jake bridled Scar and rode him to the back porch. Griffin had made a leather carrier for the milk jar so that Jake could carry it on the horse without breaking it. Mattie slipped the jar into the carrier, tied it securely, and handed the strap to Jake with her usual admonition to go slow and be careful. Jake and Scar followed the small lane by the hay barn that led to Papa Griff's house. As they reached the other side of the barn, the familiar, pungent smell of goat weeds mixed with the bittersweet aroma of bitter weeds filled the air. Rance had called the lot behind the barn the sorriest piece of dirt on the place, but Jake found it mysterious. It drained poorly and Rance had said it wouldn't even grow weeds. The drought had proven him wrong about the weeds. Standing in their gray-green splendor with soft gray, almost-blue blossoms, goat weeds defiantly poked through the rock-hard ground. Mixed with the bright yellow bitter weeds, the lot was almost pretty to Jake.

As he approached Papa Griff's house, he heard the familiar sounds of fiddle and guitar. He tapped his foot and hummed as he tied his horse to a fence post in the front yard. Jake knew the words to Bob Wills' San Antonio Rose by heart and whistled along as he approached. On the porch, he stood outside the screen door, not wanting to disturb the performance. Papa Griff was playing the fiddle and singing a little while his friend Bob Gant played the guitar and provided most of the vocals. When Griffin saw Jake at the door, he smiled, winked, and kept playing as he motioned with his head and eyes for Jake to come on in.

Jake carried the milk through the living room to the kitchen and placed it on the table. He noticed the remains of his grandfather's last meal still sitting on the small, round table. Griffin had fried something in a cast iron skillet, carried it to the table, and used the skillet as his plate. Jake admired the wooden handles on the

43

fork and spoon and the yellow bone handle on the knife. Remains of buttermilk lined the sides of the goblet beside the skillet.

"Mind putting that milk down the well for me, Bolivar?" Griffin stopped playing to ask the question. Jake knew the routine. He went out to the well, removed the holder, looped the thin rope around the milk jar's lid and dropped the jar down the well where it could hang and keep cool. When Jake came back to listen to more music, Griffin dropped a few coppers, his name for pennies, into Jake's jeans. Jake uttered his usual weak protest, and Griffin his usual insistence. Jake made a couple of song requests, including *Tumblin' Tumbleweeds* and *Take Me Back to Tulsa*.

He was absorbed in the music when he heard his mother ringing the bell at the house. That meant, wherever you are, come running. He swung up on Scar and left toward home in a run, ignoring his father's and grandfather's warnings about the large cracks in the parched earth. As he arrived at the back gate, he saw Hack's '49 Chevrolet parked in the driveway. He left his horse tied to the gate post, stood on the milk can that he kept there, and vaulted over the fence. Mattie and Hack were standing on the back porch.

"Hey, Hack," he said.

"Hey, yourself, Jaker."

Hack and Mattie exchanged smiles and continued talking, ignoring Jake.

Jake waited for a pause in their conversation before speaking. "You rang the bell, Mama."

"Sure did, " Mattie replied.

Hack winked at Mattie. "Sure is a nice day, ain't it? Good and hot."

Jake's face was almost pleading by this time, and neither Hack nor Mattie could keep it to themselves any longer.

"Looks like you're going to be a little Indian," Mattie said.

Hack pulled a mimeographed sheet from his shirt pocket, unfolded it, and handed it to Jake. It was a team roster for the Indians. Jake found his name near the bottom. He stared at the list, and relished the sight of his own name on a Little League roster. Below the list, he read the added instructions:

Practice Thursday @ 5:00PM
Uniforms at Welch's Friday

Jake couldn't hide his elation. The Delta County teams were named after the New York Giants, the Brooklyn Dodgers, the New York Yankees, and the Cleveland Indians. The Indians was his favorite baseball team. He never knew why his father and he had chosen the Indians. Jake figured it was because they were not from New York. The team had finished second in the American League in 1953. Rance had said that 1954 was going to be their year. Now Jake was going to be an Indian. Was this the flow at work?

Almost an hour past milking time, Gray Boy arrived in the Ford. The cows were already in the front lot, ready for milking. Their udders were swelled with milk, and their teats leaked fine streams, begging for relief. Jake was mounted, pretending he was holding a herd of steers on a cattle drive. Rance drove up in a flat-bed truck and parked it in the back yard. Jake closed the lot gate, tied Scar, and ran toward the house. Mattie and Trish came out to look it over.

"Looks almost new," Mattie said.

"Well, she's not new, but she's new to us. It's a '47 Chevy. Seven years old, but I think she's clean." Rance glanced at Mattie to see if she approved. Her expression was doubtful. Rance moved closer to her. "Mattie, we've been needing a truck for a long time. I can pay for it by just hauling water for folks whose wells have run dry."

With Gray giving instructions and warnings as if he owned the '47 Chevy, they all handled every part of the truck inside and outside. Their curiosity sated, they sat or stood on the bed, still mystified by the spectacle of this strange vehicle sitting in their yard.

"What's that?" Mattie pointed to a tall object tied at the front of the bed with ropes and covered with blankets. Tuck was pulling at the ropes.

Rance smiled and nodded toward the object. "Untie it and see."

Mattie untied the ropes and peeled away the blankets. A shiny white Westinghouse refrigerator appeared from its cover. She put

45

her hand over her mouth, repressed a shout of joy, turning it into a gleeful whimper, sat down on the truck bed, and began to cry. Rance laughed as he stood above her. He patted her on the head and asked, "What are you crying about. You don't like it?"

She slapped him hard on the back of his leg. "You know I love it, but how can we afford it?" She dropped her voice to a whisper. "Rance, I'm ashamed to be buying these things when we can't pay for groceries."

Rance's smile faded. "We probably can't afford either one. But you know that the iceman is going to stop delivering ice soon. We can't afford to go into town to bring back ice. The bank would loan me money for a truck because they can repossess it. They added the refrigerator to the truck note."

Mattie shook her head and looked away. "Still....."

"Mattie, you know we usually pay our grocery bills when crops come in. Harry's not worried about getting his money, and neither is Raymond Mills at Camp Lake. And don't forget that good stand of cotton in the bottom. One more rain there and we might make a really good crop."

"One more rain? Do you realize how likely that is?"

"You gotta have faith, Mattie. I'm damned tired of hearing about people all over the country getting modern appliances while we live like we did forty years ago." Rance turned to see Gray moving a dolly under the refrigerator. "We'll unload it after milking. I'll have to stretch some wire to get her plugged in." Rance turned toward Gray and Jake. "Boys, we better get to those cows."

As Jake headed toward his tied horse, he thought that he could not remember ever having had a better day. Making his first little league team, getting to be an Indian, getting a new truck and a new refrigerator. All in the same day.

Chapter 7

As he stepped out on 24, Jake felt the familiar sense of freedom he always did when he went somewhere on his own. Mattie had agreed to let him leave for his five o'clock practice four hours early. Trish had the Ford, and Rance was hauling water with the Chevy flatbed, so he would have to hitch a ride. Before walking east on 24, he turned for one more wave to Tuck, who stood on the front porch. Highway 24 was Jake's connection to the outside world. The road had taken him to Hugo, Oklahoma, once with his father on Jake's only trip to another state. Getting cars to stop and offer him a ride was usually not a problem when he wore his baseball cap and carried his glove. If no cars stopped, he planned to walk the three miles to Harry Cardwell's store's in Klondike. Harry went into Cooper most days for supplies, and Jake knew he would be welcome to ride with him.

Walking purposefully down the highway toward Klondike, Jake turned for every vehicle, lifting his thumb only if it looked like a good prospect for a ride. He never just stood on the road with his thumb in the air. Someone might see a car pass by without stopping and feel sorry for him. He did not want anybody feeling sorry for him. If he was walking, it somehow seemed that a ride was really not required. If one was offered, it would be impolite to turn it down. Even if he had to walk all the way to Cooper, he knew that he was going to get to practice on time.

He was almost at Klondike School before anything faster than a tractor passed. Finally, a fast-moving, almost new Buick slowed to a stop on the shoulder in front of him and backed up. Jake approached the passenger window. The driver was a man who looked to be in his mid-twenties. "Where are you headed, boy?"

"Klondike. You goin' that far?" Jake didn't want to say he was going to Cooper, fearing that the man might feel obligated to take him all the way.

"Going all the way to Cooper. Hop in."

Jake piled in the plush new Buick. He had sat in his uncle's Oldsmobile before, but he had never actually ridden in a car so big and luxurious. "I'm really going all the way to Cooper myself. Just thought I would catch another ride in Klondike." Jake offered this comment after seeing the inside of the Buick.

"No need to do that. I'll take you all the way. I see by your outfit that you're a ballplayer. Going to the ballpark?" the stranger asked.

"Yes sir." Jake leaned forward and took note of every detail on the Buick's dash, especially the speedometer. The speedometer hand had a little circle on the end that enclosed the speed as it made its way around. Jake had seen only pointer-type speedometer hands before. The circle was fun to watch. He watched as it quickly circled 50, then 60, 70. When it circled 85, Jake leaned back against the new upholstery and watched the fence posts sail by.

The driver, tan and lean, rested his right wrist on the wheel and hung his left arm out the door window, totally absorbed in his thoughts. That suited Jake just fine. He didn't want or need conversation. The inside of that Buick smelled like new leather and furniture polish, and he liked floating down the highway at high speed. He had ridden fast in the Ford with Gray Boy before, but it was a bumpy and rattly ride. The Buick seemed to take the contours of the road in stride, floating up, and then settling down without the slightest jolt.

The driver drove straight to the ballpark. Jake thanked him with all the enthusiasm and politeness his parents had drilled into his head. The man nodded, smiled, and drove off in a cloud of dust. Jake was alone. Not a single person in sight and still more than three hours to kill before practice. He walked to home plate and imagined himself swatting one over the fence. Then he walked all the bases, soundly tromping on home plate. He walked the inside of the fence in the outfield, tossing his baseball up as he sauntered along.

Gaining energy from his imaginings, he returned to short stop, dropped his ball and glove in the position he wanted to play, and walked to home plate again. Here, he took an imaginary swing at an imaginary pitch, then ran around the bases to the cheers coming from the crowd. Just as he rounded second base, he heard a shout.

"Hey, Jake. Whatcha doin'?"

His friend Robert Don Hooten was jumping out of Harry Cardwell's blue '51 Ford pickup along with several more boys, most of them from Klondike. Jake tried to be casual and hoped the boys had not witnessed his imaginary game.

"You on our team?" Robert Don asked.

"What team are you on?"

"Giants."

"Nope, I'm on the Indians."

"Mr. Cardwell is our coach." Robert Don said it with a little too much enthusiasm to suit Jake. He was disappointed to see most of his friends and one of his favorite adults on an opposing team. He did not know that Harry Cardwell, owner of Cardwell's store in Klondike, was going to coach and wondered why he had not been chosen for his team.

Harry guessed what was on Jake's mind by looking at his face. "I tried to get you on our team, Jake, but I was a replacement for another fella who had to back out of coaching at the last minute. He had already selected his team. The Indians didn't want to let you go. Guess I can't blame 'em for that," Harry smiled and pulled the bill of Jake's cap down over his eyes.

Jake wanted to play with his friends and wanted to be coached by Harry Cardwell, but Harry had made things almost all right with those words. Harry had played ball a few years after his dad, and they bragged on each other's play a lot.

"Jake, we practice at four. I think your team takes the field at five. Want to join us? Looks like you'll always be part Giant, anyway," Harry said.

That brightened Jake's spirits even more. He moved around the field, substituting for players as they took batting practice and shagging stray balls. At five o'clock sharp, Harry called his boys in for a skull session to plot strategy. Jake was not excluded, but he knew better than to try and listen in. After the session, the Giants and their coach left. A few more boys had arrived at the field for the five o'clock practice, but none that Jake knew. He felt lonely after Harry and his friends drove away. The other boys played a little catch, but none asked Jake to join in. He just walked around, kicking the dirt and watching the roads for any sign of a coach.

At five-thirty, he saw a rooster-tail of dust behind a car traveling at a speed Jake was not used to seeing anywhere, much less in town. The car turned into the parking lot behind the bleachers and stopped. The driver got out of the car in the middle of the dust cloud he had created, walked to the trunk, and withdrew a duffel bag full of baseball equipment. He threw the bag over his shoulder and headed toward the field. A boy fell in behind the coach as he approached. The boy was as tall as the coach and moved with the same cocksure walk. Jake still could not make out the face in the dust cloud, but he recognized the way the boy moved. If Linc Little was an Indian, Jake's disappointment at not being picked for the Giants would go away. As the man came closer, he smiled and winked at Jake. It was the driver of the big Buick who had given him a ride to town. Why hadn't the man said something about being a coach during the ride?

The man gathered the boys in a circle around him. "Name's Kirk Simpson. I'll be your coach. When I call your names, I want you to answer and raise your hand." His instructions were as confident and crisp as his walk. As he called each boy's name, the coach asked what position the boy wanted to play.

When he called Rivers, Jake answered, "Here, shortstop." Nobody had called out shortstop yet, so Jake felt his chances increase for getting the position. The next two names called, however, also answered, "shortstop." Jake felt like someone had kicked him in the stomach. He looked around at the group of boys standing around the coach and realized he was the smallest one.

Coach Simpson told them to take the field and go to the positions they had selected. Shortstop was the most overcrowded position in the park. Two were at first base, two in left field, two in center. Nobody was in right field. Starting at first base, the coach started hitting ground balls to the infield. Linc Little was on first. He easily fielded the first ball and stepped on the bag. His competitor missed, his glove never touching the skinner. Jake couldn't believe that anyone had the courage to even stand on first base with Linc Little as his competitor. Nervous, the boy on second bobbled the ball but recovered enough to throw to first.

Simpson signaled for the first boy in line at shortstop to take the first ground ball. He hit it much harder than the previous balls. It went under the player's glove. Jake breathed a sigh of relief. He was next. The ball was hit just a few feet to his right, harder than any skinner he had ever tried to catch. Recalling his father's coaching, he ran a little backward and to his right at the same time to get in front of the ball. He stuck his glove on the ground with his right hand beside the glove. Thoughts of his sore thumb caused him to take his eye off the ball for a fraction of a second. It bounced just over his glove, spun up his chest, under and over his chin, and climbed his nose, leaving a trail of red, chapped skin in its wake. It stopped at his hairline and began its descent. He caught it in the air with his right hand. The embarrassment, along with the pain in his face and chest, made him forget the thumb. He set himself, angling his body toward first base, and threw a strike to Linc Little's mitt.

Agony. He had boggled the ground ball. He was going to be banished to right field or worse, the bench. The third shortstop contender fielded another hard hit ball beautifully. It was hit to his right, and he fielded it backhanded with only his glove hand, throwing to first base in one smooth motion, both feet off the ground as he threw. If the throw hadn't been off, the play would have been almost spectacular. The errant throw pulled the first baseman off the bag a little, but not enough to keep most base-runners from being out. Jake felt the empty feeling in the pit of his stomach return.

At batting practice, he made contact with every pitch thrown. Only one made it out of the infield, and it was no more than a pop fly that a good shortstop could have picked off. The bench seemed to be his certain future. Right field was starting to look pretty good.

At the skull session, Simpson was direct again. "We'll keep it simple for the first few games. When you have the basics down pat, we'll move more into strategies. The basics of baseball are two

51

things; fielding and hitting. Fielding is catching and throwing the ball. When you are fielding, get in front of the ball." The coach picked up a glove and ball and planted himself squarely in front of the wide-eyed boys and demonstrated. "If you're fielding a ground ball, never let it get past you. Get in front of it, put your glove on the ground, and catch it. If you can't catch it, knock it down so that it doesn't go for extra bases." He paused long enough to examine the eager faces staring up at him, then added an ominous note. "I don't care if you have to stop it with your teeth or your eye, stop it."

The coach's eyes traveled down the line of boys, pausing to look each in the eye. "Make your throws good. Set your feet and your body before throwing. Better to be a little late with a good throw than quick with a bad one, especially if there are men on base. Don't be so interested in how you look as you make plays. I want solid players, not show-offs."

Simpson walked over to the equipment bag and pulled out a bat. He made a couple of level swings over home plate. "If you're batting, just make contact with the ball. To make contact, you have to watch the ball." He pointed to his eyes. "If you can do those things, we will win some games. He slapped the closest boy to him on the back and winked. "Later, I'll teach you more complicated things about this beautiful game."

He waved the boys into a circle around him and pulled a folded sheet of paper from his pocket. "Here's the starting lineup for Saturday's game. Be here at six-thirty for warmup." Mouths opened and unblinking eyes hurt as the coach painstakingly unfolded the paper and scanned it before uttering the life-or-death words the boys agonized to hear.

"Lead-off man and playing shortstop - Rivers." Jake didn't hear the second and third names called, but he did recover enough to hear the fourth. "Batting clean-up and playing first base, Linc Little."

Jake's spirits soared. He tried not to smile, but he could not contain his enthusiasm. His body made an involuntary little jump as he and the others helped carry the equipment back to Coach Simpson's car. Simpson's words were almost the same ones his father had used in teaching him to play ball, except that he had not mentioned choking up on the bat.

The coach looked at Jake as he slammed the Buick's trunk. "You think that thumb is going to be well in time for the game?"

Jake nodded. "One more day is all it needs."

"Need a ride?"

"Naw, I got somebody coming to pick me up. Thanks, just the same." Jake stumbled his answer, unable to suppress the wide smile on his face.

As the coach drove away, he wondered why he had said that. Maybe he just did not want to take a chance on messing up his good fortune by saying something stupid to the coach on the way home. Nobody was coming to pick him up. Rance and Gray Boy were milking, and Trish wouldn't be home with the car yet. He wasn't worried, though. He felt he could fly home. He wanted some time alone. Time to let the elation soak in. Time to throw up his arms and shout for joy. Time to visit his own baseball heaven, where he hit only home runs and made miraculous catches and impossible throws from shortstop. Time to think about the flow.

As he reached downtown Cooper, baseball heaven gave way to Texas heat, and he was dreading hitching home. It would be dark soon, and he wasn't supposed to stand out on the highway after dark. Just as he headed out of town, the Ford pulled up beside him.

Gray Boy shouted, "Get in, Piss-ant."

"What're you doing here?" Jake asked as he stepped on the running board.

"Now what do you think I'm doing, Dipstick? I'm picking up your scrawny little butt."

Jake had barely closed the door when he felt himself thrown back against the seat as Gray slammed the floor shift into first, popped the clutch, and made the tires squeal. Gray Boy practiced speed shifting as he went through the gears, missing most of the time, causing the gears to grind, and the old Ford to jerk spasmodically. Jake put his hands on the dashboard and tried to see out the front window. If he was going to die in a car crash, he wanted to see it coming. Gray kept the footfeed all the way to the floor, and <u>Jake felt the Ford try for the speeds he had reached only a few hours</u>

earlier in the Buick. The smell of grease and brake fluid contrasted with the pleasant smell of new upholstery in Coach Simpson's car. He felt smug and decided to keep that ride a secret.

Jake was brimming with excitement when he and Gray Boy entered the house, but he did not let it show. Tuck wanted him to roll the ball back and forth to him, so Jake sat in the living room floor and played with his little brother. Rance came in from milking chores, stood in the doorway, and stared at the two boys playing on the floor. "How did it go with practice?"

"Fine," Jake answered.

"Fine," Rance repeated with sarcasm. He put his calloused hands on his hips and rolled his eyes. "That all you got to say, boy?"

"I think I did pretty good. I'm starting shortstop for the first game, at least." Jake kept his eyes on his little brother, trying to repress a smile and his excitement.

"You're starting shortstop? Well, Mama, what do you think about that?" Rance smiled as Mattie lifted his arm and put it around her shoulders.

"Tell us some more about it, son," she said.

"It seemed like he hit the hardest skinners to the three of us trying for shortstop. I bobbled mine a little, but managed to stop it with my face." Jake warmed up to the story. "Coach Simpson told all of us to stop the ball just like you told me to. Then he pretty much said the same thing you have always said about batting." Jake had stopped playing with Tuck to give full attention to his parents.

Rance winked at Mattie. "He probably hit the ball harder to the three of you in order to decide on a starter quickly and to weed out the weak one. You still have to compete with the other boys. If that coach is smart, and sounds like he is, he'll leave you in the infield because of your speed." Rance walked to a corner of the room and picked up a bat. "How big were the bats? Any your size?"

"Good, brand-spankin' new Louisville Sluggers. They have from twenty-eight ounce to thirty-six." Jake was building enthusiasm as he filled in his father. Baseball was one subject where they spoke each other's language.

Jake stood and looked up at his mother. "I think I'm the littlest one on the team, though."

Mattie nodded her head. "Well, that's a big advantage, I think. You can probably run faster and move quicker than the bigger boys."

Rance poked his fingers lightly into Jake's chest. "You stick to the twenty-eight or twenty-nine bat until you get a little bigger." Rance moved his hands up the bat handle, away from the knob, to demonstrate the choke-up position. "And remember to choke up. Don't swing for the fences. Your job is to swing level and make good contact with the ball. You'll be able to place the ball where the fielding is open or weak if you don't try to swing too hard." Rance took a slow, level swing at an imaginary ball. "I know that Ted Williams says to swing up a little, but you and I ain't Ted Williams. You can't get on base by missing the ball. Your job is to make it to first base safely. Everything else will take care of itself."

Jake had heard the instructions since he was old enough to walk, but they had new meaning today.

"Well, let's get washed up for supper, boys."

As Jake headed for the back porch and the wash pan, Rance called him back. "Come here, Jake." He pointed to a spot just in front of his wood chair.

He put a hand on each of Jake's shoulders. "Be sure to come and tell me when you are in the Rivers' flow."

Jake felt a tingle run up his spine, nodded, and smiled. "I will, Daddy."

Mental images etched in his brain from repeated telling by his grandfather played in Jake's head. As a young man, Rance had made a leaping catch at shortstop, turned a full circle in the air, and delivered a strike to first to catch a runner off the bag for a double play. Papa Griff said Rance seemed to be flying when he caught the ball and turned in midair, then floating as he returned to earth.

Jake turned toward the kitchen when Mattie called them for supper, but paused at the door to listen when she approached Rance.

"Are you telling the kids about the Rivers' flow again?" Mattie smiled as she kneaded his shoulders from behind the chair.

Rance closed his eyes and breathed deeply, then opened them

55

and smiled up at her. "You see any harm in that?"

"If you believe it, that's good enough for me. Don't see what harm it can do unless they start telling their friends that only Rivers can do it."

"I don't see any harm in telling them that it's our family's little secret. In a way, it is. They'll find out soon enough that others can do it if they're of a mind to."

After supper, Rance went outside to sit in the swing under the chinaberry tree. Jake followed him. "Tell me about it again, Daddy. About my great-grandfather and how he discovered it."

Rance smiled as the swing moved slowly. "You ought to have that story memorized by now, but I'll tell it one more time." Rance looked toward Griffin's house, as if seeking confirmation from his father. "Grandpa Lev, your Papa Griff's daddy, fought for the South in the Civil War. He was mostly a foot soldier, but, being a ranch hand before the war, he always wanted to be Cavalry. At Gettysburg, his outfit was taking a beating on the ground. About dusk on the second day of fighting, he found a Yankee horse without its rider and climbed aboard, determined to fight the rest of the battle horseback."

"Was that old Yank?" Jake asked.

"You're getting ahead of the story, Jake. This was the first Yankee horse. Old Yank comes along later. Before Grandpa Lev got set in the saddle good, the horse and him were shot at the same time." Rance thumped the left side of his chest with two fingers. "Grandpa was shot in the chest, close to his heart. The horse and him fell together, and he wound up under his mount." Rance leaned toward Jake as he warmed to the story that had been told and retold. "He was unconscious until after dark." Rance's voice dropped to a whisper. "Shortly after dark, his eyes opened as if he was coming back from the dead. He felt the blood oozing from the hole in his chest and looked at the dead horse that had him pinned to the ground. He panicked and wanted to scream, but was afraid of alerting Union soldiers. He tried to dig himself free, but the more he dug, the more he bled. Finally, he gave out and decided he was going to die right there under that horse."

"Then he remembered the flow?" Jake asked.

"Then he heard his daddy's voice. Lev's daddy had told him about the flow, but he had never believed in it, never experienced it to that point in his life. Now, he knew it was his only chance. As his daddy whispered in his ear, he concentrated on slowing the beating of his heart and the bleeding. By morning, he had willed the bleeding to stop. His heart kept beating slowly. He said he sort of allowed himself to die so he could live."

Rance rose from the swing and walked toward the barn, away from Mattie's hearing. Jake followed close behind, knowing the end of the story but not wanting to miss a word. "The battlefield was strewn with dead bodies, so soldiers passing him assumed he was dead. Finally, two Yankee soldiers put a rope on the horse's legs and rolled it over to use as a shield. He had to lie perfectly still with bullets landing all around him until the Yankees left at dark. When they left, he just got up and walked off."

This was the part that Jake could not understand. "With the bullet still in him?"

Rance chuckled. "Yep. He had no idea where his regiment was, so he kept walking until he couldn't hear any sounds of soldiers or battle. He had matches in his pocket, so he found a little draw and built a fire. He held his knife over the fire until it was red hot, then seared the place where the bullet had gone in." Rance stopped to let Jake ask his usual question.

Jake winced and whistled. "He just left it in there? Just burned the hole shut without screaming?"

"Papa says it was there until the day he died some fifty years later. As for screaming, he willed himself to take his mind off the pain by using the flow."

"Then what happened?"

"Then you get into bed. You know what happened."

"I remember most of it, but I like to hear about Old Yank."

"We'll save that for later."

As they started back toward the house, Jake stared at the stars. The story was exciting, but did not explain anything. Each time he heard it, he expected to hear something that would explain the flow, something that would allow him to experience it. The story only increased his frustration and fear. He was not likely to be in a war.

He was not likely to be shot. He could not will pain away, could not even keep from being nervous when he stood in the batter's box. He felt unworthy of the flow.

Chapter 8

"Do you suppose I could get a ride to Cooper tonight after milking? Our uniforms and caps are ready to pick up at Welch's." Jake didn't dare to mention cleats. One subject at a time. Rance was under the Ford, draining the oil. Jake heard nothing but the sound of the drain plug dropping into the catch pan. Rance rolled the creeper out from under the car.

"They'll be there tomorrow night. Can't see making two trips into town. Your mother can take you to the ball game a little early. You can pick yours up then."

Jake felt that hollow feeling again. He wished he had asked his mother instead. He could have argued and pleaded with her, but knew better than to try that with his father. Now it was too late. The decision had been made and it was final. His mind took him to Welch's, where all the other kids were picking out uniforms, caps, and cleats. He saw himself arriving tomorrow to an empty store.

Jake gathered eggs on Saturday, caught a pullet with his rope, penned it for Sunday frying, and helped with feeding calves. When milking started, Mattie called him in to get cleaned up for the big game. He usually took his summer baths outside, in the dairy barn or in the pasture pool, but she insisted that he use the washtub inside today. She wanted to check the results. After he was dressed in his best jeans and shirt, they examined his shoes. Last year's Converse shoes had holes in the tops and the bottoms were worn lopsided. Except for riding in boots, he went barefoot most of the summer and shoes waited until fall.

"Any chance of getting baseball cleats?" Jake asked.

"We'll just have to see," Mattie replied. "Trish and I are going to take you. We need to go right now. I made a bacon sandwich that you can eat on the way. Gray Boy and your daddy will be along after milking."

Mattie and Jake found pandemonium when they entered Welch's store. Jake's excitement subsided when he saw the new uniforms scattered across two big tables, some dangling off the sides, some dropped on the floor, dirty footprints soiling their brilliance. His daydream was coming true. He was going to have to play his first game in shoes with holes and without a uniform. Parents and children were frantically searching for complete uniforms, socks, and caps. The uniforms belonged to the Little League association, but caps and cleats were paid for by each player. Jake saw his mother's face lose some of its color. She looked through scattered tops and pants, holding them up to Jake for size. Jake was mesmerized by the activity. He had never seen Welch's store so full of people and as disorganized. Mattie finally got Mr. Welch's attention.

"What team is he on?" he asked.

"Indians," Jake answered for Mattie.

Mr. Welch made a sweeping gesture with both hands, his face showing the exasperation he felt. "You need to look for the uniforms with red piping. I'm sorry for all the mess, but everyone came at once, and there are only so many uniforms to go around. The kids that live here in town came in yesterday and picked theirs up, but all of the country kids seem to be coming in at the same time tonight." He looked down at Jake's worn-out cap. " I can get you a cap, though. I have to crease 'em, so I 'm keeping 'em in boxes in back. What size do you think?"

Jake took Tuck's hand and followed Mr. Welch over to a big steam iron and ironing board. The store owner found a cap that fit, placed the crown on the board, pulled the steam iron down, and put a permanent crease in it just above the white "D." Jake looked around at the other boys to check their creases and decided that his cap had not been destroyed. He wished for Gray Boy to help him round the bill. Jake had broken the bill on his only other baseball cap trying to get it to look like his brother's.

"Want me to roll the bill?" Mr. Welch asked.

Jake was hesitant until he felt Trish's hands on his shoulders. She knew as much about baseball as their father did. "Yes, he wants it rolled," Trish answered for him. Mr. Welch had fashioned a creasing pad for the bills out of an old can wrapped in canvas. He sprayed the bill with steam from the iron, then neatly folded it over the can. He held it for a few seconds, then handed it to Jake. Jake thought it was just about the prettiest thing he had ever seen. The look in his sister's eyes said it was. It must have been evident in his face because Mr. Welch laughed out loud. Jake looked around the store for his mother. Not finding her, he reached into his empty pocket and asked, "What do I owe you?"

Mr. Welch laughed again. "Go find your mother. Get your uniform and shoes and we'll settle up then."

When he found Mattie, she had located a uniform with red piping. "This is the only uniform in the store that comes close to your size, Jake. It may be a little big, but it's the best we can do. I'll alter it tomorrow."

Tomorrow? The game starts in less than an hour, Jake thought. He and Tuck went into the makeshift dressing room and Jake put on the uniform. The top came to his knees, but he thought it might not show when he stuck it into his pants. The pants, however, were another story. They would not stay up. He peered around the dressing room curtain and motioned for his mother. Mattie put her hand to her lips and shook her head. "We'll figure something out. That's all there is. Everything has been picked over."

Jake thought about his daydream, but said nothing. Disconsolate and not willing to walk out holding up his pants, he dressed in his regular clothes and left the dressing room carrying the uniform. He and Tuck found Mattie and Trish at the checkout counter. The store was almost empty. Jake worried that he was going to be the last boy to arrive at the ballpark. Mattie paid fifty cents for the cap and signed a receipt for the uniform, agreeing to return it at the end of the season.

"Did you get socks?" Mr. Welch asked.

"No. Does he have to have special socks, too?" Mattie was bewildered.

"Yes, they come with the uniforms. Jake, go get yourself a pair of red socks; they're all the same size."

Just as Jake was returning to the counter with his socks, Rance and Gray Boy walked into the store. Rance surveyed the situation quickly. He knew they were running out of time. "Have you got cleats to fit him, Mr. Welch?" Rance asked.

Jake's heart jumped.

"What size?"

Jake heard no more of the conversation. He just felt a new pair of cleats slung over his shoulder and his father's hand on his back shoving him out the door. He never knew how the cleats were paid for.

Gray Boy left in the truck, while Jake climbed into the car with his parents, Tuck and Trish. "Why don't you have your uniform on?" Rance asked.

"They didn't have one my size." Jake choked out the answer. He could barely suppress the tears and the resentment he felt toward his parents for not bringing him earlier.

Mattie turned in the front seat. "Put that one back on. I picked up some safety pins from Mr. Welch. He was sold out of belts."

Jake's face brightened a little. A belt? Of course . . . that was the answer. He had not worn a belt since school turned out in the spring. Safety pins? Was he going to have to play with safety pins in his pants? After instructing Trish to turn her head and look out the window, he struggled out of his clothes and into the uniform. Mattie reached across the seat, grabbed the waist, tucked it, and inserted a safety pin. Sensing his distress, she said, "Nobody will ever see that."

Easy for you to say, Jake thought. He took off his shoes and put on the cleats. A little big, but all of his shoes were big at first. He laced them up tight and started to feel like a ballplayer. He looked toward his sister for approval. "Where are your baseball leggings?" Trish asked. Jake took off the cleats and his regular socks, replacing them with the baseball socks. But the baseball socks had no feet, just straps that went up under the elastic in the bottom of his pants. Rance looked back to check his progress and smiled at Jake's predicament.

"The baseball socks go over your regular socks, son."

Jake punched his sister lightly in the back. "Why didn't you tell me before I took off my socks?"

"You're the one who told me not to look. You'll learn someday that I can help you a lot with baseball."

At the ballpark, Jake got out of the car with his glove on. His pants immediately dropped, the top folding over the elastic in the bottom of the legs. He dropped the glove and frantically pulled them up. Rance opened the car trunk and retrieved a rope that he used for starting small engines. He threaded it through Jake's belt loops and tied it in the front.

Rance, Mattie, and Trish stepped back to examine the finished product. His cap looked good and fit good. His uniform top was too large. Mattie folded it into tucks and stuck it back into his pants. The blouse bottom reached almost to his knees, but at least it couldn't be seen. The pants were held up by one safety pin and a small engine rope with grease on it. The worst part, however, was that his regular socks did not come to the top of the baseball socks. Bare legs showed on each side of the leggings. Rance pulled the elastic in the pant legs down below the shorter socks.

"That's the way the old timers wore them, anyway. You look good, son. Get out there."

Tuck smiled at his brother and slapped him on the leg, as if affirming what their father had said. Tuck looked deep into Jake's eyes, and Jake felt better. The parking lot was full as he made his way through the cars and people to reach the field. The lot was lighted only by moonlight, but the baseball diamond stood out in the summer night brighter than the downtown square on Saturday night. Jake had never played under lights before nor on a field with chalk lines or real base bags.

Across the field, he saw his team gathering. As he entered the boundary fences and approached the north dugout, he saw the green stripes and green D's on the Giants' caps. He heard some good-natured teasing from his friends on the Giants as he crossed in front of their dugout in his enemy uniform. All of the boys in his team dugout were bigger than Jake, but Linc Little stood head and shoulders above them all. As Jake joined his team, he was pleased to see Bo Randall, the boy he had met on the first day of tryouts. He had not practiced with them during first practice.

"Hey, Bo. You on our team?" Jake asked.

"Yep," Bo said. "Started out on the Yankees, but they had too many players, so I got traded." The Indians took the field for warm-up.

The first year of Little League baseball in Delta County would have made the founders of Little League proud. A few feet back of the first base line, two large tables had been set up for score-keeping and announcing. Four people sat at the tables, busily poring over score sheets and lineups. Bleachers ran parallel and just behind the first base dugout. Across the road behind the third base dugout, withering corn stalks seemed to be anticipating the game. The stands were full, and people stood along the entire length of the outfield fence.

As the Indians returned to their dugout after warm-up, the loudspeaker started to emit static and crackling before a voice came through. "Ladies and gentlemen, welcome to the first game of Delta County Little League Baseball. My name is Lundy Clark, Jr., and I will be your announcer this evening."

The loudspeaker startled Jake and Bo and set their hearts racing. They removed their caps, placed them over their hearts, and reverently stared at the flag for the playing of the national anthem. Heads were bowed for the opening prayer, but the words did not penetrate.

"The first game this evening will be between the Indians and Giants. Will the home team take the field," Lundy's professional voice boomed through the assemblage. Jake could not believe the quiet that enveloped the ballpark as the Giants took the field.

"Batting first and playing shortstop for the Indians will be Jake Rivers. He has the honor of being the first batter in the first game of Delta County Little League Baseball." Lundy's announcement signaled the start of the game.

Jake knew the game was about to start - knew he was batting first, but the sound of his name over the microphone made him freeze. He had never heard his name over a loudspeaker before. He didn't expect such a large crowd. Standing in the chalk-lined on-deck circle, he continued to swing two bats for warm up. He surveyed the groomed field, with its white chalk lines marking the

64

base lines and boundaries. He couldn't bear to look at the crowd, so he stared at the lights and the bugs of summer that swirled around them. Glancing toward the corn field, the envy he felt toward the small kids darting in and out of the corn rows surprised him. Carefree. No pressure in their play.

The home plate umpire looked at him pointedly and yelled, "Batter up!"

Jake tossed the extra bat to the bat-boy, strode to home plate, and stood stiffly in the batter's box. Muscle memory let him take a couple of awkward practice swings before the first pitch. Nothing felt right about his swings. He was grateful that good friend Robert Don Hooten was pitching. Robert Don was a control pitcher, and most of his balls were down the middle at good, but not blinding speed. Robert Don kicked the rubber on the pitcher's mound. True to form, he threw the first ball down the middle.

"Strike one!" Jake flinched and turned to see the umpire bend and point his right arm down the line toward first base. He had violated his father's teaching already. Never stand and watch a ball down the middle unless you are told to take it by a coach. Get a piece of it. Robert Don smiled at him from the pitcher's mound. Jake started to wave, but thought better of it. For the moment, Robert Don was the enemy.

The next ball was also down the middle. Jake watched it all the way, lunged at the ball, and punched a line drive between short-stop and third base, just where his father had taught him to time his swings.

"A well-hit line drive will be fielded by left-fielder McDonald, and Rivers will be held at first with a stand-up single. Delta County Baseball is underway," announced Lundy Clark, Jr. Jake knew it had not been a well-hit ball. He had jumped at the ball early and had not hit the sweet spot on the barrel of the bat, but he was on with a single.

The Indians loaded the bases in that first inning. When Jake advanced to third, Coach Simpson and Linc Little discussed strategy before Linc stepped into the batter's box. Linc slammed the first pitch twenty feet beyond the left field fence for a grand-slam home run. Without realizing it, Jake had just scored the first run in Delta

County Little League history. The Indians went on to defeat the Giants 9-1. Jake went one for three in batting, but he made contact with the ball each time he was at bat and never struck out. He threw three men out at first, and was the first half of a successful double play. Jake's desire to play on the Giants with most of his friends had subsided. His pants had not fallen down once.

Chapter 9

The Indians continued their winning ways the following Tuesday, shutting out the Yankees 8-0. Jake's spirits soared. At practice on Thursday, Coach Simpson talked to them about the next game with the Dodgers. The Dodgers had a 1-1 win-loss record, defeating the Yankees, but beaten by the Giants.

"I don't want to rattle you, but I also don't want you to go into this next game overconfident," Kirk Simpson began his pep talk. "The Dodgers have a pitcher most of you have not seen yet. I think Linc Little may be the only one on our team who has seen Charlie Wagner pitch. He'll be pitching against us Friday night. You may have noticed the big guy that has been playing first base for the Dodgers."

Jake had noticed that the Dodgers had a couple of really big boys playing, but he was too concerned with his own games to pay much attention. He did know that the Dodgers had shown weak pitching in both of their games.

Coach Simpson clapped his hands to regain their attention. "Charlie throws his pitches very fast and is very accurate. His pitching will be different from anything you have faced yet. Don't let his size or speed rattle you. Just keep your swings level and make contact with the ball. Remember. . .a ball thrown hard will go farther when you hit it."

Jake and Linc Little rode home that day in the back of Harry Cardwell's pickup. Linc knew a lot about Charlie Wagner. Charlie's brother Floyd, just a year out of high school, was already playing for a farm club of the Cleveland Indians. Everyone seemed to think that Charlie was better than his older brother had been at the same age. Charlie was only twelve, but he had already played in many adult and high school baseball games. He had pitched four perfect games in his short career - no runs, no hits, no errors. Not a man had reached first base.

"You worried?" Jake looked to Linc for some encouragement.

"A little. I only played against him once, and he struck me out three times," Linc answered as they piled out of the pickup at Cardwell's store. Jake couldn't imagine anybody striking out Linc Little three times in one game. Jake followed Linc into the store and down the aisles as they both wished for money to buy candy or a coke. The cold wood stove attracted almost as many sitters in the summer as it did when it was putting off needed heat in the winter. A slab of bologna, some crackers, and a slab of cheese rested on a butcher block close to the stove. The board floor had turned a dark red from continuous sweeping with oiled sawdust. Jake stopped to take in the wonderful aroma of pipe tobacco, grape drinks, and bubble gum. Both boys knew where every item they most longed for rested. Jake was relieved to find the new Rawlings glove he had been admiring since it arrived at Cardwell's a month ago. He slowly put his hand inside the glove and brought it to his nose, feeling the softness and inhaling the aroma of new leather. When he noticed the stove sitters watching, Jake returned the glove and headed for the door. Hitchhiking home from Klondike, he concentrated on the terrible Charlie Wagner so much that he forgot to tell the driver where to let him out until they were almost a mile past the driveway. As he retraced the journey down 24, he continued to think about Wagner. If Linc Little could not hit Charlie Wagner, how could the smallest boy on the team expect to? Jake's father had been a good player; his brother was good, but was he? He had only two base hits for six at-bats, and those had both been singles. He had never been tested.

By Friday afternoon, Charlie Wagner had taken on superhuman qualities for Jake. As he walked toward the Indians' dugout, his teammates' eyes were on the pitcher's mound. Bo looked toward Jake, then nodded his head toward the mound, a solemn look on his face. Jake watched a boy taller than his father throwing warm up pitches off the mound. He seemed to be throwing effortlessly, but each pop of the catcher's mitt made the Indian team jump. Every throw was fast, and every throw was over the plate. And this was only warmup.

It suddenly occurred to Jake that his team was first at bat and that he was lead-off man. Considered to be an honor before, batting first now struck terror in his heart. He felt a trickle of sweat run down the middle of his back, and his face grow hot. By game time, he was paralyzed with fear. Coach Simpson walked with him to the on-deck circle. He seemed to know that Jake had little chance against this formidable pitcher.

"Just remember what I told you, Jake. Watch the ball all the way from his hand. Choke up on your bat and don't try to swing hard. Just meet the ball and run like hell when you make contact. If you hit it solid, it will go a long way."

He could hear his teammates shout half-hearted encouragement. "Get a bingle going, Jake. Be a hitter. Watch 'em down, baby."

Even Jake could hear the lack of confidence in his coach's voice. Coach Simpson had seen this guy pitch. Frozen with fear, Jake handed the extra bat he had been swinging in the on-deck circle to the bat-boy and made himself walk into the batter's box. He forced a look at the ominous Charlie Wagner. Charlie was a good-looking fellow. His face showed nothing sinister, just deep confidence. Jake had heard that he could pitch with either hand but didn't believe it. The infield chatter seemed fuzzy and remote in Jake's ears. He could hear the catcher repeat "eeezy out" over and over. Jake made a couple of weak, stiff practice swings, set himself, and prepared to die.

Charlie picked up the resin bag, tossed it around in his hand, dropped it in the dirt beside the mound, kicked the rubber, tucked the ball behind his back away from Jake, leaned forward with his glove hand on his knee, and looked for the catcher's sign. He shook off the first signal, then nodded on the second. His first pitch lived up to Wagner's reputation. Jake tried to follow the ball as it left the pitcher's right hand, but Charlie's arm seemed to begin at short-stop and wind up along the third base line as he delivered the pitch. The ball seemed to be coming directly at him from somewhere in the vicinity of third base. Jake instinctively jumped back, watching the ball come over the inside corner and pop loudly in the catcher's mitt. His face grew even hotter as he heard the umpire shout "steeeee-rike" much louder than necessary. Jake had jumped completely out of the batter's box.

Adding insult to injury, both of the umpire's feet left the ground as he gyrated his body to point his right arm down the first base line. Obviously, the umpire was caught up in the excitement of calling strikes for the famous Charlie Wagner. The big catcher stood up with the ball in his mitt, looked Jake in the eye, spat, and smiled before returning the ball to the assassin on the pitcher's mound. "Fast, ain't he?"he said. Charlie threw two more balls exactly like the first one. Jake took the second one just as he had the first. On the third, he made a feeble swing that went well over the ball.

"Yer' out!" the umpire shouted as he pumped his right hand, thumb up. The catcher had been right. Easy out. The loudspeakers bellowed, "Rivers goes down swinging. Next up and playing third base, Randall."

Jake had never had to hear those words before. He had been out before but never at home plate. He had not struck out in six at-bats in two games. He knew his father and brother were ashamed of him. Bo suffered the same fate, watching three straight strikes come over the plate without lifting the bat from his shoulder. Complacent about it, Bo dragged his bat back to join Jake on the bench. "I don't see how they expect a Little Leaguer to hit a Major League pitch. I heard this guy can pitch 90 miler per hour. They say his brother has reached 100." Jake nodded, figuring that was an exaggeration. Even Bob Feller could pitch only at 100. He just knew that the pitches were faster than anything he had ever seen before. He watched Wagner's confident movements on the mound, watched him keep the ball behind his back, then behind his knee as he went into windup, then behind his glove. The ball seemed to magically appear for a split second as it headed toward the batter at menacing speed.

The third batter managed to tip the ball into the catcher's mitt on the third strike. The inning ended with three up and three down. Only one hitter had even touched the ball. As Jake and his team-

70

mates threw the ball around the horn, Jake was heartened when Linc Little strode to the pitcher's mound. Coach Simpson had been saving his best pitcher for this game, too. Linc delivered the same medicine to the Dodgers that Wagner had delivered to the Indians.

The pitcher's duel continued for five innings with only slight interruptions. Little had let four runners reach first base. Two reached first on errors, one was walked, and the other was hit with a wild pitch. Wagner had not allowed any Indians to reach first base. Linc Little made the lone smudge on Wagner's perfect score-sheet by hitting a strong fly ball to left-center. It was caught by the left-fielder.

In the bottom of the sixth, however, Linc served up a fast ball that was low and outside. It was hit over the right field fence. The batter - Charlie Wagner. He hit the home run standing on the south-paw side of the plate. He might not pitch with both hands, but he sure was a switch- hitter. Dejection showing on his face and in his movements, Linc dropped his glove on the pitcher's mound when he saw the ball clear the fence.

With the score at 1-0 at the top of the seventh, the Indians were back to the top of their batting order. Jake's nervousness had subsided a little. On his second trip to the plate at the top of the fourth, he had made contact with the ball. His swing was weak, but the shortstop had to run backwards to catch it. It almost dropped in for a Texas-leaguer-hit in shallow leftfield. Coach Simpson was right; a ball thrown fast goes farther.

As he headed for the on-deck circle to warm up for his third at-bat, he heard a familiar voice yell, "Show him what you got, Jake. You can hit this guy. He ain't Superman." Jake turned to see Gray Boy and a few of his friends, boys and girls, hanging over the fence just behind the dugout. Still swinging two bats for warm-up, Jake glanced farther down the fence line at the spectators. Just beyond third base, he saw the rest of the Rivers. Mattie and Trish stood with their arms wrapped around themselves, their nervousness showing. Tuck was sitting on his father's shoulders, happily clapping his hands. As his eyes met Jake's, he stopped clapping and smiled. Jake felt almost ready to face Wagner again.

Rance called out, "Hit the first thing he throws, son. He

doesn't think you can hit, so he'll serve one up for you."

The first pitch was just like all the other ones he had been thrown, but this time Jake watched it all the way from Wagner's hand. He knew where it was headed. He swung evenly, but firmly, hearing the satisfying crack that the bat makes when the ball is struck in the sweet spot. The ball went over the pitcher's mound and bounced just past second base. Jake never saw it hit the ground. He rounded first base and was heading for second when Joe Daniels, the first base coach and Simpson's assistant, called him back.

As he stood safely on first, breathing fast and deep to catch up to his racing heart, Jake took a second to look at his family. Gray had both hands in the air and was shouting and swapping licks with his friends. Rance was smiling and holding Tuck's hands as they clapped together. Mattie and Trish hugged each other. Jake tried to remain calm but couldn't keep the smile off his face. He had never had a crowd cheer him like this before. Charlie Wagner's no-hitter was gone.

Joe patted Jake on the butt. "Atta-boy, Jake. Now we're gonna' try to steal second. That may be the only way we can even this thing up. Take a good lead off first and watch for any chance, but wait until I say go before you take off. If this kid's got a weakness, it's his ability to pick runners off first base." Jake took good leads off first with each pitch to Randall. Bo managed to make contact with the ball, but the spinning pop fly was caught by the second baseman. One out. No chance to steal.

Jerry Smithers batted third in the line-up. On his second pitch to Smithers, Wagner finally felt the pressure, throwing a ball into the dirt at the catcher's feet. When the catcher fumbled it, Jake left before Joe could say go. His good slide into second was not required. The catcher knew there was no chance for a play. Buoyed by Wagner's loss of invincibility, Smithers took a good but late cut at the third pitch, hitting a line drive to first base. Two out.

It was fitting that it came down to this - the pitchers' duel ending with the two great players facing each other. Jake was confident that Linc Little, the clean-up man, was going to bring him in. With two outs, Joe gave unnecessary instructions to Jake to run on anything. On the first pitch, Linc drove the ball over the left field fence just outside the foul line. He hit an identical shot on the second pitch. Jake had rounded third before he was called back on each foul ball. Just move it over a little to the right and we will pull ahead, Jake thought. On the third pitch, Wagner served up an unusual curve ball that was outside. The catcher had called for it and was waiting on the right side of the plate. Linc went for it and foul-tipped it into the catcher's glove. Jake died on second. Indian fans let out a collective moan as their hero was pronounced out. The Dodgers went on to beat them 1-0.

Stunned, Jake walked away from the dugout toward the family car when the game ended. How could such happiness turn into gloom in a matter of minutes? His little single could have been a game winner. Now, it amounted to nothing. Still, he had eked out a single against the un-hittable nemesis from Pecan Gap who might play professional baseball someday. As he crossed the field, he saw Charlie Wagner approaching him. Jake was wary, but he looked the big pitcher in the eye. Charlie stuck out his hand to Jake and said, "Nice hit."

Jake managed a smile and a weak, "Thanks, great pitching." Jake had stolen his no-hitter, but Charlie was still nice enough to congratulate him. Just being noticed by Wagner made Jake feel a foot taller. He caught up to the family before they reached the car. Mattie and Trish gave him a big hug and told him what a great job he had done. Even Gray Boy managed a slap on the head and a "Not bad playing out there, whistle-britches." Tuck, of course, was like a faithful puppy, always glad to see him, win or lose.

Jake stared at his father and said, "Yeah, but we lost."

Rance smiled and put his hand on Jake's neck, drawing him close to him as they walked clumsily together. "Bet you can take 'em next time. Now you know that Wagner is not invincible."

When they reached home, Jake sat down on the old wooden sawhorse table outside. He was in no hurry to remove his uniform. The stains and dirt from play were badges of honor. His mother had altered the pants and shirt to fit him. He now had socks long enough to keep his bare legs from showing and was comfortable in the uniform. He didn't want the night to end. When he heard Rance coming out the back door, he assumed it was to tell him to get to bed. Rance, however, seemed to be in no hurry. He sat down on the table beside Jake. They marveled over the speed and accuracy of Charlie Wagner's pitching. "I was lucky to even make contact with the ball, much less get a hit." Jake was fishing for a compliment.

Rance whittled on the twig he had picked up. "I think it was little more than luck, Jaker."

They sat in silence for a few minutes more before Jake asked what he had wanted to since the game. "Do you think I was in the Rivers' flow?"

Rance continued whittling without looking up for so long that Jake was sure he had asked a stupid question. "Only you can know that, Jake. The flow is all about knowing what is going to happen before it happens." Rance answered.

"How will I know for sure?"

Rance turned toward him. By the moonlight, Jake could see into his father's eyes. "Jake, I think you may be worrying too much about it. Maybe I should never have told you those stories."

Jake felt a lump rise in his throat. He kept his head down to conceal the tears that were coming to his eyes.

Rance stood and rubbed his forehead as if he were clearing his head looking for the right words. "Jake, you stole a hit from one of the best Little League pitchers in the state tonight. "That's enough for me. Isn't it enough for you?"

Unable to speak, Jake kept his eyes down and slowly shook his head.

Rance put a hand on Jake's shoulder. "You come on in and get ready for bed in a few minutes."

Jake lay back on the table and looked up at the stars and the moon. Rance had said that experiencing the Rivers' flow was like having God lay His hand on your shoulder. Since God had not whispered into Jake's ear at church or Sunday school, maybe He was keeping him from experiencing the Rivers' flow. Maybe Jake did not deserve special treatment. He woke an hour later, still on the table. When he started to step down and go to bed, he heard his mother's voice drifting through the kitchen window.

"Guess you're going to keep filling him full of the same stories about the flow that you did the older two."

There was a long pause before Rance answered. "He's trying harder than the other kids did, and I think that's why it isn't happening. There's plenty of time, but he wants it now."

"Aren't you forgetting that baseball is supposed to be fun?"

Chapter 10

The second game between the Indians and Dodgers was the talk of the county. The Wagner-Little match-up had made all the local newspapers. When Floyd Wagner advanced from the minor league farm club to play in the major leagues for the Cleveland Indians, sportswriters from Dallas newspapers were rumored to be coming to Cooper to see his little brother play. Reporters had already speculated that Charlie's speed was better than his brother's had been.

Every afternoon just before or just after milking, Rance pitched to Jake. With Gray or Trish catching, Rance steadily increased speed until he was pitching as hard as he could. Jake started to hit a few out into the pasture and to make dents in the smokehouse wall with balls from his bat. On the night of the second meeting between the Indians and Dodgers, Jake stepped in the batter's box to face Wagner again. The tension in the air was palpable, and Jake couldn't chase away the fear. Infield chatter was mostly "batta, batta, batta, eeezy man." Jake looked down to third base where Coach Simpson stood. Simpson touched the bill of his cap with two fingers, the hit-away signal for tonight. Wagner's first pitch was a curve. Determined to hit the first pitch and end his agony, Jake squibbed it off the end of his bat. It dribbled out between the pitcher's mound and first base. Wagner strolled over to pick it up, looked at Jake racing toward first, smiled, and threw him out.

In the fifth inning, with both teams scoreless and a Dodger on first base, Jake ran to second to take a short throw from the second

77

baseman for a double play. He dropped the ball, reached down to get it, and fumbled it. He managed to pick it up in time to tag second, but the throw to first was too late. The field umpire had taken his eyes off Jake when he dropped the ball and didn't see him tag second. Both runners were called safe. The runner at second went on to score the Dodgers' only run. One run was enough. Linc and Charlie had allowed one hit each, but Jake's fumble had cost them the only run of the game. To make the night even worse, Jake was the last batter in the ninth inning. He struck out to end the game.

Dejected, he stood at the plate after striking out, wishing he could have that last swing over. He had been talking to God, asking to be in the Rivers' flow. Tonight, he was anywhere but. The catcher casually tossed the ball out to the pitcher's mound, where it was picked up by the right-fielder returning to the dugout. He threw the ball toward home plate. Out of frustration, Jake stepped across the plate and hit the ball as hard as he could. The angle of his swing hooked the ball over the boundary fence just to the left of third base. As soon as he made contact, Jake knew he had made his third big mistake of the night. The ball was headed in the direction of the cornfield, toward the spectators that were heading for their parked cars or home. Jake stood frozen at the plate for a few seconds, wishing he could take back that swing. He looked around to see if anyone had seen him hit the ball. Nobody seemed to be watching. Maybe he could just drop the bat and walk to the truck. Instead, he ran toward the ball.

Just behind his team's dugout, on the street next to the cornfield, Jake saw a group of Indian uniforms. He slowed his run to a trot, then a slow walk, as he saw Coach Simpson holding the ball he had just hit. Linc Little, Danny Lawler, Fred Choate, Jack Poteet, Billy Whitlock, the biggest and best players on his team, watched Jake approach.

Coach Simpson tossed the ball to Jake. "You hit this ball, Jake?"

Caught off guard, Jake dropped the ball. He answered the question while he was reaching down to pick it up. "Yes, sir."

"Well, it must have been hit like a girl. It bounced right off my windshield. Didn't even crack it."

Jake felt the blood rush to his face as he scanned the faces of his teammates, counting the seconds he had remaining as an Indian. Coach Simpson stepped a little closer to Jake. "I don't know what to say to a boy who does such a stupid thing, so I'm gonna leave it up to your teammates and your daddy." The coach got in the Buick and left.

Linc Little gave Jake a quizzical look. "What about it, Jake?"

Jake shook his head. "I lost the game for us twice tonight. Then I did something else stupid."

Linc nodded and stepped closer to Jake, towering over him. "Did anybody say anything to you about the bungled play on second?"

Jake shook his head.

"Did we say anything when you struck out at the end of the game?"

"Nope."

"Coach says we're a team, so we got to play like a team." Linc turned to his other teammates. "Right, guys?" They all nodded.

"If you plan on hitting any more into the crowd, you should discuss it with us first." Linc turned to walk away, the other players following. As the lights went out on the field, Jake heard him shout. "Be here on time for practice next week, Rivers. We'll work on that double play thing."

Jake's arms hung limply, the ball in one hand, glove on the other, as he watched his teammates walk away. He stood there until he heard his father's stern voice. "Jake, let's go."

They rode home in silence. As the family left the car, Rance called Jake to the smokehouse. Jake braced himself for a razor strap whipping for hitting that ball into the crowd. Rance opened the smokehouse door and motioned Jake inside. Moonlight and starlight filtered through the cracks in the cracked roof, keeping the room from being pitch dark. Jake could see the outline of the razor strap hanging on the wall. Rance leaned against the workbench and motioned for Jake to sit on an old stump used for preparing hog meat to be cured. Jake inhaled the distinct aroma of smoke and curing salt that permeated the wood in the little shack. He could hear his father's breathing and his own. Finally, Rance spoke. "Jake, you did several dumb things tonight. I can tolerate the errors, but I should whip your little ass for putting people's lives in danger with that dumb stunt. You could have killed somebody."

"Yes, sir."

"I should whip you, but I won't because it may be my fault. I don't know how to get you to do it, but I want you to forget about the flow. The flow is a good thing, meant to motivate you and give you extra strength so that you can perform at the peak of your abilities. You're turning it against yourself, playing below your ability and doing stupid things."

Jake stared at the hard dirt floor and said nothing.

"Before you can experience the flow, you have to have confidence. You have to know you're going to catch a ball before it's even hit, know you're going to hit it before it's thrown. That takes confidence and confidence takes practice. Stop pressing it and just enjoy the game."

Chapter 11

As Delta County's first Little League season neared the final game, Charlie Wagner remained undefeated as a pitcher and was batting .418 with six home runs. Linc Little was 1-2 pitching because he had to pitch against Charlie Wagner. He was batting .389 and had seven home runs. It was appropriate for the two biggest and best pitchers and batters to meet in the last game of the season. Little League baseball had changed the whole county, taking people's minds off the drought. On the night of the final game, streamers and colorful posters decorated the stadium and field. Merchants and other business people had purchased advertising on the fences. Recorded organ-baseball music came through the loudspeaker as the crowd started to gather. In the first game, the Giants stopped the Yankees. The Yankees had the youngest team, and the boys were mostly from Cooper. They ended the season without winning a game.

The Indians and Dodgers gathered in opposite dugouts with little of the usual chatter and catcalls across the field. The teams had mutual respect. The Dodgers were the only team to have beaten the Indians, and they had done it twice. Both times, they had needed only one run to back up Charlie Wagner's scoreless pitching.

The Dodgers were designated home team and took the field first. Their infield warm up was quiet as Wagner threw his usual heat into the waiting catcher's mitt. The catcher was almost as big as Wagner and had huge hands, helping him to absorb the impact of Wagner's throws.

As lead-off hitter, Jake stepped into the batter's box to face Charlie Wagner again. He had one hit in six tries against Wagner. Knowing that Jake usually went for the first pitch, Wagner threw him a curve, and Jake let it go outside. He was relieved to hear the umpire grunt "Baw" and hold out his left arm. Jake felt the tension ease with that first pitch. He felt his body limber up as he stepped out of the batter's box to take a couple of practice swings. His teammates had gone from silence to loud chatters of encouragement. "Good eye, Jake. Watch it down, baby. Be a hitter. Let's get a bingle going. You're the man."

Jake took his time, lifting each shoe and using the bat to knock off any accumulated clods that might be lurking in the cleats to trip him up. It was unnecessary, as the field was dry and dusty, but it gave him time to think. He looked at Wagner, waiting patiently on the mound, face expressionless; then he looked down the third base line toward his coach. Coach Simpson pulled his left earlobe, the hit-away signal for tonight. As Jake nodded his head to affirm the signal, he saw Tuck standing just behind the boundary fence near third base. Tuck's small fingers were entwined in the cyclone fence, his eyes smiling at his big brother. A voice echoed in Jake's mind. Just imagine that you are in the driveway at home, and Daddy is pitching to you. The voice sounded like Tuck's, but the words were enunciated clearly.

Jake barely had time to set his feet inside the batter's box before Wagner delivered a fast ball down the middle. Jake recognized the same pitch that had struck him out before, following it all the way from Wagner's hand. He took a good cut; he felt and saw the bat strike the ball in the sweet spot, driving it over the shortstop. Jake had never hit a ball any harder or better. Joe Daniels, the first base coach, was down with his knees bent, his body and his arm pumping and pointing toward second, yelling, "Go, go, go, take second!"

Jake made sure to touch the corner of the base as he rounded first and headed for second. His body leaned far left, making it seem as if his left hand was going to strike the ground as he pumped his arms and dug his cleats into the infield. He followed the progress of the ball as it bounced between center and left field. Unaccustomed to having any balls hit in the outfield when Wagner was pitching, both outfielders were caught off guard and had to chase the ball as it bounced toward the fence. Jake rounded second and headed for third, but he was given a hold-up signal by Coach Simpson standing at third base. He returned to second and caught his breath as he stood on the bag.

His teammates had left the dugout and were on their feet shouting. Half the crowd was on its feet. Most didn't know Jake Rivers, but they knew that Charlie Wagner had been hit. Jake had slammed a stand-up double against the best pitcher in the league.

He took good leads off second as he watched the next two batters go down under Wagner's heat. Both, however, made contact with the ball. The mystique had been broken. As Linc Little stepped up to the plate, the crowd grew quiet again. Everyone in the stadium, especially the adult men, knew that this event was significant. Even in boys' baseball, seeing two great players go head to head in the final game of the season for the championship was something they felt honored to witness. Everyone wanted to be able to say that they saw these two future big league players battle it out before they were famous. Writers from local papers were furiously taking notes. Jake studied Linc's face for signs of tension and saw none. He seemed confident and calm.

The first pitch was high and inside, Linc's weak spot. He let it pass for ball one. The second pitch was a fast ball that didn't exactly curve; it just seemed to come toward the batter, clipping the inside corner at the last split second. Little calmly stepped back and let the ball pass at his knees. Strike one. The third pitch was thrown with all the speed that Wagner could muster, low and inside. Linc probably expected it, because he had positioned his body a little away from the plate. Jake heard the beautiful crack of the bat and watched the ball go over his head as he headed for home.

Linc Little took his time, gently dropping his bat on the baseline as he headed for first. He knew that he could take his time and trot slowly around the bases. The ball went over the fence and into the windshield of a car that was supposed to be parked out of danger from hit balls. Indians two. Dodgers zero.

After eight and one half innings, the score remained the same. If the Indians could hold the Dodgers at their last bat, they would win the game and be the first champions of Delta County baseball. Jake had gone two for three and scored one of the runs. An almost perfect night, if they could hold on to the win.

The Dodgers were at the bottom of their batting order. The Indians thought it was all over. Little retired the first batter. The second batter made contact with a late swing that sent the ball along the first base line past first base. It should have been an easy out, but the first baseman was playing wide of the base and was caught off guard. The batter took a lucky single. The third batter laid an excellent bunt down the third base line. Bo, playing third base, made the throw to first, getting the batter out, but the man on first advanced to second. The game had gone from being a certain win to a possible loss in minutes. The Dodgers were now at the top of their batting order with a man on second.

"The tying run is now at the plate with two out," the loudspeaker crackled with Lundy Clark's voice. With the Dodgers lead-off batter at the plate, the tension was like hot ice on the field and in the stands. Linc Little looked tired. He served up a hard fast ball down the middle of the plate. It was hit over second base to drop in for a single. The center fielder threw to home, trying to stop the runner from second base, but he was too late. The hitter advanced to second when the try was made at home plate. Dodgers one, Indians two. Runner on second. Two out.

Jake felt adrenalin sending messages to every nerve ending. His body tingled with anticipation; his heart beat rapidly in his ears. He tried to take in all the possibilities. The runner on second was taking a big lead and obstructing his view of the boy coming to the plate. He looked around the base runner and saw the big catcher for the Dodgers, Jerry McFadden, a power hitter. Worse, Charlie Wagner was standing in the on-deck circle. How could that be? Charlie had always batted fourth, the cleanup position. The coach must have known that not many batters would get on in this pitching duel and moved him to third in the lineup. Jake had not noticed that until now.

Excitement could be heard in Lundy Clark's voice as it crackled through the speakers. "The tying run is on second, and the winning run is now at the plate.... Wagner on-deck."

Jake was aware that the ballpark had suddenly grown quiet. People were moving their mouths, but no sounds came out. The

84

crowd was on its feet and seemed to be yelling, but he couldn't hear. He found his little brother in the sea of faces, sitting calmly on his mother's lap, his eyes focused on Jake. As blood rushed to his face and ears, Jake felt warm and loose. A comforting pleasant tingle ran up his spine, across his shoulders and down his arms all the way to his fingertips. The hair on his neck stood up. He heard one repeating, soothing sound, the sound that ocean waves make. His breathing was deep and rhythmic, and he felt the cadence of his heart change from fast to slow.

Jake searched the faces of his teammates to see if something had come over them, too. From the pitcher's mound, Linc Little gave him a tired stare and a slight nod. From first base, Billy Whitlock stared directly at Jake, his expression determined. Jack Poteet, the Indians' big catcher, looked at Jake as he crouched behind the plate to take Linc Little's first pitch to Jerry McFadden.

As the huge power hitter stepped to the plate and positioned himself, Jake moved to his right. He seemed to be moving in slow motion, yet his body felt light and alert. His father had taught him to judge where a ball was going to be hit by the batter's stance, history, and swing pattern, but he had never been so certain before. He had traveled all the way behind Bo at third base by the time the ball was hit. McFadden hit a blazing line drive, shoulder high, down the third base line. The ball zoomed past Bo Randall and toward Jake, but it seemed to be moving in slow motion. Jake saw it come over third base, saw the chalk fly from the marked boundary line as the ball touched down behind third.

The flying chalk left no doubt that the ball was fair. It was fair and it was going for extra bases. Jake saw the runner who had been on second rounding third. The game would be tied if he reached home. As Jake expected, the ball had some spin on it and took a sharp turn to the right toward the boundary fence after touching the ground. He reached over with his glove, watching as the ball pushed the pocket to its limit. Calmly removing the ball with his right hand, he felt the seams as he positioned his fingers around the ball, set his feet and body, and threw.

He seemed to float above himself on the field, watching his shoulder, arm, wrist, and hand fully extended, cooperating together in a splendid dance as the ball left his hand. Moving a strong step toward first base with his right foot, he watched the ball leave slowly, then gain speed until it dropped perfectly into the glove of the first baseman. When the ball left his hand, his arm followed through completely and seemed a foot longer as it almost touched the ground. Head down, composed and serene, he strolled back to his position at shortstop as he heard the first base umpire shout, "Yer out!" Jake and Charlie Wagner stared at each other as Charlie walked away from the on-deck circle. This game was over.

Jake began to hear the sounds of the crowd again as his breathing became faster and adrenalin pumped. He realized that his team had won the championship. All of the team members were being congratulated by the coach, shaking hands and patting butts and backs. The loudspeaker announced that the Indians had won the game and the season, with the Dodgers second, Giants third, and Yankees last. Linc Little, Danny Lawler, and Billy Whitlock shook Jake's hand. "Nice catch, nice throw." There was no surprise in their praise, as if they had expected Jake to come through in a clutch situation. Not too much, but just enough.

Lundy Clark turned up the volume on the speaker system. "Folks, don't anybody go home yet. We have tallied the results of the voting for the Delta County All-Star team, and we will announce them in about five minutes." Jake looked at Bo Randall and the other team members. They all seemed as surprised as he was. What all-star team?

Ballots had been distributed among the crowd during the game with blanks for each position on the field. The ballots had been collected and were now being counted. With adrenalin still rushing, Jake and his fellow players thought this just added to the excitement.

Bo nudged closer to Jake and whispered. "Dad said the Cooper Review mentioned something about an all-star team to play other leagues in the area."

Players from all the teams were asked to gather in front of both dugouts while the all-star team was announced. Fifteen players were to be chosen from sixty. Jake looked around for his family and found his father standing alone along the fence beside first base. Jake was in front of the third base dugout, so he could not read the expression on Rance's face.

Players receiving the most votes for each position were called first. They would be the starting line-up for the all star team. The first name called was Charlie Wagner as pitcher. The crowd erupted with applause as he strode to the pitcher's mound As Jake watched Linc Little trot toward first base amid shouts and applause, he felt a ripple of fear enter his stomach and grip his heart. He had to compete at shortstop with three other starters. Was he good enough? The starting shortstop was already standing on the diamond before Jake realized what was about to happen. Being on the championship team was not enough. He wasn't going to make the all-star team at all. He began to feel eyes on him, stares of pity. As the blood rushed to his face, he wished to be somewhere else, anyplace else at all. By the time nine names had been called, four of his teammates had taken their positions on the field, including Bo Randall at third base. Two alternate pitchers were called, then four substitute players completed the fifteen. Jake was not chosen.

When he walked through the gate beside the dugout, he felt two hands on his shoulders. Harry Cardwell turned Jake around to face him. He bent down to look at Jake face to face. Jake didn't want to talk to anyone. He was barely holding back the tears and thought he might burst if Harry said anything at all.

"Jake, I know you're disappointed. I think you should have made that team. If the coaches had been the ones to choose, you would have made it. But we weren't. You just hold your head up. You made the best defensive play tonight that I've seen made all year. Shoot, you just about won that game and the championship for your team."

Jake could not take the chance of saying anything, knowing that any word could break the dam that was building up inside him. The votes were cast before that play was made; he couldn't help but think it. Jake nodded his head as he stared at the ground. He saw his father's brogans walk up and stand beside Harry. When he looked up, the look in his father's eyes caused an involuntary spasm in his throat. He could feel his eyes start to fill.

"Let's go home, son."

The rest of the family had already left for home. They had not been in the stands and did not know about the all-star team selection. Riding home in the truck, Jake was silent and morose. He was grateful that his father seemed to know he could not talk about it, so they both rode home without a word. Jake left the truck as if escaping from a trap. He avoided the back of the house, where he knew his mother would be waiting, ran to the front, through the dog trot, through Trish's room, and into the room he shared with Gray. Thankfully, Gray was not there. He threw off his cap and uniform, crawled into bed, pulled a pillow tightly over his head, and let the water break the dam.

When Jake had no more tears, he continued to heave from suppressed sobs until midnight. As he pulled the pillow from his head, he saw his cap, uniform and cleats lying in a crumpled heap. Strange how the once proud evidence of his athletic ability now served as a rude reminder of just the opposite. He rose from the bed, careful not to wake Gray, and walked into his parents' bedroom. He stood quietly by their bed, in his underwear, barefooted.

Rance was not asleep. "What is it, Son?"

"I was in the Rivers' flow tonight." Jake's voice was solemn. "It's something that kinda comes over you when you least expect it, ain't it?"

Chapter 12

Trish and Gray stepped on the school bus with Jake following a step behind. As he stood on the second step, he stopped, backed down one step, jumped to the ground, and motioned for the bus driver to go on without him. Jake had done it before, and the driver was not inclined to wait until Trish could persuade her brother to board the bus again. He closed the door and drove away. Through the bus window, Trish wagged her finger at Jake, but he ignored her. It was Monday morning after Friday night's all-star team selections, and Jake needed a little more time to consider whether he would ever return to school. He started walking down 24. Maybe he would hitchhike to Oklahoma instead. When people stopped to offer him rides, he explained his preference for walking with white lies.

Klondike held school for six weeks in mid-summer, so that farm kids could be out of school for cotton harvest in late summer and early fall. Jake hated school anyway, and the prospect of facing his friends after failing to make the all-star team made it unbearable. As he drew close to the school, he crossed 24 and hid behind some weeds in the pasture west of school. Squinting east into the morning sun, Klondike schoolchildren still looked like small ants scurrying around an ant bed. Jake heard the first bell sound. The fear of his father's wrath clutched him like an invisible arm and propelled him into a run for the schoolyard, overpowering his urge to run away.

Mrs. Thrasher was not pleased at Jake's late entrance and pointed him to a desk in the rear of the room. Not a good start with his new, stern teacher. The inkwell in the small desk was dyed dark blue from overflows, and the desktop was scarred from many pocket knives. Jake was searching the carvings for names he might know when Mrs. Thrasher made her first announcement. "Will all the Klondike boys who made the Delta County all-star team please stand?" It was going to be a long summer.

Jake stared at the floor while the children gave their heroes a round of applause. He forced himself to think of other things, trying to reach the flow once more. His mother had told him to think of how fortunate he was. His eyes traveled the aisle between desks and studied his classmates' feet. Jake wore last year's gym shoes in spite of the holes in the bottom and sides, but most of the other boys and some of the girls were barefoot. Some of their feet could have used a good washing. He had a dime in his pocket, and his jeans did not have holes. His shirt was faded, but not threadbare like some of the others. Most had better houses than he did, but some fared worse.

***

Jake pulled bolls for other farmers the first few weeks after summer school was out. Cotton was sparse, and a picker had to cover a lot of ground to fill his sack. Jake managed to put back a little money for fall school clothes, but he expected to make most of his cotton money off the bottomland patch. It was late in the season before Rance took him and Gray Boy to the bottom.

Jake sat on his heels, leaning against a truck wheel, as he and Gray Boy watched the sun rise over the mound of dirt that made a semicircle around the bottomland cotton patch. Early morning dew was rising from the weeds growing on the embankment that was supposed to keep this section of bottomland from flooding. Scrub oaks, willows, and locusts stood like silent sentinels on the embankment.

This cotton patch had been the beneficiary of three isolated thunderstorms; one had moistened the ground for planting, one two weeks after the plants emerged, and a third on July 4. The rains came with almost perfect timing. Rain had come with each of Tuck's visits to the field. Soil in the forty-acre patch was black gumbo, highly fertile dirt that could produce a bumper crop of cotton in a good year, sometimes more than a bale per acre. In a county replete with fields of shriveled cotton stalks, this leased patch looked like a bumper crop.

Jake had been pulling bolls since he was six, long enough to develop a healthy dislike for the job, especially for tall cotton. He could occasionally feel a breeze in short cotton on sandy land. In the bottom, air was sparse and heavy. Oxygen seemed absent between the rows of tall cotton stalks. Huge mosquitoes prospered in this humid, still environment, and they attacked any exposed part of the body.

It was already hot and humid this morning. No air stirred in this bottom hollow. Beads of sweat appeared on Jake's and Gray's foreheads and upper lips. They might argue and disagree over a lot of things, but they joined in their dislike of bottomland cotton patches. Rance was walking the rows of cotton, checking to see how many bolls had opened enough to be pulled and how many were still green.

Jake and Gray waited, resigned to their fate. Jake's Rat Terrier, Shy, lay resting on Jake's cotton sack, his big eyes watching and hoping for any opportunity to play fetch or just walk around. The little black and white terrier had been Jake's present for his eleventh birthday a week earlier. His last adopted stray dog, like all the ones before him, was caught killing chickens. Jake was glad to have Shy with him. Timber rattlers and other snakes liked tall cotton. Copperheads were prevalent in the surrounding woods, and water moccasins ventured out of the Blue Bottom. He counted on Shy to warn him and kill any snakes they might encounter.

Rance emerged from the field, several yards away from the row he had entered a half-hour earlier. He pushed his hat back on his head and stood long enough to roll a cigarette. "She's ready, boys. Give it about a half-hour to dry a little more, then start filling those sacks. I'll leave you the water while I go get the cotton trailer and bring you some dinner." Rance unloaded the water cooler from the back of the truck and drove away.

Jake played fetch with Shy until he thought the half-hour was up. Reluctantly, he pulled on his new brown cotton gloves, put his cotton sack strap over his head, and headed to the end of the patch to begin on the first row. After he was a safe distance away, he threw a green boll to wake Gray, who was snoozing on his cotton sack. He did not necessarily want to work beside his brother, but he waited until he arrived to start. Gray Boy squinted as he scanned the cotton patch. "Hell, we'll still be pulling bolls down here at Christmas." Jake was not tall enough to see beyond a few rows, but the patch looked like a thousand acres to him. Gray might have been joking, but Christmas seemed optimistic.

Jake encouraged Shy to sit on his cotton sack at first, but had to shoo him off as the sack grew heavy with cotton bolls. Jake and Gray were almost at the end of the return row when they filled their sacks. Without a trailer to empty them into, they left them in the field and were returning to the shade tree when they saw their truck, cotton trailer behind, pull into the patch. Jake's spirits lifted when he saw his mother and Tuck in the front seat with Rance. A car pulled in behind the truck.

Jake smiled as he looked at Gray Boy. "That's Uncle Seth and Aunt Tillie's car, ain't it?"

Gray nodded his head and laughed. "Looks like Shep is gettin' to use his new steering wheel knob." Jake watched Shep back the old Chevy under the shade of a tree using exaggerated turns of the red, shiny knob. Seth, Tillie and Brenda piled out of the car as Jake broke into a trot to welcome his aunt, uncle and cousins. He felt a hand on his shoulder as he came around the truck.

"You ain't gon' speak?"

Jake recognized the familiar voice of Runkin Slater, a colored man from Klondike who had helped them clear this cotton patch of stumps and pulled bolls with them every year. "Hey, Runkin. Didn't see you. Where did you come from?"

Runkin flashed a white, full-toothed smile and pointed to the bed of the truck. "Sat up next to the cab to keep down the dust."

"You helpin' us pull this patch?"

"Naw. I just gon' sit under the trailer and weigh yo' sacks when you brings 'um in. Much cotton as you pick, that keep a old man like myself busy 'nuff."

"No, you ain't, either. Gray says we might be here till Christmas without any help."

Tillie's voice interrupted their teasing. "Y'all come on to dinner. Rance says there might be as many as forty bales here, so we don't want to attack it on an empty stomach."

Jake had expected to eat a cold bologna sandwich for lunch, so his mood was lifted even further when he saw what Mattie and Tillie had spread on a quilt under the shade of the cotton trailer. A platter of Tillie's cold biscuits, a gallon jug of Mattie's cold red beans, three purple onions, two pans of fresh cornbread, and two mince meat pies made his mouth water. They sat cross-legged around the quilt and passed around the food.

Mattie made her way around the circle, pouring iced tea into glasses for everyone. "Don't expect to eat this good every day, folks. Tillie and I are going to be pulling bolls, too, you know."

Jake watched his mother and her sister as he and Brenda helped with Tuck's plate. Reflecting a lifetime of shared experiences, Mattie and Tillie worked comfortably together, making sure everyone had a plateful of food and a glass full of tea. Jake listened a little as Rance discussed the cotton patch and cotton prices with brother Seth, wondering if he would ever have such comfort and closeness with Gray Boy. Seth and Rance bore strong resemblances to each other and to Papa Griff. To Jake, Gray Boy looked like all of them. Jake wished he did, too.

Gray Boy and Shep sat a few feet back of the circle, giggling about some shared story. Jake was startled when he heard Runkin speak his name. "Mistah Jake, how long you figure it gon' take to pull this patch?" Runkin winked at Rance.

Jake was embarrassed because he had no idea. "Gray Boy says it might have taken just me and him till Christmas. As much cotton as you can pull, I expect we'll be done in a week."

Rance laughed. "With the Rivers family pullin' together, no telling how quick we can get this cotton to the gin. We just about got the whole clan here. All the hard-workin' ones, anyway. Trish would be here if she wasn't working in that cafe."

Seth put his hand on Runkin's shoulder. "Well, Runkin, I guess if these Rivers are so hard workin', you might as well go on home. We probably won't need you."

Rance shook his head. "Heck, Runkin is a Rivers, too. Shoot, he's worked around us so long, he's just about inducted. I think he's even startin' to turn white."

Runkin rose slowly, shaking his head. "Nosuh. Just tother way around. I thinks you folks turning my color. Not as far to go, you see."

Mattie walked away from the group and motioned for Jake and Gray to follow.

"Do you boys understand how important this crop is to us? Without it, we don't make it."

Gray and Jake nodded.

Mattie touched each of them with her finger. "Your daddy might not say it, but I will. Without water, we will lose the dairy. This is the only thing we have going for us. We'll go down without this cotton, so I want no horseplay, and I want you both to be serious whether your daddy is here, gone to the gin, or milking. Understand?"

It did not take until Christmas to harvest the bottomland patch. Jake and Rance pulled away from the patch with the fortieth and final bale from the small patch less than three weeks from that first dinner-on-the-ground. Jake fidgeted with excitement as he thought about the end of cotton picking, the buying of fall clothes, and the World Series. The Cleveland Indians had knocked off the Yankees to win the 1954 American League Pennant but were down three games to none in the World Series against the New York Giants.

It was traditional that Rance and Jake would listen to at least one World Series game on the radio each year. Because of the cotton harvest and an early start for the Series, they had been unable to listen to their favorite team's chance at the world title. Jake knew that the fourth and possibly final game was to be played today in Cleveland.

Jake wondered if his father had forgotten today's game. "You think the Indians can pull it out?"

Rance shook his head. "I think it's all over but the shoutin'. Even if they win today, they'll have to win two at the Polo Grounds in New York to take the Series."

As they entered the gin office, Jake heard the sounds of a

baseball organ and a baseball broadcast. He followed the sounds, expecting a radio, but found a television instead. He had seen televisions before, but never watched a baseball game on one, much less the World Series. The gin manager, Bill Whitworth, winked at Rance. "You boys pull up a chair. The Indians are already down three to nothing, and it's the top of the fourth. Bob Lemon hasn't got his stuff today." Caught up in the magic of seeing players actually move that he had only seen before on baseball cards, Jake paid little attention to the score until the TV announcer proclaimed the Giants' sweep of the series by winning the final game 10-6.

On the way home, Jake sat on the front seat of the truck, balancing a Coke and a Snickers bar. Rance took the last bite from his peanut pattie and touched the check in the bib of his overalls. "Might as well go on to Enloe and give this to the bank before I get too fond of it."

Jake took a sip of his Coke, keeping his eyes on the road ahead. "All of it?"

"Most of it, but not all. The grocery stores and feed store will get the rest." Rance took his eyes off the road long enough to see that Jake's expression had turned grim. "Oh, it's not that bad. Lots of people around here didn't take a single bale to the gin. They won't make a dent in their notes at the bank, much less pay off grocery or feed bills. We're lucky we got those rains when we did. That little cotton patch will carry us through till the drought is over."

Chapter 13

They blew smoke rings with their breath as the bus slowed to a stop on the shoulder of 24 on the first day of the real school year. The school bus passed the Rivers' house twice each day, empty on its first pass and full of kids on the return trip. Trish and Gray Boy decided to make the full route on the first day back. Jake reluctantly stood beside them, dreading school, wishing he could stay home and play with Tuck, who stood on the front porch waving.

Jake entered the bus wearing everything new except his coat, clothes paid for with money he had earned pulling bolls. None of his friends were on the bus yet, so he sat in an empty seat to watch students board. Some kids picked up along the bus route were cheerful, laughing as they renewed old friendships. Some were defiant and surly; some were afraid; some smelled of bacon grease and hair oil; some of fresh soap. The Applegates lived along the bus route in a shack that was worse than the Rivers' home. They usually smelled of a combination of wood smoke, fried sausage, and grease guns. The mean kids, the bullies, seemed to smell of cold bologna. Jake imagined their homes never warmed, even with wood smoke, with no hot meals.

Most of the kids who rode the bus were as poor as the Rivers, but poverty seemed to affect some families more. Some kids were threadbare. Some were still barefooted and many wore clothes that could not keep them warm on this crisp day. Few had coats as good as the hand-me-down Jake wore. He had not seen any of those kids in the cotton patch. Did they not pull bolls for their clothes as he did, or did their money have to go for food?

As they stepped from the school bus into the Klondike schoolyard, Jake's eyes turned toward the gym. Although he was thirty yards away, he could feel the tradition surrounding that old gym, smell the hardwood floor, new rubber from shoes, basketball leather, dust, and locker room sweat. He could hear the squeak of new tennis shoes and the roar of the crowds. He could see his team's picture hanging in the school halls, see their names on the trophies inside the trophy case. He had heard his parents recite from memory the names of championship teams and their players from as long as forty years back. These players became community legends. Trish, Gray, and Jake all wanted their place in that history. Gray wandered away with Shep, and Jake followed his sister into the schoolhouse. As she did at the beginning of every school year, Trish stopped at the trophy case in the front hall.

Jake read the names and the years on the trophies, trying to recall the stories his parents had told about each team or player. "There's your team and your trophies." The girls' team had won district and bi-district last year and the trophies were displayed in the front. Beside them, Trish's name was engraved on her personal all-district trophy and the tournament MVP ribbon hung from the small statuette.

"Yep. We'll put another one in there this year. State championship this time, Rivers' flow willing." She gave Jake a firm punch on the arm and walked down the hall to the Senior room for class. Jake headed in the opposite direction toward Mrs. Thrasher's room, thinking about the flow, but glad that basketball would be taking the place of baseball.

When Jake returned home from school, a feather bed was set up in the dog trot. Mattie was making it up as Jake entered the front door. "What do you think, Jake? This will be yours and Tuck's room. Your aunt Lilas gave me the bed." Tuck smiled at his brother through the iron railings at the head of the bed.

"What do you think about it, Tuck?" Jake plopped down on the feather mattress. Tuck copied his brother and plopped beside him. Staring at the ceiling, he said "Good."

Jake was happy to change roles and be the big brother. Mattie and Rance feared that Tuck might be reluctant to leave their bedroom, but he welcomed the chance to sleep with his brother. Jake no longer had to worry about touching Gray as they slept. Tuck liked to snuggle on cold nights. Jake could feel himself grow and become wise as Tuck peppered him with questions every night until they drifted off. Jake was determined to give him the patience he had always wanted, but never received, from Gray Boy.

All the Klondike basketball teams, including Jake's, seemed destined to win district championships as the end of the year drew near. Gifts were never abundant at Christmas, and Jake was worried that the drought might take them away completely this year. Just after Thanksgiving, Mattie began cautioning the children not to expect much from Santa Claus. When Jake was younger, he never understood how Santa Claus, the very essence of abundance and generosity, could come up short some years. What caused the shortage? Why did it seem to happen with some of his friends and not with others? Mattie explained it away with some vague reference to poor children in foreign countries. "So don't be greedy and expect too much," she would say.

Rance loved Christmas as much as the children and had cultivated gift exchange to an art form that lasted most of December. Mattie did the "basic" shopping, but Rance always came in two or three weeks before Christmas with his own gifts. They were wrapped in unique ways with strange things like old newspaper and baling wire or twine. Mattie and the children had learned that the size or weight of the package was not a clue as to its contents. Everyone in the family knew the routine and looked forward to it. Rance always waited patiently for the time when everyone was together around the stove in the living room before bringing in a present for examination.

They listened to Fibber McGee and Molly, Dr. Sixgun, Amos and Andy, or Gunsmoke on the radio while the present was discussed. The parade of stories and riddles was continued every couple of days until Christmas Eve. The riddles were repeated every night as the family sat around the Christmas tree and the wood stove. Rance's excitement with the process was exceeded only by the children's. He knew how to raise their curiosity to a fever pitch over a single gift.

Early Christmas Eve morning, a blue norther rumbled in and

dropped the temperature from the sixties to the twenties. With the wind blowing in gusts up to thirty miles per hour, it felt like it was zero in the drafty house. The house faced due north, and Jake and Tuck's bed looked toward the front door. The dog trot where they slept was designed to attract breezes. All well and good for the summer, but not for the winter.

Jake woke shivering. "You froze yet, Tuck?" Tuck had drawn himself into a ball and tried to bury himself under Jake. The tattered remains of wallpaper and the cheesecloth backing that clung tenaciously to the pine board walls struggled against the north wind. The front door had blown open with the first gust from the norther, and Jake could see dark clouds rolling in from the north like an approaching freight train.

Still in his underwear, he ran to the door and shoved it against the jamb. Either the door or the jamb had warped too much for it to completely close, so he shoved a big chair against it. Shivering, he watched through the glass in the door as the blue clouds approached. Maybe that was why they called it a blue norther. Gray had told him it was because people turned blue from the cold. He dug Tuck out from the light covers and led him to the kerosene cook stove in the kitchen. Mattie was not in her usual place by the stove, so they huddled against it in their underwear and waited.

Mattie arrived, carrying quilts. "I couldn't find you two. Are you about to freeze to death? We weren't expecting this norther, or I would have piled on some more covers for you last night." She wrapped them both in one of her quilts.

Jake could hear the cows bawling. He looked out the kitchen window and saw the light from the dairy barn.

Mattie sensed the question Jake was reluctant to ask. "Daddy decided not to wake you this morning with the cold and all. He said you could clean up the barn and lot a little later. If you clean them real good today, you can have the whole day off tomorrow." Music to Jake's cold ears. He went back into the cold dog run to retrieve some clothes for himself and Tuck.

The wind and cold increased during the day, driving temperatures into the teens, with the wind making it seem even colder. As she had in years past, Mattie draped cotton rope through the quilt-

100

ing rings in the ceiling and pulled it through some hooks along the wall. The rope was strung to make a circle around the wood stove. With Trish and Jake's help, she hung sheets, ragged quilts, and blankets across the rope, trying to capture the heat in a smaller area of the room and block out the wind. She made sure that the Christmas tree was inside the temporary cloth wall.

Jake got in extra wood for the stove from the pile by the smokehouse and put it on the front porch. As he brought his last armload to place beside the wood stove, Mattie smiled and said, "The radio says it might snow. We may have a white Christmas." Jake had never seen a white Christmas. He had seen snow only once before and it had been just a light sprinkling.

Gray Boy and Rance returned from milking with faces and eyes red from the wind and cold, but in festive moods. The cold and the promise of snow pulled the Rivers closer. This was the best day of the year. They had to put out extra hay for the cattle later and do the afternoon milking, but no more work than that. Dairy inspectors were not likely to come on Christmas Eve or Christmas Day, so they could relax a little bit on cleanup chores. They washed up and sat down to enjoy hot buttered biscuits, oatmeal, eggs, and a special treat of ham with red-eye gravy. The Rivers children ate hearty breakfasts, but their minds were on the presents waiting under the tree. They teased Tuck with Santa Claus sightings. All the children looked forward to opening their own gifts, but especially wanted to see Tuck open his.

The unexpected cold weather kept everyone busy during the day. Mattie tried to plug as many cracks in the old house with rags as she could. Rance wrapped water pipes at the barn and cut off the water at the house after Mattie had filled every container that would hold water. Jake cleaned the barn and lots and helped Rance, Gray and Griffin put out extra hay for the cattle. Rance maintained a happy countenance, but Jake sensed his worry about the cold and its effect on the cattle. Being out in the wind and cold made Jake feel a sense of closeness and equality with his father, brother and grandfather.

Mattie insisted on baths for everyone before supper and gift exchange. She had saved enough water to warm several teakettles and pots on the stove and had two washtubs ready. One was placed in Trish's bedroom for the girls and one in Gray's for the boys. Nobody complained about having to share bath water or argued about who went first. Steam rose off the warm water into the cold rooms. Tuck took his bath in the kitchen sink because the room was warm.

Mattie fried some ham and fresh pork tenderloin for sandwiches made with skillet toast. She also had mincemeat, coconut, pineapple, and chocolate pies ready. Tuck sat on the counter as she rolled the dough for fried apricot pies, Gray Boy's favorite. He came into the kitchen first, fresh from his bath and dressed in faded, soft Levis and a green shirt too faded for school. He put his chin on his mother's shoulder and watched her as she closed the dough over the apricot filling. As Jake came in from his bath, Mattie was protesting, but laughing, as Gray Boy picked her up and swung her around the room.

Rance started a pot of cowboy coffee as they heard the familiar sounds of Griffin scraping his boots on the porch before coming inside. Jake relished the sight and smell of the chocolate and mincemeat pies blending with the aroma of fresh coffee. He was dressed in a favorite soft red corduroy shirt that had faded to pink. The boys had already started building their fresh pork sandwiches when Trish entered, wearing a red sweater with a green scarf. Instead of her usual ponytail, she wore her hair down. She flushed as Jake and Gray stared.

Everyone helped Mattie and Trish clean up the kitchen while Rance stoked up the fire in the wood stove in the living room. For this cold night, the wood stove was not enough, so the Dearborn butane stove hissed only a few feet away. The wind came defiantly through the cracks in the walls, announcing its presence with loud whistles and stirring of the quilts Mattie had draped around the room. The hanging quilts forced the wind to slow down and creep under, but even the foil icicles on the Christmas tree waved in the breeze that was only partially slowed by the pine and fabric walls. On the couch, Jake and Tuck kept their feet folded under them and off the cold floor while Gray Boy and Trish backed up to the stoves. The cold outside and the sound of the wind entering the house did not chill the Christmas spirit. Jake felt that the whistle of the wind made the room seem even cozier. It was the best Christmas the Rivers would ever have.

Chapter 14

Jake sneaked out of bed to avoid waking Tuck, pulled the quilts snugly around his little brother, and walked into the living room. His clothes lay by the fire where he had left them the night before. Sitting on his mother's Christmas-present rocking chair, he pulled the clothes on, enjoying their warmth. No sound came from the kitchen, so he assumed his mother was making beds. He rocked in the chair a few minutes and looked at the spot where the Christmas tree had been. Dragging the dry and brittle little cedar behind Scar the day after Christmas, Jake contrasted the joy of cutting and dragging the tree to the house with the sadness of taking it back.

He walked into the kitchen, trying to recapture the Christmas spirit through the sights and smells of holiday food. The meringue on the pies was turning a little sugary and sticky; the mincemeat was cold. Life was returning to normal. Jake's melancholy mood grew darker as he thought of returning to school. Why did he dread it so? Why was he in constant fear of failing and getting into trouble at school? Tuck walked into the living room wearing his Christmas flannel pajamas with little cowboys and Indians running up and down the legs and sleeves. Without speaking, he crawled into the chair beside Jake.

When their father came into the house from the dairy barn, Jake and Tuck were working on the shards from the Christmas morning peppermint stick. Rance took off his hat and sprinkled snow from the hat's brim onto their bare heads. "Is that snow?" Jake asked. He and Tuck ran to the window and saw light snow falling. Jake ran outside in his shirt sleeves, Tuck close behind, still barefoot and pajama-clad.

Rance whistled to get their attention. "Hey, get back in here. Don't you boys have sense enough to put on clothes before you go out in the snow?" Mattie returned from making beds and layered Jake and Tuck with clothes and galoshes before sending them back out to play. She had to bribe them with cinnamon toast and snow ice cream to get them to come back in for breakfast. By afternoon, the strong north wind had pushed the snow into drifts tall enough for Jake and Tuck to build tunnels. Mattie found them in a tunnel when it was time to milk that afternoon.

"Is the drought over?" Jake asked his mother.

"Not by a long shot. It looks like a lot of snow because of the drifts caused by high wind, but we really haven't had much moisture."

The snow made milking almost fun. Cows came into the barn with snow on their backs and tails, a sight that Jake had never seen. As the last cow left the dairy parlor, Rance smiled and rubbed his hands together. "You boys want some Dutch oven biscuits cooked on the wood stove?" Jake felt good all over when his father showed such high spirits. The presents were opened, the tree was gone, but eating buttered biscuits together in the living room was consolation, somehow. Life could be good, even with Christmas over and school starting soon.

Bright sun and a clear sky greeted Jake and Tuck the next morning as they stepped out on the porch to take it all in. The sun made the snow sparkle. As they stood out in the road and stared up at the house where they had lived all of their lives, Jake began to see what his father saw in their house with no paint. The snow had given it a white roof, at least, and changed it into something strangely beautiful. More impressive than the drifts, the house, or the sparkle, was the quiet. Tuck tugged on Jake's hand. "Listen." Tuck's big eyes and small body made a slow circle, trying to take in the spectacle that nature had created. Jake stopped his snow play and listened. Why did the snow make things so quiet? It was dark when Mattie made them come inside for supper.

When Jake walked into the living room from his morning chores the next morning, Tuck lay on a quilt pallet by the wood <u>stove. He had awakened during the night coughing and Mattie had</u>

taken him into her room. Tuck smiled at Jake, but seemed reluctant to talk, so Jake trudged back to the dogtrot to prepare for school. He looked out the glass in the north door as he pulled on his school clothes. Wind whistled at the other end of the dog trot. He knew it was a warm wind and it was melting the snow fast.

Drops from the house ceiling had turned into steady streams in every room as the rooftop snow melted. With no rain, Jake had almost forgotten how much the roof leaked. Mattie seemed to know in advance where the leaks would be and had placed pots and pans to catch the water. The serenade from the splattering water inside contrasted with the clear skies and sunshine outside.

Dressed for school, Jake returned to the living room. Mattie rocked in her new Christmas chair and stared at Tuck on the quilt pallet. Bills from Christmas lay on her lap. She seemed lost in her thoughts and did not acknowledge Jake when he plopped down on the divan. The house had a mildewy smell that seemed familiar to Jake, but he did not know why. The water dropping against metal pots and pans or splashing into almost full receptacles and the creaks of his mother's rocking made Jake's mood even darker. He pictured God laughing as He made them dodge water on the inside while they prayed for rain outside.

Rance returned from the morning milking and looked at Tuck's flushed face and touched his forehead. The odor of Vicks salve filled the room. Mattie patted Tuck's chest and motioned for Rance to follow her out of the room. The children all moved closer as Mattie whispered to Rance. "I'm afraid he's really sick. He doesn't usually willingly lie down like this. His little throat is sore and he has a fever."

Rance ran his fingers through his hair. "Have you given him anything?"

"Paregoric and baby aspirin are all I have in the house. Even the sally rag didn't seem to do any good last night."

Rance nodded. "He seems too listless for just a sore throat. He's not even talking, and he's always got something to say." He walked to the doorway and stared in at his son. "I just lack a little in the barn. I'll be back in a few minutes and we'll take him to Dr Olen."

Gray Boy and Trish had already started down the road to meet the school bus when Jake walked over to say goodbye to his little brother. He noticed a red rash on his neck. "Mama, come look at this." Mattie opened Tuck's pajamas. The rash had spread to his chest. Jake rubbed his hand across Tuck's chest. "Feels sort of like sandpaper."

Mattie put her hand on Tuck's head. "I'll crank the Ford and turn on the heater. Go tell your daddy to hurry. We're taking this boy to the doctor."

"Can't I go with Tuck and see how he is?" Jake was ashamed as he heard the whine in his own voice.

Rance entered the room and pointed his hand toward the road. "You know better. Go on to school. Tuck will be fine."

As he and his friends stood in line at the school cafeteria, Jake confided that his little brother was sick. As he described the symptoms, someone mentioned polio. Jake left the line, walked out of the cafeteria without opening his sack lunch, crossed the barbed wire fence in the pasture across the road, ducked down in the weeds, and ran for home.

The wind had shifted again and the sky was gray. It had been warm when he left the house this morning, so he had only a blue jean jacket for warmth. The north wind took his breath as he broke out of the weeds and ran down the highway toward home. As he left 24's shoulder to enter the driveway, he slowed his run to a walk. The Ford was still gone. He knew that nobody was home the minute he stepped onto the back porch. The house was cold. Breakfast dishes remained on the table and in the sink. The beds were not made. He found no note from his father or his mother.

Changing into work clothes, he put a bridle on Scar and rode him toward Blue Bottom Creek. He had all the diary cows in the lot, ready for milking, when Gray Boy and Trish returned from school. He did not mention that he had left early and they did not either. A light mist was falling, and ice was forming on the fence lines when he and Gray left the dairy barn after milking. Jake was pleased to see the Ford in the driveway.

"How long you been here?" Jake spoke to his father, but looked toward the living room for his mother and little brother.

Rance was at the kitchen table, sipping a cup of coffee. "Just sat down. I'm much obliged to you boys for milking. Everything go all right?"

"Yes sir." Jake and Gray both answered.

Gray looked outside. "Looks like we're gettin' some ice. May be tough milking in the mornin'."

Jake sat down, put both hands on the table, and tried to study his father's sad, tired face. He finally blurted out the question. "Where's Mama and Tuck?"

Rance ran a hand through his coarse hair before reaching out to stop Jake's hands from bouncing on the table. Jake was afraid his father was going to cry. Rance looked at each of their faces before swallowing and speaking. "They're both still at Dr. Olen's."

Before his father could go on, Jake heard his own whispered voice. "Why?"

"Tuck is pretty sick. Dr. Olen says he has scarlet fever." None of the children knew what scarlet fever was, but it did not sound as terrible as polio, so there was a collective release of tension. "Jake, you know that red rash you found? That's a sign of scarlet fever. It used to be real bad, but Doc says he can fix Tuck right up with penicillin." The release of their held breaths filled the room. Nobody wanted to hear more. If Dr. Olen said Tuck was going to be alright, then he was.

In an hour, Trish had warmed up some left-over red beans and fried some potatoes, her specialty. Jake was disappointed to find no cornbread, but the Ideal light bread was fresh and almost as good. When the meal was over and dishes washed, Rance stoked up the wood stove in the living room and lighted the Dearborn. Trish did her homework, and Jake pretended to read a book, hoping his father would not notice that he had no homework. Trish had promised not to tell about his skipping school and Jake was armed with too many stories about Gray for him to tell.

As bedtime neared, Rance shifted in his chair. He seemed ill at ease without Mattie to announce bedtime. "About time for bed. Tomorrow, Dr. Olen wants me to bring all of you in for shots and examinations. What Tuck has is a little contagious."

They all stared at each other until Rance continued. "We'll

109

leave just after milking in the morning." Jake felt comforted and went happily to bed. Tuck was going to be all right, and his day of reckoning for skipping school was going to be delayed. Maybe it would be forgotten by the time he had to return.

The house always made lots of creaking noises, but Jake was awakened several times with unusually loud popping and cracking during the night. Rance called him at 4 a.m. "Get up, Son. We had an ice storm overnight and we need to get started milking."

Jake looked out the window and saw a sheet of silver and icicles hanging from the porch. As he stepped off the back porch, his feet went out from under him, and he fell flat on his back into the yard. Gray Boy had been watching and waiting from a few feet away. Jake could hear him laughing as he landed. Sleet began falling as they milked. The barbed wire fences around the cow lots had changed from rust to a glistening silver. Tree limbs were bending under the weight of the ice and a limb from the chinaberry tree scraped the top of the Ford as they left for the hospital.

In Cooper, Jake was comforted when he saw Dr. Olen's new 1955 Ford sitting just outside the hospital. The doctor looked down their throats, listened to their chests, and gave them all shots before allowing them to go upstairs to visit Tuck. Trish and Gray Boy went directly to Mattie for a hug, but Jake was drawn to Tuck. As they gathered at the side of Tuck's bed, they tried to say something cheerful, but were awkward. Tuck opened his eyes and smiled at them, tried to move his mouth to say something, but his swollen tongue allowed only unintelligible sounds. His appearance, especially the swollen tongue, frightened Jake. He felt the sense of confidence that Tuck had always given him ebbing away. Even though Jake had always done most of the talking in their many conversations, he now realized that Tuck had really inspired most of what was said. Jake reached out and touched Tuck's arm. Mattie made a signal not to get too close.

"I miss my bed partner. I need you home. You get better and get out of this old hospital," Jake whispered. He moved back and turned his face away.

Gray Boy stepped up closer to Tuck. "When you get home, Jake and I will play with you more together and we won't fight...

it'll be just like you always wanted."

As Gray stepped back to join Jake, Trish, already crying, looked at her parents before stepping closer. Mattie encouraged her with a nod. Trish couldn't keep her voice from breaking. "I miss my little sweetheart. I'm sorry your throat hurts. If I could take that sore throat on myself, I would. You're going to feel better soon, though. Dr. Olen will see to that."

The three of them walked down the hall where Trish's weeping intensified into sobs. Seeing her cry, Jake looked to Gray for strength, but found his brother's eyes watery and the corners of his mouth drooping. Mattie caught up with them before they reached the stairway. "You have to be strong for Tuck. Dr. Olen thinks he will be all right. I want each of you to say a prayer for him, though. Can you take care of yourselves while Daddy and I stay with Tuck?" They all nodded. "Trish and Gray, I'm counting on you to look out for Jake."

"We will, Mama. Do you want us to wait in the waiting room?" Gray asked.

"You can go outside as long as you're not gone more than thirty minutes. We might need you, and we don't want to have to look for you. Tell you what, it's not long till dinnertime. Go on down to Welch's and get some hamburgers." Mattie reached into the pocket of her dress and handed them a dollar.

Having a simple duty to perform and hearing instructions from their mother brought some degree of normalcy to them that was comforting. The streets and sidewalks of Cooper were still mostly covered with ice and sleet, and Jake could not suppress a sense of excitement as they walked the block downtown to Welch's. As he sat with Gray Boy and Trish at the lunch counter, he felt a different kind of bond than before . . . a bond of shared worry and pain. Although their parents were only a few yards away and their mission was simple, he felt a deeper sense of maturity and responsibility. Jake was included in their conversation, almost as an equal. It lessened the worry about Tuck.

After finishing their burgers and Cokes at the counter, they returned to the hospital with a sack containing two hamburgers and two Cokes. Grease had already streaked the sides of the paper sack by the time they entered the hospital waiting room. The sack's contents greeted the other waiting patients with the delicious aroma of hamburgers and fried onions. Jake and Gray started up the stairs with the sacks when Trish stopped them. "Better let me go up there and tell Daddy and Mama that the food is here. You know how Tuck likes hamburgers, and he won't be able to eat one."

Mattie came down first to have her dinner in the waiting room. Jake stared at his mother, wanting to be strong, but could think of nothing to say. Trish broke the silence. "Did you have breakfast?"

Mattie shook her head and seemed afraid to speak. She sank into the closest chair.

Trish tried again. "I saw the roll-away bed in Tuck's room. Did you get any sleep?"

Mattie shook her head again. "I catnapped in the chair. Couldn't seem to make myself lie down." She jumped suddenly out of the chair and opened her arms to Trish. Weeping, they all circled Mattie and hugged. Jake was frightened. He had never seen Gray Boy cry before.

Again, Trish broke the silence and snuffed back the tears. "Your food is getting cold, Mama." Fear and worry evident in her eyes, Mattie returned to the chair. Weariness was reflected in her slow motions as she nibbled at the hamburger. Gray took her Coke to the opener behind the receptionist's counter and removed the cap. She finished less than half of the burger but drank all of the Coke. The children stared and worried. They looked to her for consolation, but saw that she needed comforting more than they did. Few words passed between them before she trudged back up the stairs.

A few minutes later, Rance came down and sat in one of the low gray chairs in the waiting room. All of the waiting room furniture had little padding and sat very low to the floor. Even Jake's knees reached higher than his seat. The children sat on a matching gray divan and watched as Rance reached into the sack for his burger. Jake knew that his father had never really cared for hamburgers. He opened Rance's Coke and set it on the table beside his chair. Rance did not appear to notice. As he was wont to do at mealtimes when he was troubled, he drummed his fingers on the arms of the chair, staring at the floor with dazed eyes.

He looked up to see his children watching him. "I hate this damn furniture. I told Doc that if a man wasn't sick when he walked in here, this furniture would probably kill him." Any other time, this would have brought a smile to Rance's lips, and they would have all laughed, but not today. He walked slowly back through the waiting room door and up the stairs, leaving most of his burger untouched.

Left alone, the children leafed through the outdated magazines. Bored to the point of torture, Jake wandered down the hall, past the examining rooms and Dr. Olen's office. Emboldened when nobody noticed his presence, he started opening doors and peering inside. He was reasonably familiar with the hospital. Dr. Olen's son, Jeff had taken him on guided tours of the backrooms after scrub baseball games, but never into the north end of the old building. Without knowing where he was, he wandered into the colored waiting room. It was furnished just like the waiting room Rance had complained about except the furniture seemed to show a little more wear and tear.

Jake was startled to see Runkin Slator sitting in one of the low, hard, gray chairs. Runkin showed no surprise at Jake's presence. Jake felt like an intruder.

"Hey, Runkin."

"Hey yourself, Jake. How's Lil' Tuck?"

"You know about Tuck?"

"Everybody in whole county know about Lil' Tuck. Everybody prayin' for him," Runkin answered.

Jake looked at the chairs in the room, but remained standing, not sure of what to say or whether to stay. "You sick?"

"Nope, my sister's in a room upstairs. You remember meetin' Nellie at my house last winter when you and your daddy brought us a tin of syrup?" Jake nodded. He did remember Nellie. She wore more makeup than any woman he had ever seen. She was pretty, but sad -looking. Rance had said she was a little "rough around the edges."

Runkin interlaced his fingers and pulled up one knee. Jake noticed the yellow color of his nails. "She's sick. But I came to see about Lil' Tuck, too. Set down and visit a spell." Runkin patted the seat next to him.

"Trish and Gray are up front, don't know how long I can stay." Jake sat beside Runkin, watching the sidewalk through the glass door and listening for the approaching footsteps of any unfamiliar colored person who might catch him where he did not belong.

They sat in silence for what seemed a long period of time. Jake wanted to talk, but could think of nothing to say. He looked around the room for other signs that distinguished this colored waiting room from the one he had just left. He read the painted words on the outside of the glass door backwards. Colored Entrance. "We sure got that cotton picked before Christmas, didn't we?"

Runkin smiled his familiar broad smile and nodded. "Sho did. You pulled more bolls that I ever seed you do befo'. 'Spect you even out-pulled ol' Gray Boy." His face took on a serious expression that Jake had never seen as he put a hand on Jake's shoulder. "I be praying for Lil' Tuck."

The serious look scared Jake a little, but he managed a smile and a nod. "Thanks...Well, guess I better get back. I didn't tell 'em I was leaving." As Jake started to retrace his steps, he saw Dr. Olen's nurse in the hall, leading a patient from the waiting room to the doctor's office. Afraid to be seen in the colored waiting room, Jake ducked into an open door across the hall and found himself in a stairwell closet. The small room held cleaning supplies and rags and smelled like stale mop-water.

This second set of stairs was new to him. The narrow stairs were little more than an almost vertical ladder leading to a hole in the first floor ceiling that was covered by a small door. Jake wondered if the door would open and where it led. He put his ear against the hall door and listened for footsteps, then climbed the steps and pushed open the small door at the top of the stairs. He found himself looking down the second floor hall, a few feet from Tuck's room. With his back to Jake, Dr. Olen was walking into Tuck's room. Jake lowered the door just enough to see but not be seen.

"Get out of this room, Nellie. Don't you know you can't be in here?" Jake heard Dr. Olen raising his voice to address someone. The doctor came out of Tuck's room escorting Runkin's sister, Nellie Slater, by the elbow. Her makeup was gone, and she seemed to have aged a lot since Jake had seen her last summer. Dr. Olen walked her all the way to her room at the end of the hall and closed the door. Jake had never seen Dr. Olen angry. He watched as the doctor returned to Tuck's room.

Mattie's voice drifted out into the hall. "Dr. Olen, I didn't mind her being in here. We've been in her brother's home many times, and she and Runkin have eaten at my table."

"I didn't run her out of here because she's colored, Mattie. I ran her out because she has syphilis." Jake heard his mother's sudden intake of breath as Dr. Olen continued. "She was instructed to stay in her room, but she's a little out of her head now. Did she touch Tuck or get close to him?"

"No, thank goodness, she stood really far back. Could he get anything from her just by her standing there?" Mattie asked.

"No, but I don't want her in here at all. I'll warn the nurses. If she leaves her room again, I'll have to lock her in."

Jake knew he had heard some important information, but he did not know what syphilis was. He made his way back down the stairwell, out the back door, and slid on the ice all the way around the building to the front entrance. Gray and Trish were leaning against the wall inside the front door as he entered the waiting room. "Runkin's sister is in a room a few doors down from Tuck's, and she came into his room awhile ago." He waited for Gray and Trish to react.

Trish looked up from the schoolbook she had brought along. "Really? Guess she wanted to see Tuck again. I remember that she came to see him at the house when he was just a tiny baby. She held him and rocked him forever. Mama said she almost had to pry Tuck away from her."

"Dr. Olen ran her out and took her back to her room. He said if she came out again, he would lock her door." Jake presented his new information with authority.

This got Gray's attention. "Wonder why he did that?"

"Cause she's got syphilis."

"What's that?" Trish asked.

"I don't know, but it must be real contagious. I never saw Dr.

Olen so mad."

Rance's appearance at the door abruptly ended their conversation.

"Do y'all want to come upstairs and see Tuck again before we go home? It's almost time to milk."

The mention of milking and seeing his sick brother again jerked Jake back from temporary escape to harsh reality. Oppressive sadness and fear enveloped him as he followed his brother and sister up the stairs. He wanted to take his little brother and all of the family and fly out the window toward home. Dr. Olen was outside the door, leaning against the hall wall, his thumb and index finger rubbing the bridge of his nose.

"Any change?" Rance asked.

Dr. Olen smiled at the children before turning back to Rance. "Yes and no. His scarlet fever symptoms are going away. His tongue is not as swollen, and the rash is fading." Olen jingled the change in his pocket and looked down the hall. "But his sore throat seems to be getting worse. I don't like the look of his throat. I'm going to take a throat culture and see if there is something I missed. Don't know if I can get it to a lab with this ice storm, but maybe I can get a technician down here tomorrow to look at it."

Jake didn't understand anything except that the scarlet fever might be going away. He hated for Tuck to have that awful swollen tongue. Rance put one hand against the wall and leaned in closer to the doctor. "I need to get these kids home and milk. This ice storm may have dropped some power lines down, and we may not have any electricity. That means milkin' by hand. Do you think it'll be all right if I'm gone for a few hours? I plan on coming back and spending the night so Mattie can go home and rest."

"Yes. He's sleeping now and needs his rest. This may drag on for longer than I thought. It will be better for Tuck if you and Mattie both get some rest."

Jake peeked into the room and saw that Tuck was asleep. He felt better, but wondered how long it would take to milk by hand.

Chapter 15

Jake held his breath as Trish pulled the chain on the light bulb that hung over the kitchen table. They both smiled when the naked bulb bathed part of the room in glaring light and created shadows in the rest. They would not have to milk by hand. Jake built a fire in the wood stove, and Gray lighted the butane heater before they left to milk. Trish warmed leftovers for supper and prepared a sandwich to send to Mattie. With their father running things and the electric milkers working, the milking seemed almost easy for Gray and Jake, a relief from the gloom at the hospital. Hack Gentry and Seth were waiting in Seth's pickup when Rance and the boys left the barn. They offered their services for milking the next day.

Rance looked into the eyes of his best friend and brother. "Thanks, men. But let's save that offer until we absolutely have to have it." Rance nodded toward Gray and Jake. "Besides, I've got two of the best hands a man could have right here." Jake felt a little tingle of pride at the rare words of praise from his father. Rance returned to the hospital after supper. Anticipating that Mattie would refuse to leave, Trish packed a bag of toiletries, a gown, and a change of clothes for her.

The next morning, Gray Boy and Jake stood outside the barn under the small porch where the cows entered and left the milking parlor. They watched the last cow drift out of the lot toward pasture and the hay already scattered on the ground. Each propped a single boot on the lowest board of the fence dividing the entrance and exit lots, their arms dangling across the top rail. Both stared down at the bottom board, heavy with scraped manure and mud. Milking was complete for the morning, but cleanup remained. Their father had not arrived to help. Several layers of clothing and the exertion from milking protected them from the cold.

The persistent north wind had died some, but its whistle could still be heard coming through cracks in the barn windows and sneaking around the sides of the barn. The cows had tromped the remaining ice in the lots into an ugly brown slush, but ice still clung to the trees and the house top. An icy fog rolled from the south along the banks of the Blue Bottom toward Jake and Gray Boy, inching its way toward the Rivers' home like a giant cat stalking its prey.

Gray dragged his boot across the rail to remove clumps of ice. "Even with this ice, you can scrape down an inch or two and find dry dirt. Seems strange to think we are still in a drought and our pools are about to dry up. We got all the trouble that goes with something wet coming from the sky, but none of the benefits."

Jake looked up at his brother, surprised to hear him sound so much like their father. They were lallygagging again, Jake knew, but one more day without school would not hurt much. He didn't like school, but knew that staying away made him dread going back even more. Looking south, he caught a glimpse of something moving through the ice fog. A man horseback was slowly emerging from the mist. Gray had seen him, too. The man's hat was pulled down tight to keep it from blowing away, and his head was ducked low to avoid the wind. No word passed between the brothers as they recognized Papa Griff and Buddy, gliding effortlessly through the ice and fog, the breath of horse and man coming in regular, visible gusts now. The sight of Papa Griff and Buddy riding out of that silver mist was both beautiful and frightening to Jake.

"Daddy and Uncle Seth say that nobody sits a horse like Papa Griff. Wonder why he's coming from that direction?" Jake said more to himself than his brother. As the horse and rider came closer, Jake could see the ice that had formed on Griffin's flowing moustache. He was wearing a sheepskin-lined coat that Jake could not remember having seen before. The ever-present wild rag was wrapped snugly around his neck for warmth, not for flair. Jake had never seen him wear a black one before. They were surprised when he headed straight toward the old hay barn instead of the back porch

118

of the house. He rode Buddy into the barn hall and dismounted.

The boys kept their posts, almost afraid to move, as Griffin unsaddled the horse and rubbed his back with a worn-thin but dusty-dry horse blanket from the corn crib. Steam rose off the horse's back and hips. The boys glanced at each other, not speaking the questions. Why was he so warm? Where had Papa Griff been to get his horse this warm and collect ice in his moustache? Griffin tossed a small bucket of shucked corn into the feed trough and headed toward the house, avoiding the muck in the cow lots on his way. As he neared the back porch, a black '48 Chevrolet drove onto the driveway between the barn and the house. The boys recognized Hack Gentry's car. Gray and Jake stayed under the barn porch, somehow wary of greeting their visitors, watching as Seth and Hack left the car. Griffin joined them without speaking and all three started toward Gray and Jake.

"Didn't hear you come up," Gray spoke with anxiety in his voice, as if he wanted to be the first to break the silence that was starting to be uncomfortable.

Seth scraped the edge of his boot through the grass, keeping his head down. "Boys, we been waiting out front till you finished milking."

Jake heard what was being said, but his eyes never left his grandfather's. He could see something in those eyes that he had never seen before and it frightened him. "What's goin' on, Papa Griff? Why is Buddy so warm, and why were you coming from the Blue Bottom?" Jake was surprised to hear his own voice sound so frail.

Griffin ran the back of his index finger under his moustache, causing the icicles to bounce over his upper lip. He met the stare of each grandson and held their eyes with his own. "I was just riding a little to clear my head." Griffin removed his hat and looked toward Seth and Hack. Jake noticed the neat line the hat had made on his thick gray hair. The hat had caused it to reach a little over the tops of his ears. Papa Griff needed a haircut. The smell of Buddy mixed with the inside of Griffin's hat drifted on the wind and under Jake's nose.

Griffin turned again to Gray and Jake. "I won't lie to you, boys.

You're nearly men, doing men's work." He hesitated as he heard his voice start to grow thin. Swallowing hard, he began again. "It's Tuck. He had a bad night. He's worse this morning. Your daddy and mama want his brothers and sister to come in and see him."

Seth put his hands on both the boys' shoulders. "Tillie is already in the house. She and Trish have breakfast ready. You need to eat quick and jump into a hot tub. Mattie gave us instructions to get you cleaned up before bringing you to town."

Gray shook his head firmly. "I don't want to eat, and I don't want to clean up. I want to go now." His voice seemed to come from deep within, sounding hollow and hoarse.

Seth took off his hat, put his fingers inside the sweatband, and bounced it on his fingers. His ears were red from the cold. "I know you do, son, but you don't want to upset your mama today, and she wants you to have that bath."

Jake was scared and felt an anger he didn't understand. Had his little brother died and they weren't telling him? Afraid to ask the question he wanted to, he asked another. "What about the barn? We ain't cleaned it up yet."

Hack smiled at Jake. "We'll take care of that for you later." That scared Jake more.

As they entered the kitchen, Trish sat at the table, staring at her breakfast. She looked up at her brothers, and her eyes filled with tears. Jake walked past the table toward his room, but Tillie blocked his exit from the kitchen. She took him in her arms and hugged and patted him. Jake felt himself start to cry and jerked away to try to regain his composure.

Tillie put on her best smile. "Boys, it will take me a few more minutes to draw the water and heat it for all of your baths. I brought along an extra tub, so I have one ready for all of you. Mattie gave me my instructions. I am to feed you and get you clean. Then we will all go see Tuck."

They all sat down to fried eggs, bacon, and hot biscuits. Jake stared at the eggs, never his favorite, then the bacon, but could not summon the will to choke them down. Tuck always sat on his knee at the breakfast table and finished his eggs and bacon for him. Jake did love Tillie's biscuits. At her urging, he ate one with some plum preserves and butter. Fed and bathed, they climbed into the back seat of Hack's old Chevrolet. Griffin sat in the front with Hack. As they left the driveway to head down 24 toward Cooper, Jake looked out the rear window and saw Seth and Tillie head the opposite way. He wondered if they were going to pick up Shep and Brenda before coming to see Tuck.

They rode without speaking, avoiding eye contact. Jake stared at the back of his grandfather's head and realized that he had never seen him in a car before. Had he ever owned one? Did he know how to drive? The hat line in Papa Griff's gray hair seemed more pronounced in the car. Papa Griff's being there scared Jake. He knew that his grandfather had a strong dislike for hospitals and distrusted doctors, even Dr. Olen. His wife had died at a young age in a hospital, and Griffin blamed it on her doctor and the hospital. He had vowed to never walk into a hospital or doctor's office again. If he was going today, then things with Tuck must be very bad. The heater in the car churned valiantly, combining with body heat to warm its occupants. It stirred the smell of soap, Vitalis hair oil, and Old Spice aftershave.

Hack parked the car on the street in front of the hospital door. Griffin left the car, stood on the sidewalk, and put on his hat, pulling it down a little firmer than usual. He stared at the hospital for a long time, his eyes traveling up to the second floor and back down to the entrance. It was not the place where his wife had died, but Jake could still see his body stiffen. Hack held the door open while the children formed a line behind their grandfather. Griffin stared up at the sign that read Bartlett Hospital & Clinic for another uncomfortable period, then strode firmly through the door. Without pausing, he walked through the reception room, through the door that led to the stairway, and up the stairs. Hack remained in the waiting room while Trish, Gray, and Jake followed their grandfather. Griffin seemed to know his way around, and Jake wondered if he had been to the hospital before.

Filled with a terrible sense of dread, they used their grandfather as a shield, as if he could protect them from what they might find. Griffin entered Tuck's room and looked into his son's eyes. Rance met his stare with a knowing expression of hopelessness and

121

then turned toward the children. He hugged each of them and then put his arms around them all, gently herding them to the rocker, where their mother sat with Tuck in her arms.

Tuck was pale as he lay against Mattie's breast. Jake looked at him and at his mother. Dark circles under her eyes accentuated the lack of color in the rest of her face, but he was more frightened by the expression in her eyes. Rance had always said that Mattie could say more with her eyes than most people could by shouting. Today, those eyes showed sadness and fear. More disturbing, they showed resignation. She seemed to have surrendered.

Jake reached out to touch and speak to Tuck, not sure of what to say or how to say it. At home, he always secretly kissed his brother good night and snuggled him to sleep. He wanted to wrap him in his arms now and take him home to their shared bed in the dog trot. Trish kissed Tuck on his forehead and ran her fingers through his hair, softly whispering words that Jake could not hear. Even Gray tried to embrace Tuck as he spoke soothing words into his ear. Jake stood back, awkward, feeling trapped and helpless, tears now coming in spite of his efforts to control them.

Mattie saw his distress. "It's all right, Jake. You can kiss your little brother. The swelling in his tongue went away yesterday, and he told me how he wanted to go home and crawl in bed with you. I know you love on him all the time, and that's nothing to be ashamed of. It's something to be proud of. Dr. Olen says he's not contagious now, so give him a hug. He needs it." Mattie's quivering lips smiled. Her eyes did not.

Jake got down on his knees and kissed his little brother on the cheek, and then took Tuck's hand in his. Tuck's eyes barely opened and he whispered, "Jake, dog trot."

Jake took that as a good sign and began to talk to Tuck as if they were alone. He talked about how smart Shy had become, learning to shake hands and to howl and bark on command. Tuck closed his eyes again, but a smile crossed his face. Mattie's eyes filled with tears as she squeezed him tighter. Jake's body twitched when he felt a hand on his shoulder. He turned to see Dr. Olen smiling above him.

"Well, Jake, you got him to smile and talk a little. That's really good. Now we need to see if we can get him to take some of this medicine." Dr. Olen stood above them with a bottle and a spoon.

The children huddled into a corner of the room as Rance took Tuck from Mattie. The routine was wordless; they had obviously done it many times before. Rance had told them about the medicine. It was foul-smelling and foul-tasting, and it hurt for Tuck to swallow, so he had been unable to get it down without retching and spitting it back up. Rance whispered gently to him, apologetic for the taste and pain he was asking him to endure once more. Tuck opened his mouth and swallowed both spoonfuls, swallowing repeatedly to keep it down. He opened his eyes, looked at Rance and said, "I did it, Daddy, I did," then closed them again and lay back in his father's arms. Rance felt Tuck's body grow limp. He looked at Dr. Olen, who walked over and put his finger to Tuck's throat, then his stethoscope to his chest. He looked at Rance, then at Mattie, and shook his head. Mattie and Rance held Tuck between them, softly swaying together in the middle of the hospital room, both crying and speaking their last words to their son.

Dr. Olen walked over to Griffin and the children. "I'm sorry, Mr. Rivers . . . Gray Boy, Jake, Trish. Little Tuck is gone."

Griffin visibly stiffened when he heard the doctor's words, his eyes fixed on his youngest grandson, still held in his son's arms. He acknowledged Olen Bartlett with a nod of his head and a handshake. With voice breaking, he said, "Rance said you did all you could."

The enormity of what had just happened swept through the room like a fire hungry for oxygen. Jake's eyes burned and he tasted something bitter in the back of his throat. As he watched his parents gently sway with Tuck, his vision blurred and he felt detached from the room and its other occupants. Jake had heard Mattie's father speak of the angel of death. The black angel Jake had pictured in his mind seemed to have entered the room, taken his little brother and all of the air at the same time. He watched helplessly as his main sources of comfort and strength seemed to crumble before his eyes. Even his grandfather, always calm in the face of adversity, seemed to be stricken numb.

Jake bolted from the room. In the hall, Seth reached out for him, but he broke free and ran toward the stairs. He had to get away from this awful place that had taken his brother, the purest part of his family. As he reached the stairway, he heard Gray's voice call out to him. It was not a command, the sort that Gray usually addressed to him, but a plea. He stopped just before reaching the stairway, leaned his back against the wall and allowed his body to slide to the floor. Seated on the cold floor, he wrapped his arms around his knees and dropped his head. He had never felt such despair. Nothing could change what had just happened. Nobody, not even his parents, could make it better. He needed to cry again, but the tears wouldn't come. He wanted to recapture the tender feelings he had expressed to Tuck a few minutes before, but he could only find fear, anger, and dread. Why had God sent the angel of death to tear the heart out of his family? Jake's worst fears and dread seemed to be coming true all at once. What had happened to the flow? Had it finally turned against them?

Chapter 16

Jake felt Aunt Tillie's hand in the small of his back, ushering him downstairs to a small room beside Dr. Olen's office. They sat in silence for a few minutes, with Tillie alternately hugging each of the children. Trish was heaving with sobs, Gray stood huddled in the corner, and Jake sat on the floor, arms wrapped around his knees, afraid and angry. Griffin and Seth walked in together.

Griffin hugged Trish, then pulled Jake from his sitting position and put both hands on his shoulders. "I'm sorry you kids have to grow up so soon, but I know you can take whatever comes. You've already shown me that." Griffin took a deep breath and swallowed to regain his voice. "Your daddy and mama need you more than ever for the next few days, maybe weeks. You have to suck it up and put on your best face before they come down here. If they see you like this, it's likely to make a bad situation worse." Griffin walked over to the high window and looked out on the street. " Tuck is gone. There's nothing we can do about that now. But we can go on living. We have to reach down deep to try and be worthy of the courage that little fellow showed us trying to beat this thing." Griffin put his arms around both boys and drew them to him.

Against his grandfather's chest, Jake could feel the old man's ragged intake of breath and hear his heart beating. He smelled of tobacco, soap, and aftershave. He had never seen his grandfather cry. Muted footsteps could be heard outside the office. They turned to see Carl Leslie coming down the hall carrying something that looked like a large basket. A gray blanket covered the contents. When they saw Rance and Mattie following behind, they knew that Tuck was in that basket. Carl was the owner of the funeral home.

Seth ushered them outside and opened the door to Carl's black station wagon. Carl gently placed the basket on the front passenger seat.

A small crowd had gathered across the street, standing at a respectable distance in the cold air. Men had removed their hats in spite of the cold, their breath visible in uneven puffs. Children big and small hovered close to their siblings and parents, forming an imaginary barrier to the grief they were witnessing across the street.

Jake had never seen his parents so drained and weak. They even seemed to be smaller and a little stooped. They walked over and hugged each child before getting into the back seat of the station wagon. With his eyes, Jake followed the tracks made by the hearse in the leftover ice as it pulled away toward the funeral home. He knew it was only three blocks away, but it seemed that the car was taking away all the stability in his life to a faraway place, never to return. The crowd began to disperse, but kept their eyes on the Rivers family as they walked. Ashamed and angry at being the object of others' pity and curiosity, Jake suppressed the urge to walk across the street and be a spectator.

"I can't believe it's already dark," Gray said as he looked up at the stars in the clear sky. They had lost all sense of time in the hospital.

He and Jake seemed to realize simultaneously that they were already late for milking. Jake visualized the cows waiting at the gate, milk streaming from swollen udders. Seth seemed to read their minds. "Don't worry about milking tonight, boys. Hack is getting started right now, and I'm on my way to help him. You two and Trish are going to spend the night with us. Tillie will take you home and cook us all a big supper."

The words brought an immediate sense of relief to Jake, and he felt guilty that it took so little to make him feel better. How could he ever feel better when Tuck was under a gray shroud in that basket, never to wake from his sleep? "What about Daddy and Mama?" Jake needed to be near them.

"They'll be along as soon as they make arrangements for Tuck," Seth answered softly.

Jake felt good when Gray put his arm around him when he spoke to Seth. "What about the cows? They'll mess up the whole barn and not give as much milk with strangers in there."

Seth put a hand in the middle of each of their backs and nudged them toward the car. "They know Hack and me a little bit, and we ain't exactly strangers to handling milk cows. They'll probably be a little problem tonight, but by morning, we'll have 'em all straightened out. You boys are going to get a few days off from milking."

Gray and Jake willingly crawled into the back seat of Seth and Tillie's old car, leaving Trish the seat beside Tillie in the front. Jake had always felt almost as safe with Tillie as he had with his own mother. Today was different. He needed to be close to his parents. He looked out the back window toward the funeral home as they drove away. Carl Leslie's black station wagon was out of sight.

They passed their home on the way to Tillie's. Lights were on in the dairy barn. Hack already had the milking underway. Cars lined the driveway all the way from 24 to the house. "Who's at our house?" Jake asked.

Tillie looked at the line of cars. "Everybody loved that sweet baby," she whispered to herself. Then she turned her head so that Jake might hear her from the back seat. "Friends and relatives. They've come to pay their respects and help with getting the house ready. They're bringing food mostly. Our sisters and brothers are there, and it looks like your daddy's family is, too. Want to stop?"

"No," they all answered in unison.

Tillie laughed softly. "I don't blame you. Seth and I figured you wouldn't want to be with a crowd of people right now. We'll get you fed and a good night's sleep before we face that group."

Jake didn't understand the resentment he felt about people being in his home. He knew they were trying to help, but it seemed intrusive to him. He didn't want anyone disturbing his own things or those of his little brother.

Tillie's driveway was almost full of cars too, more of her sisters and their families. Nine girls and three boys in the Pelt family made for a crowd at both Rivers' homes. Jake groaned, and Gray didn't hide his displeasure either. Mattie and Tillie's sisters were pleasant enough, but Jake did not want to see them just now. He wanted to hide in Tillie's house and find comfort in her food and care. As they entered the front door, they were swarmed with tearful women and stared at by men wringing the brims of their hats, unable to think of anything to do or say. Gray, Jake, and Trish took their hugs and teary kisses dutifully from their aunts, looking over their shoulders at the stares of their cousins.

The meal was not the quiet one that Jake had looked forward to. He was handed a plate of food brought by the sisters and neighbors and had to eat with several aunts clucking over him. He heard them say that a poisonous kind of diphtheria had taken Tuck's life, not the scarlet fever that he had thought. Hearing this conversation, Tillie quietly worked the room, whispering to her guests before urging them outside to their cars.

Left alone, conversation was awkward with Shep and Brenda, with each muttering awkward "I'm sorrys" through their tears. Trish led the way with stories about Tuck's life. Telling those stories had a consoling effect and strengthened the bond that existed between the double cousins. Soon, they were laughing softly as each interrupted the other with the large stockpile of memories that Tuck had left in less than three years of living. They cried together as the story of his final minutes of life was told. Tillie found them all asleep in the living room. She covered them with quilts and added wood to the fire.

Jake awakened at dawn and moved Shep's arm off his own. His arm was asleep, and he couldn't move it. The useless arm reminded him of Tuck. He brought himself to a sitting position on the couch and stared at the wood stove while he massaged his arm. The room was still warm, but he felt cold. The stove popped as the coals inside it began to cool.

Sleep had not taken it away. Had it really happened? Was Tuck really gone? He still couldn't imagine God stealing his little brother. Was the unnamed presence that continually frightened him to blame? He rubbed his eyes and tried to erase those thoughts. Stumbling to the breakfast table, he was surprised to find Gray and Trish already awake, sitting with his parents and Seth and Tillie. Jake went willingly into his mother's outstretched arms. He could think of nothing to say that might stem her flowing tears and felt guilty that he wanted to be comforted himself.

Rance hugged Jake and managed a smile. "Too much company at our place, and we needed to be with you three. People mean well, but we need our time to deal with this." He was still gaunt, and deep sadness had replaced the fear and panic that Jake had seen the night before. He drew strength from his father. Rance seemed to be growing strong and taking charge of the family again. Mattie looked extremely thin, and dark circles were still under her eyes. They still held a look of terror, a need to run and escape.

Rance poured his already cold coffee into his saucer. "We decided to go ahead with Tuck's funeral today. It'll just be a graveside service at four this afternoon. He will be buried at the New Klondike Cemetery, beside Mama. All our brothers and sisters will be here by then, so we don't see any sense in waiting." The kids just stared in numb silence. "Is that all right with you kids?" They nodded silent approval.

Mattie wrung her hands and looked at Tillie. "None of us have any funeral clothes."

Tillie took her sister into her arms. "The kids have new school clothes and that will be good enough. Between all the brothers and sisters, we can surely come up with something for you and Rance."

Mattie insisted that they all ride together in the funeral car with Tuck. Seth and Tillie followed behind with their children and Griffin. Sisters and brothers of Rance and Mattie were next in the large caravan of cars that left Seth and Tillie's headed toward Klondike. The clouds seemed to part for them as they left the car, revealing a blue sky. It was turning into a clear, crisp winter day. Jake thought about how much he and Tuck loved to play outside on such days.

Carl Lester's funeral home staff had set up a green tarp shelter supported by poles at the cemetery. The Rivers sat on cold folding chairs under the unnecessary shelter. It would have been warmer under the sun. Jake tried not to, but he could not keep from staring at the grave. He knew that friends and neighbors had dug the small grave this morning. Some of those same people had stayed with Tuck through the night at the funeral home. The grave was discreetly covered with a black tarp, but Jake could see large dry clods, a grim reminder of the drought and the coldness of the hole that his little brother would be placed in.

Jake kept his eyes on the ground, trying not to make eye contact with anyone, lest the tears escape. He felt a hand on his shoulder and turned to see Papa Lee and Big Mama Pelt, Mattie's parents. He left his seat to embrace his grandparents. Pearl Pelt was a large woman who had given birth to eighteen children. Phlebitis had made it almost impossible for her to walk more than a few feet at a time, and Lee was her faithful caretaker. Jake could not remember the last time they had been seen together outside their home in Klondike. Pearl's usual stern expression had softened today. Lee, a hail-fellow-well-met, was clearly in agony for his daughter and her lost son. Mattie reached behind her chair and held both their hands.

Back in his cold metal seat, Jake looked at his two grandfathers seated on the same row of chairs. He had never seen them together before, though he had been told that they were good friends in their earlier years. Lee was the quintessential grandfather, a jolly, rotund, slightly balding man with a perpetually cheerful expression and a hearty laugh. Today, he wept unashamedly and profusely for his grandson. Griffin sat erect and motionless. Pain showed in his eyes, but his tears would be shed in private. With a kind, generous, jolly, affectionate grandfather like Lee, Jake wondered why he identified and tried to please Papa Griff more.

He turned to scan the crowd behind him. A lone black face stood out. Runkin met his gaze and smiled. Jake nodded and turned as the preacher called for bowed heads. He kept his eyes on the small red wreath sitting atop the tiny casket and the ribbon that said "Little Tuck."

Jake heard the droning voice of Brother Lake, preacher at the First Baptist Church of Klondike. Nine weeks of that voice had not moved Jake from his pew during invitation. His head remained bowed until his neck hurt from the strain as the preacher prayed incessantly, trying in vain to find words that explained the situation. Finished with praying, he launched into a full-fledged sermon entreating his captive audience to "get right with God, before your day of reckoning arrives." Brother Lake strung out the end of each word that ended with a hard sound, making God into Godd-uh. Each sentence seemed to start with a low drone and end with a shout.

Jake heard little of what the preacher said, his mind returning to the time that he and Tuck had played in the snow. He first realized that the service was over when people began hugging him and whispering nice things about Tuck in his ear. Jake acknowledged the hugs and words of the well-wishers with wordless nods, but kept his eyes on a flock of white cowbirds as they circled the cemetery. As the crowd began to disburse, the birds swooped over the tent and came to rest next to the boundary fence, a few steps from Tuck's grave. Jake was still watching them when Gray tugged his sleeve and waved him toward the black car that would take them home. With his nose pressed against the window of that car, Jake saw a mockingbird glide under the tent and come to rest on the red wreath.

Chapter 17

In the dogtrot that night, Jake watched the naked, dark, light bulb over his bed after pulling the string to turn it out. Suspended from the fourteen-foot ceiling by a long cord, the bulb's movement was barely perceptible. He had loved telling Tuck scary stories about what made the bulb move. Now, those stories frightened him. Was there a presence moving that bulb? Was it the same presence that had taken his little brother? What had he done to cause Tuck to be taken away? What had the family done to deserve losing their best? If God gave them Tuck as a gift from the flow, then why did he take him away so soon? Maybe God did not like the flow. Was Tuck cold in that hard, dry, ground?

***

The Rivers seemed suspended in time as spring arrived. Their talk had shriveled into communication that was required to live together in the same house. They seemed afraid to extend it beyond what was essential and felt guilt when a rare laugh interrupted their determined march from one hour to the next. Rance knew that the family needed his strength, Mattie his comfort, but he believed that his failure as a father and head of his family had caused Tuck's death. If their house had been warmer, their living conditions better, Tuck might never have contacted scarlet fever and diphtheria. If he had mastered the flow himself instead of depending on Tuck's magic to carry the whole family, Tuck would still be alive.

Gray Boy and Jake did not understand the depth of their parents' wretched states, but sensed that Tuck's death had left them on their own. The loss of their brother had cast a pall over their own relationship. Gray's teasing and torment of his little brother escalated and Jake's resistance stiffened. What could have brought them closer together tore them further apart. Unwilling participants in a tragedy they resented, captive members of a family that God had chosen to visit his wrath upon, the brothers first internalized their grief, confusion, and fear, then began taking it out on each other. Their behavior grew verbally abusive, then physically violent.

On a Saturday night in May, Rance did not show up for milking. Jake resented his brother's bossing in the dairy barn, and Gray chided him for every mistake he made. When the last cow left the parlor, their anger spilled out into the cow lot. Jake was grasping for air, but didn't dare breathe. Breathing meant ingesting the mixture of dairy barn muck and slime that his face was buried in. "Breathe, you little smart-ass."Gray Boy shouted as he pressed Jake's head into the honey wagon mess.

"What the hell?" Rance grabbed Gray's shirt collar and the seat of his britches and pulled him off Jake. He crawled into the muck wagon and pulled Jake to his feet as he spoke to Gray. "You trying to kill him?"

Jake staggered to his feet and wiped the muck from his face. He was pleased to hear his father's voice, but could tell that his speech was slurred.

"What's wrong with you boys? You fight all the time now."

From the ground, Gray pointed his finger up at Jake, still standing in the muck wagon. "He started it."

Rance turned toward Jake. "That right?"

"I may have started the fight, but he's the one that started callin' me names. I'm tired of him pickin' on me."

Gray turned away from his father and raised his voice. "What business is it of yours who started it? You show up late for milking most days, smelling' of whiskey. Looks like today ain't no different."

Rance was taken aback by Gray's sass. He looked at his elder son, then turned toward his younger. Jake looked away. With his hands on his hips, Rance stood in the boot-top-high muck inside the trailer, slowly shaking his head. Gray seemed to draw courage

134

when he did not receive instant rebuke. "Hell, you're drunk as a skunk right now. What right have you got to say anything to either one of us?"

Rance stared at Gray for what seemed like a long time to Jake, then suddenly jumped from the trailer, grabbed him by the front of his shirt and pulled him so close that their noses were touching. "I may have been drinking, but that doesn't give you the right to talk to me that way." Jake watched as Gray's defiant stare turned into one of fear, but he refused to give in, refused to look away.

Jake picked up a blob of muck and slung it at both of them. His voice cracked. "I'm leaving this damn family." He stalked into the dairy barn, threw his filthy clothes onto the floor, washed himself down, put a towel around himself and ran to the house. He managed to avoid his mother while he dressed. In a few minutes, he was on 24 with his thumb out.

Since Tuck's death, Jake had found his own home increasingly cold and uninviting, and he sought frequent refuge at his grandparents' house in Klondike. Jake felt alone and defenseless against his older brother and resorted quickly to any weapon available to strike back at Gray. When the violence became too much, he found refuge in Papa Lee's small book collection and read himself into the worlds of Tom Sawyer, Jack London, Huck Finn, and Will James' cowboys. Little was expected of him at the Pelts' home, and his maternal grandparents seemed to understand his need for privacy and escape.

In the Pelts' Klondike backyard, under a mulberry tree and behind a honeysuckle hedge, Jake found a place that seemed to capture the same feeling that he and Tuck had enjoyed under the porch at home. Tuck returned to him in this new place. He imagined that Tuck was with him as he sucked the sweet liquid from the honeysuckle blooms of spring. From his hiding place, he imagined his grandmother making lye soap in the large, cast iron black pot that still leaned against the house.

Rance found him there the next day. He was smiling his crooked smile, but Jake was comforted when his words were not slurred. "You about ready to come home?"

Jake shook his head. Rance took out his pocketknife, leaned

down on one knee, picked up a twig and started to whittle. "Your mama sent me to get you. If I don't come back with you, I'll be in a lot of trouble." Jake did not answer.

Rance stood and offered his hand to pull Jake from his sitting position. Jake did not take the hand, but rose to face his father. Rance folded the blade, dropped the knife into his pocket, and looked into Jake's eyes. "Truth is, I need you to come back home, son. I'm having a hard time getting over losing Tuck, but that's no excuse for not being a proper daddy to you and Gray Boy. If you come home, I'll try to make it up to both of you." Jake was ready to go home, and what his father said was enough.

"Well, what do you think?" Trish, dressed in her new prom dress, was showing off for her mother in the living room when Jake and Rance returned. Still looking at Trish, Mattie hugged Jake and chose to ignore his overnight absence. She had known where he was. Jake resented the intrusion when Gray swaggered in wearing his white sport coat and pink carnation. It was hard for anyone to sparkle when Gray was in the room. His dark complexion, white teeth, and dark eyes with long eyelashes were the perfect complements to the white coat. Jake suppressed the urge to tell his brother that the coat was secondhand. He had been with Mattie when she bought it from a friend. Gray gave Jake a tentative nod. A nod was all that Jake used to need from his brother to forgive any transgression.

Trish, always humble, was proud of Gray and did not resent his sharing of her spotlight. "That coat looks really good on you, Gray Boy," she said.

Mattie ushered them to the front yard for pictures with Trish's new Brownie camera. Jake sat on the picnic table beside his father as pictures were taken in the swing under the chinaberry tree. His big sister was going to graduate high school. Jake had not seen her take down the state championship poster that had hung in her room for almost two years, but knew that it was gone. The fire left her belly when Tuck died. Her team barely won district and was eliminated in the first play-off game. She was getting serious about Pete, the young soldier from Commerce. Jake liked Pete and envied Trish her pending escape from the Rivers' cold house.

Mattie waited a respectable time before leaving for the prom at Klondike school. She planned to sneak in to observe Trish's crowning as prom queen. It was traditional for mothers to do that. Everyone knew they were watching, but pretended they were not. Fathers did not usually attend, so Rance and Jake headed for Dad Flannigan's store. Dad's store was at the end of the only business street that ran down the center of Klondike. When Cardwell's moved out on state highway 24, only the post office and Dad's store remained of the once thriving downtown. Charred bois d'arc stumps used for foundations were now ghostly reminders of the depression and fires that had destroyed the bank, livery stable and general store.

Dad's small building was covered in rusted sheet metal. Two small windows in front looked out on the front porch. The sign above the porch, read C. P. Hollon---General Merchandise---Est. 1886. Jake did not know C. P. Hollon and could only imagine Dad as the owner of this small store. Dad stayed open most days and nights, never closing until everyone left. Sometimes that was midnight; sometimes it was as early as eight. In defiance of Texas Blue Laws, he was always open on Sundays, selling whatever was on his shelves to people he knew. Strangers, however, could buy only groceries on Sundays.

Ironically, the man everyone called Dad was a bachelor with no children. He lived alone. Store patrons were his only family. Jake liked Dad. He was the only adult he could look directly in the eye when they were both standing. Dad's head sat squarely on his shoulders with no sign of a neck to hold it. In order to look left or right, he had to turn his whole body.

Several men, including Jake's Uncle Seth, were gathered on the benches and empty nail kegs under the porch of the store when Rance and Jake left the truck. Some were regulars, men who seemed to be sitting on the same bench or nail keg every time Jake came to Dad Flannigan's. He wondered if they ever left. When he asked his father what they did for a living, Rance had dismissed him with a vague answer. Rance and Seth seldom chewed tobacco, and neither dipped snuff, so they smoked roll-your-owns while most of the other men dipped and chewed, spitting on and off the board

137

floor of the porch.

When the stories became repetitions of ones he had heard before, Jake wandered down to the railroad tracks running across the middle of town to look for pennies that he had left on the tracks beside the old depot when he had visited the Pelts. Pennies crushed by the wheels of a train were rare and highly valued by himself and his friends. The pennies were not on the tracks. He looked inside the windows of the abandoned depot, trying to imagine what it must have been like when passengers arrived and departed from Klondike. The sound of a screen door slamming shook him from his thoughts. He looked up to see Lee Pelt take a seat on the front porch swing. Jake looked toward Dad's, then ambled in the opposite direction to join his grandfather.

"Hey, Papa Lee."

"Hey, Jake. Come sit beside me."

Jake's feet barely touched the ground as they swung in silence, listening to the sounds of spring. Jake's grandfather always smelled of pipe tobacco and green pecans, no matter what the season. His legs were not much longer than Jake's. Lee Pelt broke the silence. "How's your Grandpa Griffin? Haven't seen him in awhile."

"Ok, I guess."

Only the squeak of the chain that held the swing interrupted the silence of the evening until Lee spoke again. "Playin' baseball again this year?"

"Suppose so."

"You know I can't leave your grandma to attend the games, but I keep up on how you're doing. Rance and Mattie and folks around Klondike say you're making a fine little ballplayer."

Jake shifted uneasily in the swing and walked to the porch steps to sit. "Papa, do you know about the flow?"

Lee Pelt laughed his hearty laugh. "Your mama asked me that same question right after she married your daddy." He looked down and nodded his head slowly as he continued to swing. "Yes, Jake, anybody that knows the Rivers men as well as I do knows about the Rivers' flow. Why?"

"You believe in it?"

"Doesn't matter if I believe in it or not. What matters is if you do."

Jake stared at his grandfather. He did not understand the answer.

Lee Pelt chuckled again. "I see that I have confused you. What I mean to say, Jake, is that if a man believes in something strongly enough, then it becomes true for him, regardless of what others may think." Seeing that Jake's questioning was intense, he reached into his vest pocket for a cigar. He rolled it on his tongue, pulled a match from another pocket, and lighted it. Smoke came out with his words. "Sometimes, Jake, the things that are the hardest for a man to believe in are the things he needs to believe in the most."

These were questions Jake had been wanting to ask someone a long time, so he pressed on. "If the flow is real, then why is Papa Griff so poor? I mean, why didn't he use the flow to get more money?"

Lee chuckled softly. "I don't know any men richer than your grandfather, Jake. Ever noticed how he just seems to glide along with life? How he enjoys his fiddle and singing and good friends?"

"Yeah, but he's real poor. He doesn't even own a car and lives in a three-room shack."

"If you mean poor in terms of material possessions, then I guess you're right. But have you ever noticed how your grandfather relates to that old horse? Why, I hear Buddy's shoes clopping down this street two, three times a week. When I look out, your grandpa is in that saddle, relaxed but ram-rod straight, like he's sittin' in an easy chair with wheels. Buddy's head nods with each step, his ears justa twitching. People along here watch to see what color his bandanna is."

"Wild rag." Jake said.

"Huh?"

"Wild rag. It's not a bandanna. Papa calls it a wild rag."

"I see."

Jake thought about those things for a minute, then pressed on. "How come, if he has the Rivers' flow, he didn't become a champion roper like he wanted to be?"

"That's an easy one. When he was young, he chose his wife and family over traveling the rodeo circuit. He was still a good hand with a horse and rope, but he found the flow at home with his wife and family. When his wife died, he fell away from roping and from the flow for a good while. Then he found it again." Lee rose from the swing and joined his grandson on the porch steps. "You see, Jake, your Papa Griff drifts along in the flow most of the time now. He doesn't care about material things. He cares about family, people, and things you can't see. He tells me he hears fiddle and guitar music in his head most of the time, whether anybody is playing or not."

Jake nodded as if he understood, then rose and walked down the porch steps. "Guess I better get back before Daddy misses me."

Tree frogs were squeaking and the dusty, wet smell of twilight had arrived when Jake left to return to Dad's. It was dark when Jake reached the store. He heard voices and saw the shadows of the men inside. Dad was carving slices off a block of rat cheese and passing it and saltines among them. The men passed around a bottle to chase down the crackers and cheese. Jake sat on one of the benches outside and stared at the Old Klondike Cemetery down the street. Clouds crossing swiftly across the moon made the shadowy outlines of tombstones seem to dance.

Jake was startled when Dad Flannigan followed Rance, Seth, and the other men out of the store. Some of the regular bench-sitters left their vigils and headed down Main Street toward home. Rance and Seth joined the others as they walked around the side of the building toward the rear of the store. Dad hesitated as he turned to lock the door.

"Jake, would you mind watching the store for a little bit? Probably won't be any more customers, but sometimes folks need something late at night." Jake nodded. "If they come in, just tell 'em to get what they want."

"How will you know what they got?" Jake asked. Dad's squat frame reappeared at the corner of the store. "There's a ticket book on the counter. Ask 'em to write down their names, what they got, and the price. Help yourself to a Coke and a candy bar for helping me out. When you get tired or when it reaches ten, you just close up and put the key under this nail keg. I left it in the front door."

"Sure, be glad to."

As the men started to leave, Jake watched his father and uncle closely. Both offered a guilty, crooked smile in his direction, and he could tell from their eyes and expression that both had been drinking. He called out a last question to Dad. "What if somebody wants to pay?"

Dad's nasal, high-pitched laughter could be heard through the empty streets of Klondike. "If that happens, come and get me. I want to take a picture of those customers." He hesitated and turned again toward Jake, his expression more serious.

"If somebody offers you money, you take it. You've seen me open that old cash register enough to know how to open it, haven't you? You know how to make change?" He was shouting over his shoulder as his short legs moved quickly to catch the others. The canebrakes behind the store seemed to swallow him.

"Yes sir," Jake called after him.

With the men taking their smells of sweat, smoke, and tobacco away, the store greeted Jake with the welcoming smells of rat cheese, bologna and fresh bread. Having control of the whole store gave Jake a sense of power. He took a Snicker from the glass shelves under the front counter, then pulled a Coke from the cooler and snapped its lid in the opener. Walking over the plank floors, he began examining each shelf in the dim light. He found peanut butter jars in which the oil had separated and risen to the top. A layer of dust that must have taken years to accumulate sat undisturbed on their lids. Jake was surprised at how little merchandise was on the shelves. Flour sacks were filled with weevils, and roaches scattered when he moved loaves of bread. He put his candy bar under the light bulb for closer examination before taking a bite. It was fresh.

The dust levels made it easy to see that Dad sold a lot of candy and cold drinks, a small amount of feed, a few bottles of milk, and a few loaves of bread. The rest just sat on the shelves growing stale. Other kids had told him that gold was buried under the floor of the store and that the cash register contained thousands of dollars.

After an hour had passed, and the candy and Coke were gone, Jake grew bored enough to carefully open the cash register. He just wanted to find out if the rumors were true. Careful to keep the sound muffled, he softly pushed the bar he had seen Dad push many times. The drawer released against his hand, and he allowed it to gently open. Jake softly chuckled when he looked inside and saw the slots for ones, fives, tens and twenties. The twenties slot was filled with an old dirt-dauber nest. Round slots had been hand-carved for pennies, nickels, dimes, quarters, halves, and silver dollars. A single silver dollar rested in the silver dollar slot, year 1924. The drawer contained a total of nineteen dollars and twenty-seven cents. He quietly closed it, feeling a little closer to Dad Flannigan and anxious to tell his friends that the stories about the cash register, at least, were not true.

Jake looked at the clock over the door. It was already 10:45. His mother was probably already home from the prom. He turned out the lights and locked the door, removed the key, put it under the nail keg, and headed in the direction that Dad and the rest of the men had taken. He knew where they were going. He also knew better than to follow them, but wanted to see what shooting craps looked like.

Jake and his friends had sneaked around in the tall cane stalks behind Dad's store many times. Once inside the tall cane, it wasn't hard to find the trail that led to the men's little hideaway. A circle was cleared in the center of the cane where they kept a few folding chairs and stools. They had carried a lantern and built a fire for light. A tattered quilt was spread on the ground to catch the dice.

It was a windless spring night, and sounds carried in the still, thin air. "Eighter from Decatur, county seat of Wise. Fever in the whorehouse, run, whores, run." Jake heard the men coaxing the dice from deep within the canebrakes. Mesmerized by their chants, Jake found a comfortable spot to sit, leaned against a small tree, and settled in for a long lesson on gambling. The rustling of the cane as the dice game broke up awakened him around midnight. He rode home with his father in silence.

Chapter 18

"Say a big thank-you to Dr. Jonas Salk, Jake." Dr. Olen held up the needle and smiled. Jake winced as he felt the needle sting his arm, but the new polio vaccine was one shot Jake was happy to take. He had a cousin with polio and had nightmares about the crippling disease. Jake tried to ignore the sting in his arm as he and Rance stepped from the clinic office into a blazing sun. Rance jerked his hand back after touching the door handle on the '47 Chevrolet truck. "Damn. That's hot enough to burn your hand." Rance rubbed the handle with his shirt sleeve to cool it off as he looked toward Jake. "You want a ride to the ballpark?"

"Naw, I can walk. I got plenty of time to make the first practice." Jake wanted to walk around the square, peeking in store windows, before going toward the ballpark. Town somehow seemed cooler and wetter than it did in the country. It was just as dry here, but houses in town seemed somehow protected from the heat and drought. By comparison, the Rivers' home seemed unprotected, exposed to the baking sun that was shriveling the house and everything around it with each new dry, hot day.

"Jake, where are you?" His father's voice shook Jake from his daydream.

"What?"

"I don't know where you go in your head when you drift off like that. I asked if you could catch a ride home after practice."

"Yes sir."

Jake stopped in Miller's Drug to take in the cool air and smells of medicine mixed with ice cream and ladies perfumes. He had no money, so he pretended to look at the greeting cards as he watched

Mabel Wheat make a strawberry malt for a pretty high school girl. Jake's passion for baseball rekindled as he walked the familiar streets leading to Cooper School and the ballpark. June bugs singing in the trees reminded him of last summer's triumphs and failures. He wished that he had practiced more at home, but thinking about games after Tuck died seemed wrong, somehow.

Bo Randall greeted him at the backstop. It seemed to Jake that Bo came from another time, another life. Since Bo went to school in Cooper and Jake in Klondike, they had not seen each other since that final game of the previous year....the game in which Jake had experienced the flow. Tuck had still been alive then.

"Hey, Jake Rivers."

"Hey, Bo Randall." Bo had changed. Only slightly taller than Jake last year, he was almost a head taller now.

They both watched as Joe Daniels emptied a huge duffel bag full of balls, bats, face-masks, and mitts in front of the south dug-out. Joe saw them approach. "Well, Rivers and Randall, glad to see you boys are back. Looks like I'm your coach this year."

"Where's Coach Simpson?" Jake asked.

"He's off trying out for a minor league ball club somewhere." Jake was disappointed, but almost relieved that Coach Simpson was not going to be back. He was tough and demanding, and Jake was more in the mood for Joe's easy-going style.

Jake and Bo watched as a group of young players spilled out of Joe Daniels pickup bed. Many of the young players sported new gloves and caps. While Jake saved his cleats for games, these boys were wearing theirs for practice. Jake looked down at the holes in his tennis shoes and his well-worn glove. He remembered how frightened he had been at his first practice and his extreme self-consciousness the night of the first game. These boys looked and acted confident. Although all were younger, only one boy was smaller than Jake. He wondered if he was going to have to compete for his position at shortstop again.

***

Lundy Clark, Jr.'s familiar voice flowed through an improved microphone the night of the Indians' first game. Jake felt a certain pride as he stood at shortstop. The Indians were the reigning champions of Delta County Little League baseball. In a way, he almost felt that they represented the Cleveland Indians, 1954 Champions of the American League. He wanted both Indians teams to repeat as champions in 1955. His team was playing the lowly Yankees, last year's weakest team, so Jake expected victory.

When the first three pitches bounced in the dirt before reaching home plate, Jake silently groaned. The second Yankee batter, a young southpaw that went hitless for most of the 1954 season, slammed one twenty feet over the right field fence. Jake's spirits plummeted. How could this kid have grown that much, gotten that strong, in one year? He looked around the diamond at his new teammates. He and Bo were the only two returning infielders. He longed for the comfort of seeing Linc Little on the mound or at first base.

The Indians were already down four runs when Jake finally got to bat. Joe had inserted him as lead-off man again. He was surprised to see Dennis Mobley, a small boy from Cooper who had warmed the bench most of last season, throwing warm-up on the mound. Jake felt a silent chuckle of glee rise in his throat, but suppressed the smile that wanted to crease his face. He tapped home plate with the end of his bat and took his usual choke position on the handle. Piece of cake. Mobley's first pitch was a good fastball at Jake's knees. He let it pass for a called strike.

Jake felt his confidence waiver. The fastball had not been at Charlie Wagner or Linc Little speed, but it had been fast. The second pitch was a wobbly curve like none Jake had ever seen. He lunged at the ball with his bat and felt the vibration in his hands as he hit the ball close to the handle. The ball sputtered like a wounded bird as it spun between first and second. Jake's speed on the base paths earned him a single, but he died on first.

In the bottom of the ninth, Jake lunged at another pitch and punched another sputtering, spinning ball down the first base line. He hit the curve ball so close to the handle that it mashed a finger, but he still beat out a lucky single. Thoughts of last year's thumb injury entered his head as his right index finger throbbed. He man-

145

aged to steal second on a passed ball, but died there. The game ended Yankees 12, Indians 0.

Trish had come from Commerce for the first game and was there to take him home. She and Pete had married and were living in a small house close to campus at East Texas State while Pete finished his degree. Gray Boy had been at his usual spot along the outfield fence, but Jake was glad that nobody else from his family came.

"I heard that the Yankees practiced last fall and have been playing scrub ball since March. You boys will to better after you learn to start playing as a team." Trish kept her eyes on the road as she spoke.

Jake's embarrassment at the loss lessened for a minute. He looked to see who was at the Dairy Queen as they left town. "Don't kid me. Our pitcher couldn't even throw it hard enough to make it to home plate. Bo and I got the only three hits, and none of these new kids caught a single fly ball or skinner. Course, the Yankees who didn't walk hit home runs."

Trish laughed. "Ok, ok. You're right. But I think I saw a budding athlete or two out there. Just give 'em time."

Jake slumped back against the seat of the Ford. "I guess what Mama said about baseball is right."

"What's that?"

"Cows are dying of thirst, crops won't come up, and the ground's got cracks wide enough to swallow a horse. It's silly to worry about baseball."

The final game of the '55 season was half over when dust billowed across the baseball diamond like a brown cloud. The wind whistled as Lundy Clark announced a temporary suspension of the game. There was no place to get inside, and dust storms like this usually passed quickly, so the players stayed at their positions. At shortstop, Jake tried to breathe as little as possible until it passed. His eyes burned as the dust particles stung his skin. The Giants had them down only 4-0. Still time for a comeback.

Jake had to squint to see as far as first base. The pitcher and first baseman were standing together, putting their backs against the wind and using their caps to cover their faces. It had been the final game of last year's season when he first experienced the flow. Was it going to return tonight?

He tried to imagine winning the game, but it seemed hopeless. Even if he hit home runs every time at bat and made miracle plays in the field, he could not win the game without his teammates. He turned his back to the wind, sat down, ducked his head, and covered his face with his cap. The shouts of Linc Little on the pitcher's mound, Danny Lawler behind the plate, and Jack Poteet on first base drifted through the howling wind. He heard the sound of Tuck's laughter mixed with the comforting voices of his parents, Gray Boy, and Trish coming from the stands. As the wind began to die down, he lifted the cap to see his old friends and mentors on the baseball diamond, but they were not there. Nobody from his family was in the stands. The Indians finished the season without winning a game.

It was already blazing hot as Jake walked to the mailbox the next morning. He had ordered free information from Charles Atlas on how to build muscles and wanted to intercept it before his brother saw it and teased him. He thumbed through the small stack as he walked along. Nothing from Charles Atlas, world's most perfectly developed man. He recognized Harry Cardwell's name and distinctive handwriting on the return address of one envelope.

In the kitchen, he tossed the mail on the table and started to walk away. Harry's letter landed on top. It was addressed to Rance and Mattie Rivers. Jake stared at the letter. Harry had coached the Giants again this year. Maybe the letter was about Jake and Little League. Maybe there was something inside that he needed to know. He lighted a burner on the kerosene stove and set the teakettle on. When enough steam built up, he pulled the flap open and withdrew the contents.

Jake stared at the five by seven single sheet. Cardwell's Gro. and Gas, Klondike, Texas, was neatly printed at the top. Jake had seen receipts like it before in his mother's grocery sacks. Just below, Jake read Harry Cardwell's flowing script:

Balance Due $298.24. Rance and Mattie, This old drought is about to take us all down. Seems like the rest of the country is enjoying prosperity after the war, but we are stuck in the Great Depression because of the *drought. I know you are hurting like we are, but anything you can do toward this old bill will be appreciated. Sorry, Harry.*

Jake stared at Harry's handwritten note for a long time, trying to find something redeeming in it, something besides the fact that his parents could not pay for groceries. The pleading message depressed and frightened him. At the sound of his father's truck door, he rushed to re-fold the bill and stuff it back into the envelope. He licked the flap and did his best to reseal it.

Rance leafed through the mail, tossing most of it on the table or in the trash. He stopped and stared at the Cardwell envelope, then slowly opened it and read. Shaking his head slowly, Rance sat down in a kitchen chair and stared at the bill. Jake eased out of his chair and started toward the front door, hoping his father would not notice.

"Jake, come here." Rance held up the envelope. "This looks like it's been opened. Have you been opening my mail?"

"No sir. What is it?" In his rush to deny his guilt, he had gone too far.

"I expect you know already, but it's a dun from Harry Cardwell." Rance drummed his fingers on the table and shook his head. "He's never sent one before. He knows we always pay our bills in the fall." Rance was silent for a long time, and Jake grew restless, wondering if his father was through with him. Rance finally looked at him. "You just need to keep your nose out of places where it's not wanted."

"Yes, sir."

Jake already had permission to return his baseball uniform, so he decided to leave early. He was anxious to put distance between himself and his father. The slight breeze seemed to be coming from a hot stove, but Jake welcomed any movement in the air as he stuck out his thumb on 24. His baseball uniform was folded neatly in the sack under his arm. He was disappointed when Tricky Fisher stopped to offer a ride. Jake jumped into the cab and sat on the exposed springs of the truck seat, trying not to inhale the smell of puppy poop and catfish stink bait. Dropped off at Cardwell's parking lot in Klondike, he stood outside for a few minutes to allow the hot sun to take away the smell of Tricky's pickup. He looked up at the Cardwell sign and wondered if he would be welcome there. Would the dun that Harry had sent mean the end of the relationship between the Rivers and Cardwells? Was the drought now coming between friends? Was his family going to do without groceries?

Inside the store, Jake stuck his nose in the sack to check the smell before placing his laundered and folded Little League uniform on the counter. He watched Harry Cardwell sack groceries for a man Jake did not recognize and take his payment in cash. Jake had always thought of Harry as almost wealthy. He lived in a big, white house in Klondike and drove an almost new Ford pickup. Harry had always been a kind, gentle man, a war hero, and a hero to Jake. He still showed signs of his youthful abilities when he hit ground balls to the Giants or swished one through a basketball net in the Klondike gym. Were Harry and his father enemies now?

As the customer left, Harry turned toward Jake and smiled as he filled out a receipt for the uniform. "I'll take yours and the other ones I've collected to Welch's tomorrow."

Jake nodded and turned to leave. His dejection was evident as he look a last look at the uniform. Harry followed him outside.

"Want me to have 'em save that uniform for you for next year? Nine may be your lucky number."

Jake leaned against the gas pump. "Nope. I may not play next year."

Harry's face registered surprise, but he said nothing until Jake started walking off. "Need a ride home?"

"No, thanks. I'm going down to Papa Lee's and Big Mama's for a little bit. Then I can hitch home." Jake turned to start across 24.

Harry picked up the air hose and coiled it around its hook. "Jake, I know it was a tough season for the Indians, but you can't let that get you down. The team will need you more than ever next year."

Jake nodded as he recalled the unbroken string of humiliating defeats. "I sure didn't do 'em much good last year."

Harry walked a little closer. "You played pretty well last year, Jake. Your batting average was up a little, and your fielding percentage was the best of any of the shortstops." Harry jerked a thumb toward the store. "You even grew into that uniform in there."

Jake smiled halfheartedly. "I guess so. Just seems like it wasn't much fun last year. I've been practicing my roping more. Papa says I can start ropin' calves as soon as it rains enough for Daddy to buy stocker cows. Maybe I'll be better at that than I am at baseball."

"Jake, your daddy used to tell me that baseball was like life. You win some and you lose some. If you can handle both in the game, you can handle both in life. He wouldn't want you to be a quitter."

Jake thought back to the past season. Rance had attended his games only sporadically in the beginning of the season. By the middle, he was usually drinking when he did attend. By the end, Jake hoped that his father wouldn't come to the games at all. Maybe that was why Harry had sent the bill. He looked up into Harry Cardwell's eyes. "Why not? He's a quitter." Jake ran across 24 and down Klondike's main street before Harry could answer.

Chapter 19

The dog days of summer were upon them, and heat and humidity hung like a cloud in the dairy barn, holding the aroma of milk, manure, urine, and feed inside the parlor. Jake poured some feed in the stanchions, walked back to the feed room, and plopped down on a sack of bran. It was cooler and darker in the feed room and the sweet smell of dairy feed overpowered the more unpleasant odors coming from the dairy parlor. Jake heard knocking that seemed to be coming from the milk cooler room. He walked back into the parlor and listened. It could barely be heard over the din of the milking machines. Rance and Gray had not heard it. He followed the noise down the hall to the front room where milk was stored in cans that sat in cooled water inside a huge cooler. He opened the outside door and faced the excited pointing of a slight man wearing a white shirt and black shoestring tie.

"Your house is on fire!"

Jake's eyes followed the direction of the man's finger and saw flames shooting from the roof of the house beside the crumbling chimney. His mother was inside. Jake ran into the parlor and shouted at his father and brother. They followed him outside.

"She'll be gone in a few minutes unless we can put it out." Rance ran toward the house to warn Mattie. "Hurry up, boys. Get both water hoses and hook them to the faucet at the barn."

Gray grabbed the ladder and was already climbing to the roof. "Get the hoses, Jake. Hurry!"

Jake pulled the hoses from the wash room and connected one to the outside faucet. The man with the tie connected the two hoses and carried the end to Gray. Jake turned on the water and watched as Gray turned the red flames into black smoke. He was relieved when Mattie ran to the side of the house to help. Rance had crawled into the attic from inside. Gray handed the hose to him through the hole in the roof, and Rance began hosing down the attic.

"Don't turn it down yet, Jake. The fire's out, but I want to really soak this hot wood." Rance shouted through the hole in the roof, irritation in his voice.

"I didn't touch it." Jake turned to look at the faucet handle, then walked over to check it. It was wide open.

Gray looked through the hole in the roof and watched the stream from the hose turn to a trickle, then stop. He turned back toward Jake. "The water quit. Are you sure it's still on?"

Jake checked again, his fingers trembling as he turned the faucet both ways. "Yes, it's on." He thought of his and Tuck's bed and the dog trot going up in flames. If the house was gone, there would be nothing left of Tuck. He was relieved when Rance stuck his head through the roof.

"The fire's out, but I sure would like to soak down these old shingles. Hot as it is, they could flare back up. You boys get some buckets and dip some water from the pool just in case. For the next hour, Gray, Jake and the stranger ran buckets of water from the pool to the roof. Finally, Rance climbed out of the attic through the hole in the roof, down the ladder, and walked into the living room to examine the damage. Jake followed him. Mattie sat in her Christmas-present rocker, elbows propped on the arms, her head in her hands. Rance looked up at the stovepipe that fed the smoke into the chimney. He could see daylight through the hole in the roof and along the wall where the chimney had separated from the house. He glanced at the stranger who had been his wife. "Could have been a lot worse." As Rance turned to go back outside, Jake followed. He heard his mother begin to cry.

Outside, Rance, Gray, and Jake shook the hand of the young man who had probably kept their house from burning to the ground. Rance withdrew a checkbook from the bib of his overalls. "What you did for us is priceless, and I can't afford to pay what it's worth, but I would like to pay you something."

The man held up the palms of both hands. "Sir, I can't take a man's money for doing what's right. I hate to rush off, but I'm late for a class at ET."

"You go to college at ET?" Rance asked.

"Yes sir. Working on my master's. I teach one class, too."

"Where do you live?"

"Living in Cooper now. Rent's cheaper there." The man was walking toward his car as he talked.

"Let me at least buy you a tankful of gas." Rance followed him, reaching for his billfold. He seemed almost desperate to repay the kindness the man had shown.

The man reached into his car and withdrew the biggest camera that Jake had ever seen. "My thanks are all in here. I would never have seen the fire if I hadn't stopped to take a picture in your driveway. I may owe you if these pictures turn out half as good as I think they will."

Jake walked closer to examine the camera. "Are you a photographer?"

The man nodded, his pencil tie blowing in the hot breeze. "I'm studying to be one."

"What's in the pictures?" Jake asked.

The man glanced sheepishly at Rance. "Well, I got one good shot of the flames shooting out of your roof. Sorry if that seems insensitive."

Rance shook his head.

"But that wasn't what stopped me. Sounds strange, but a bird really stopped me. A mockingbird kept flying dangerously close to my windshield. It flew back and forth in front of the car for a couple of miles before I stopped to see if I could get a shot of it."

Jake took a deep breath and looked at Rance and Gray. Their faces showed interest, but not surprise. The man put the camera back into his car so that he could gesture with both hands. He used them to make flying motions. "When I got out of the car, the mockingbird flew away and circled a big group of white cowbirds sitting right in the middle of your driveway." He paused as he saw the concentrated stares of the Rivers. Mattie had walked out onto the porch to listen. "I had never seen white cowbirds before. The ones I know about are black." The man stopped again and looked toward

153

Mattie as if he were waiting for some type of explanation. "I clicked several shots. They should be wonderful pictures. Could make me famous." He laughed nervously as he opened the car door and sat down.

Jake followed him and stood as close as he could to the car window. He did not want the man to leave. As the man started the engine and put it into reverse, he leaned out the car window and spoke softly to Jake as if he were afraid for Rance to hear. "I'm almost afraid to say this out loud until I develop the shots, but there was something else. Right in the middle of those cowbirds was a cotton-tail rabbit and a squirrel. They looked like they were all playing together, and the mockingbird seemed to be watching over them."

He waited for a reaction, but Jake just continued to stare, his gaze begging for more of the story. The man shook his head. "Overactive imagination or too much coffee, I guess, but it sure seemed like that bird was trying to stop my car." Jake smiled as the man backed out to the turnaround and drove away. He watched the car until it was out of sight and then turned to Rance and Gray. Both were staring at the departing car. Mattie wiped her eyes with her apron. Rance looked at his sons. "Damn. Did we even get his name?"

Jake put on his boots and a shirt to help Gray finish milking while his father tried to find out why the water had stopped. The cows had filled the parlor with manure and washed it down with urine while Rance and the boys were putting out the fire. Done with their feed, some of the cows panicked and struggled against the stanchions to be released. It was almost noon before Jake emerged from the barn, limedust-white from head to toe. He brushed off the lime before going into the house. Mattie was still sitting in the rocking chair in the living room.

Jake looked up through the new hole in their roof. "What do you suppose started the fire?"

"Anything can start a fire anywhere, as dry as it is. Pasture fires are popping up everywhere. Probably a spark blew from somewhere." Mattie moved the rocker back and forth. "Course, it could have been your Daddy's damned old wood stove. He's got to have everything the way it was a hundred years ago."

Jake decided not to mention that the stove had not been lighted since last winter. "Where's Daddy?"

Mattie's voice was flat. "He's trying to find out why the water quit."

Jake found him inside the pump house, priming the pump for the third time. "Did you fix the pump?"

The pump house was too low for Rance to stand erect, so he stepped outside. "Pump's fine."

"What's wrong, then?"

Rance looked at Jake as if he did not see him. He slid down the side of the pump house and sat on the hot sand. "Guess that just leaves one other possibility, Jake. The well is dry."

"Oh." Jake could think of nothing else to say. He took pride in his father's ability to fix anything that broke around the place, but a dry well could only be fixed by God. Afternoon milking started again in four hours. First a house fire, then a dry well.

Jake kicked the dust with his boot. "What are you going to do?"

Rance traced lines in the sand with his pocket knife. "I don't know, son. I don't know."

Jake sat beside his father a long time before he spoke again. "I sure would like to see a copy of that picture the man took of the birds." Jake wished he could think of something to comfort his father, but he could not get his mind off the birds, the rabbit, and the squirrel.

Rance looked at him, smiled, pinched his leg above the knee, and stood up. "Let's go, Jake. I think I know how we can milk tonight."

By milking time, Rance and the boys had set up a temporary pipeline from the pool to the dairy barn and connected the well pump to it. He had even constructed a cheesecloth filter that could be replaced daily. Not as good as well water, but it allowed them to milk. They were feeling pretty good when they walked into the house after milking, carrying buckets of filtered pool water. Jake's high spirits matched his father's until he saw his mother sitting at the kitchen table. Beans were warming on the kerosene stove.

Rance lifted the bean pot lid and inspected the contents. He dipped water from his bucket and added to the beans. As he stirred them, he looked at his wife. She had cried every day for the first month after Tuck died, but the crying had been easier to deal with than this morose brooding.

"Guess the well is dry." She spoke without looking up.

"Yes, but I rigged up a line to the pool. We probably won't pass inspection, but maybe the inspector won't come for awhile."

"How long will the water in the pool last?"

Rance took a deep breath and made the whistling noise he always did when he uttered a big sigh. "Not long. Three, maybe four weeks."

She kept her eyes fixed a few inches in front of her feet. "Where's your Rivers' flow now?"

Chapter 20

Northeast Texans were glad to see the summer of '55 depart. The Rivers began depleting the water in their pool to operate their dairy. Cattle all over Delta County were dying from lack of water and grass. Little hay was left, and livestock had become too cheap to feed grain. Many cows broke their legs falling into the huge cracks in the earth. Ironically, some drowned in bogs trying to reach water in pools almost gone dry. Usually, their carcasses were left to rot. The smells filled the dense air for miles. Rats and other rodents invaded homes, looking for water. Rance let his lease lapse on the bottomland cotton patch. The cotton he planted there in the spring had not come up.

Even with little cotton to harvest, Klondike School had held a summer session, but heat and humidity hung over the school like a wet saddle blanket. The end of cotton harvest was usually followed by cooler weather and better chances for rain, a new season and new beginnings. Honking geese flew in formation over Delta County as they headed south, and mountain breezes from the north replaced sultry Gulf winds. Hope was rekindled. Memories of falling leaves washed by water and burnished to a soft glow by autumn sun flooded the senses of people old enough to remember what it used to be like in Northeast Texas in the fall. But these were only sensory memories. The north winds carried only dust, and shriveled leaves fell too soon, drifting on the wind to finally settle on hard, dry ground.

Few families in Delta County could afford the new television sets that were entering homes across the rest of the nation. Families who bought them found their living rooms full on Wednesday nights as neighbors joined them to watch boxing. At his cousin's house, Jake watched episodes of Ozzie and Harriet and Father Knows Best and marveled at how these families' lives contrasted with his own. He was fascinated by the big homes, green lawns, new cars and appliances, mothers who wore pearls while cleaning house, maids, and especially by Robert Young of Father Knows Best. This father came home from work in a suit and tie, walked to the closet and promptly changed into a corduroy jacket with suede elbows for supper, or dinner as they called it on television, always eating the evening meal in the tie he had worn to work.

Only a few days remained before the official start of the 1955-56 school year at Klondike. Alone at home, Jake counted the money he had earned to buy school clothes. With cotton pulling jobs scarce, there was considerably less than last year. Mattie would take him shopping the next day, and he knew that tough decisions would have to be made about what not to buy. The worry about clothes added to his general dislike of school. Disconsolate, he bridled Scar and rode toward Griffin's house. The sun was mid-morning high as Jake tied his horse to the hitching rail outside and walked into Griffin's kitchen.

His grandfather was saucering a cup of coffee, staring out his kitchen window at the chickens scratching around the edges of Buddy's little shed. "Mornin' Bolivar." Without asking, Griffin poured Jake a cup of coffee. Jake sat with him at the small table, brooding as he sipped the coffee. He grimaced at the taste. Griffin broke the silence. "Seems sorta' cruel of Mother Nature to give us this damn humidity without the rain that's supposed to go with it."

Jake did not want to talk about the weather. "Things are bad at our house, Papa."

Griffin's cup and saucer clicked as he scraped the spilled coffee from the bottom of his cup across the saucer rim. "How so, Jake?"

"Everybody's sad at home, includin' me, I guess." Jake stood and pushed his hands deep into his pockets. "Papa Lee says you live most of the time in the flow. How do you do it, Papa? You seem to even enjoy just watching those chickens scratch."

Griffin stared at his grandson with a bemused expression. "He does, does he? Well Jake, assuming your Papa Lee is right, I guess

158

the only answer I have is practice . . . you can't be good at anything without practice." Griffin nodded toward the rope Jake had left on the wood floor. "When you started throwing that rope at things, you weren't very good at it. Now, you can catch what you throw at. I've practiced enjoying life long enough to be good at it." They both walked out to Griffin's front porch and stared at the empty pasture where cattle used to graze. Jake picked up his rope and followed as Griffin walked to Buddy's shed. The horse stood quietly as Griffin brushed him.

"Tell me about Grandpa Lev and Old Yank again. Daddy told me the story again last summer, but he always stops when Grandpa gets up and walks off the battlefield with the bullet in him."

Griffin threw the blankets and saddle on and looked over the horse's back at Jake. "You've heard about Old Yank most of your life, Jake. We've squeezed that story till it's drier than a corn shuck." He winked at Jake. "But I still like to tell it. Papa stole the horse from a Yankee soldier and rode him all the way home. Kept that old horse till he was twenty-four years old. I rode him when I was a boy."

"How far was that ride, Papa?"

"About thirteen hundred miles, I think. Took Papa and Yank a little over two months." Rance paused and looked into Jake's eyes. "You don't really believe that story, do you, Jake?"

The question startled Jake and he answered abruptly. "Sure I do. It's just that I told some of my friends and they didn't seem to."

"Jake, I'm sure that stories about the flow have grown with retellin' over the years, but the fact is that a man has a lot more control over his thinkin' and his body than most folks ever use. The flow's all about using that power more. Simple as that."

Jake tugged on the brim of his straw hat. "It's still confusing, though. We Rivers have the flow, but we seem to be having more hard luck than anybody right now."

"Life kicks everybody in the butt once in awhile, some more than others. You just have to get up and keep walking." He flipped the stirrup across the seat and buckled the cinches. "Jaker Ridge, you can't wait for everything to be perfect to start enjoying life. It's

159

the little things in life that make a man happy. Don't just drink your coffee in the morning. Enjoy it - smell it - taste it - let the smoke curl around your face and into your nose - experience it."

"To tell the truth, I don't like coffee much."

Griffin chuckled softly as he pulled the stirrup back down, stepped into it, and mounted. Looking down from the horse, he smiled at his confused grandson."If there's ham and eggs, that's even more to smile about. "

Jake put his hand on Buddy's hip and looked up at his grandfather. "You're saying that all it takes to make you happy is a good cup of coffee and some ham and eggs to go with it?"

Griffin pulled his hat down a little and squinted into the east sun. "On some days, you bet." He crossed the reins and allowed them to rest on Buddy's neck. He used his hands to play an imaginary fiddle. "Other days, it's the feel of a good fiddle and bow, the sound of a guitar being strummed slow and easy, sharing a laugh or two with a good friend, a hug from a grandchild. Griffin touched Jake's shoulder. "Sometimes, it's the touch of a good-lookin' woman.".

Jake had never heard his grandfather mention women before. It gave him a good feeling, like they were talking man to man. Griffin shifted his weight in the saddle and it squeaked a little. Jake could smell the leather mixing with Buddy, already starting to sweat under the blankets. "I especially like the feeling you get when your hand is resting in the middle of a woman's back before the music plays. Then the sound of music courses through your blood and sweeps you both across the dance floor." He lifted the reins from Buddy's neck. "Or the feel of a good horse between your legs in the morning." As Buddy eased off, Griffin held him up and spoke over his shoulder. "You see, that's what I'm trying to tell you; it ain't just any one thing; it's every little thing." Griffin's face lost its mellow look and took on an expression of almost pleading. "You remember when you first experienced the flow, how crystal clear everything seemed? That's how life is supposed to be. Jake, you need to look at what you have to be grateful for...not at what you lost." Griffin squeezed his legs against Buddy's sides and rode away.

"When can I start roping calves?" Jake called out his daily

question. Griffin just waved his hand in the air without turning to answer. Jake watched as his grandfather rode off with the warm autumn sun at his back.

Chapter 21

Gray used a rake to smooth the dirt, and Jake stepped on the large clods over Tuck's grave. Strange that Tuck visited him in the dog trot, but not here. Was he watching them from heaven or from below those awful clods? Jake looked around the cemetery for signs of a mockingbird, squirrel, or rabbit, but saw none. Only black crows interrupted the soft whistle of the wind through the trees bordering the cemetery.

"It's been more than eight months, and I still look around to see if he's coming in when the screen door slams," Mattie said as she stared at the marker. Her eyes were dry, and her voice did not break; surrender could be detected in the flat tone. She had no more tears, but the terrible sadness and fear remained in her eyes. Rance put his arm around her, and they walked to the car together. Jake and Gray knelt to run their hand across the words on the marker, trying to communicate with their little brother, imagining that they did. The lonesome, gray, humid day added to their melancholy moods as the Ford carried them down 24 toward home.

Rance's mood lifted as a few drops of rain splattered on the windshield. He spoke without taking his eyes off the road. "Today's the seventh game of the World Series. We have an open invitation from Raymond and Christine to drop by Camp Lake store and watch it on their television. It's an all-New York Series, and it may be about over, but we can root for the Dodgers against the Yankees. What do you say?" Watching anything, anywhere, on television drew enthusiastic approval from Jake. It was a good sign when Gray did not object or ask to be dropped off at home. Even Mattie smiled and nodded.

Rance pushed the old Ford up to seventy as they passed their driveway, headed west. Camp Lake was only three miles west of their home. Camp Lake Store was a store very much like Cardwell's, but it had more feed and farm supplies and less groceries. Jake had never understood the name, since there was no camp and no lake anywhere around. He was first to enter the store. He spoke to Christine and looked around for the television as the rest of the family came through the screen door. Christine laughed when Jake's face betrayed his disappointment. "It's in the house, Jake. Raymond is in there watching the Series now. Go on out. Mattie, you can visit with me if you don't want to watch the game."

Raymond and Christine Mills lived in a small house behind their store. Rance and the children joined Raymond in the living room and watched in awe as they put faces to names they had only heard about on the radio for years. Jake felt superior for having watched one game last year at the gin. The game was already at the bottom of the sixth. Yogi Berra sliced a long drive just inside the foul pole line in left field, just as the children plopped down on the Mills' throw rug in front of the television. Sandy Amoros made a spectacular glove-hand catch and threw a perfect relay to Pee Wee Reese at shortstop. Jake was on his feet as Reese, his hero shortstop, tossed it to Gil Hodges at second for a double play. Billy Martin died on second. Jake tried to connect the moving figures with the baseball cards that came with flat slabs of bubble gum. When the Dodgers hung on to become 1955 World Champions, Jake longed to stay and watch more television, but dairy cows were waiting.

***

With Gray staying for after-school basketball practice, Jake walked home from the first day of fall school alone. As he entered the house, he heard the familiar sounds of his mother's singing from the kitchen. She had sung before Tuck died, but it seemed that her voice had changed since his death. Her choice of songs certainly had. Her voice lilted through the house almost daily. Although the voice was nice and soft, her words seemed to be plaintive calls for mercy, a desperate pleading for escape. Her singing was disquieting for everyone, especially Jake. She seemed to sing more when he was alone in the house with her. She sang a verse or two from a few songs, continuously repeating them as if praying. She was especially fond of repeating the verse, *Please don't take my sunshine away.*

Jake knew most of the words to that short song, and he had always thought they were about a sweetheart, but it was clear that Mattie was speaking to God about Tuck. Although Jake had his own conversations with Tuck, he worried about his mother's state of mind. She also sang *Keep on the Sunny Side* a lot. Mattie seemed to be talking to herself when she sang it, as if trying desperately to claw her way out of the darkness and back to her husband and remaining children. Jake spoke to Trish about it when she visited, but she seemed to shrug it off. "That's Mama's way of coping."

The Rivers seldom sat down together for a meal. Gray Boy was gone most nights, and Rance often did not arrive until after meals were finished, bringing the smell of whiskey into Mattie's tee-totaler house. This always brought a cold stare from Mattie and a frigid atmosphere to their home. Rance's solution was to stay out later and drink more.

Mattie began taking Jake to church every Sunday, but even that was not enough to satisfy her new religious fervor. She sought out evangelical preachers and revivals whenever and wherever she could. Gray Boy always found reasonable excuses not to attend. When he did not have an excuse, Gray simply refused to go. Rance did not force him. Jake was allowed to skip revivals if they occurred on a school night, but weekends usually found him under a revival tent with his mother. He had always wanted his parents to go with him to church, but he did not like the revivals.

In November of 1955, Jake and his mother walked toward yet another revival tent on the edge of a dusty cotton field. The cotton stalks had been shredded, but the field had not been plowed. Jake figured that the farmer who planted this field had given up on cotton like his father. He watched the dust particles dance through the harsh lights set up under the tent as Mattie found them seats on metal chairs. She sat quietly and stiffly. Mattie owned two dresses that she deemed suitable for church. Tonight, she had on her navy blue dress with white polka dots. A matching round hat with dark blue lace fringing the edges perched at a slight angle on her head. It was held in place by bobby pins. Jake sat quietly and miserably, drawing patterns in the dirt with his shoes and watching the head-lights bounce up and down as cars crossed the rows and dropped down into the furrows of the cotton patch. The dust they created blew into the tent and settled. It was warm for November.

It was Saturday night, and Jake wanted to see a picture show, but Mattie had shamed him into going with her to the revival. It was just as well, because he was almost afraid for his mother to go alone. Having experienced the fervor of some revivals and heard her rendition of *I'll Fly Away*, Jake had told Trish that he was afraid their mother might just be whisked up into the sky during a revival meeting, never to return to them. The more revivals she attended, the more desperate she seemed.

Jake usually left the revivals feeling even more guilty because God had still not called him to walk down the aisle during any of the fervent invitations. The evangelists who spoke at these revivals were usually perfectly coiffed men, with hair that did not move in spite of their most violent gyrations and flailing of arms. Their faces were soft and pale. They wore shiny suits, gray or black, with a plain black tie. Everything was shiny except for their shoes, which were often scuffed, with heels worn down on the sides. Their words were spoken succinctly and with exaggeration. When it came time for the invitation to walk down the aisle and save your soul from the blazing fires of hell, the evangelists often sang or screamed their entreaties. None of these evangelists had inspired Jake to consider leaving his seat. He did not usually even like them.

A hush fell over the crowd as a man stepped behind the pul-pit. He was tall and slightly stooped. His clothing was worn and rumpled, his black hair wiry and unruly, and streaked with gray. His face was dark and craggy, with deep-set, green, piercing eyes. His eyebrows were thick and unruly. He reminded Jake of the pic-tures he had seen of Abraham Lincoln. Jake always tried to look away from the evangelists for fear of drawing their attention. He had no desire to be the object of their appeals of salvation. He knew he was a sinner but did not wish to have that fact pointed out to a group of strangers.

On this night, however, Jake could not take his eyes off the preacher. Although he intellectually understood little of what the preacher was saying, the words seemed to sink into him and comfort him. The evangelist's voice seemed to come from deep within his chest, breaking occasionally as if his vocal cords had been worn by time. They seemed to rattle and shake just behind his Adam's apple. When Jake glanced at his mother's face, the look of fear and frantic searching was gone, replaced with her former expression. Her eyes were relaxed and soft, like they used to be.

A piano sat on a piece of plywood at the front of the tent. A large lady rolled her stool to the piano and touched the keys heavily with bulbous fingers. As she pounded the keys, the evangelist began his invitation. He did not offer threats of hellfire and damnation in a loud voice; he simply offered a quiet supplication. For those who came down the aisle, he spoke softly and touched the shoulder or arm of each.

One man seated in the back of the tent suddenly bolted from his seat and ran down the aisle until he reached the back of the line just beside where Mattie sat. He shouted, "Praise God, Preacher; He has taken ahold of me. He is casting out the demons from my life." He ripped the false teeth out of his mouth as if they were vile demons and waved them in the air over Jake's and Mattie's heads. Jake imagined that he could feel the spittle dropping on his hair. The man's tongue shot out of his mouth and flopped on his chin as if his mouth now considered it an intruder. He fell backward as if pulled by an invisible rope, flopping down on his back and grinding his body against the grass. Jake was close enough to smell the dust and the bruised goat weeds and grass the man was wallowing in. He had heard of epileptic seizures and thought this must be one. He knew it was impolite to stare, but couldn't keep from it.

The man began shouting in words that had no meaning to Jake. Others in the congregation began whispering something about tongues. The preacher calmly left the front of the line, walked past Mattie and Jake to where the man was writhing on the ground, knelt on one knee, put his hand on the man's chest to hold him still, put his head near the man's ear, and whispered. The man

167

stopped writhing and shouting, got up, and took his place in line. As the preacher rose to return to his place at the front of the tent, he stopped beside Mattie, put his hand on her shoulder, looked into her eyes for an uncomfortable period of time, then whispered to her. He returned to the front of the tent to resume receiving his converts.

"What did he say?" Jake whispered.

Mattie continued to stare at the preacher, lost in her thoughts, and did not reply. But Jake had heard what the man had said. "You have nothing to fear. God is not punishing your family. Your husband and your children need you. Give yourself to them. You have the strength to go on."

After the revival meeting was over, Mattie sat motionless for a long time. The tent was empty when she finally turned to face Jake. "What does it feel like to be in the Rivers' flow, Jake?" Jake could think of nothing to say. He couldn't describe it, but more than that, it was the first time he realized that his mother had never been in the flow. She had never spoken of it as the other family members had, but he just assumed that she had experienced it. He had never considered that she wasn't a Rivers by blood, only by marriage. After that night, the fear and anguish in her eyes started to recede, replaced with grim determination. She started to become a new person.

Chapter 22

Jake and Gray were surprised to see Rance sitting on the front porch as they walked up the driveway after school. "The water pipe is stopped up again, Jake. I'm sorry, Son, but I just couldn't get it cleared. You're the only one that's small enough to get down there now." It was warm for December, but Jake knew that the water would still be cold. The thought made chill bumps come up on Jake's arms and legs. Mattie's fretting about his getting hung up in the underwater system of pipes or the fence that kept the cows away from the filtering system didn't help.

"Okay. I'll change and see if I can get it fixed." Jake hated the thought of doing the job, but was secretly proud that only he could do it. He enjoyed being needed. Rance's praise for his being able to withstand the cold and wet was always lavish. Besides, his chores would be over in less than an hour. Rance and Gray did his other work as a reward for going into the pool.

Mattie had laid out the cutoff jeans and ragged shirt that he wore when he went into the pool's muddy water. She was always waiting pool-side with a towel when he emerged shivering. He also knew that warm bath water was just inside the house. He tried to focus on those pleasant thoughts as he waded into the cold water. Clumsy and frustrated as the cold bit into his hands and body the first time he unclogged the filter, he had improved with the second. Now, in his third trip into the water, he was more adept and only had to come up for air once.

Out of the warm tub, he put on dry clothes and carried the tub outside and emptied it into the yard. He lay down on his bed, idly watching the dog trot lightbulb swing back and forth, his eyes tracing the cord from the high ceiling down to the bulb itself. Since Tuck's death, it had become almost hypnotic to Jake, seeming to accuse him of some wrong. Whenever the sorrow of losing Tuck started to overcome him, he returned to their shared bed, read, and watched the light. His thoughts were now deeper and darker than they had been before. He thought of heaven and hell and whether or not he might have been at fault for Tuck's death. He kept returning to the time he and Tuck had played in the snow. Had that caused his illness? What did God have against him? Was what they said in Sunday school true? Would he go to hell if he didn't go to church every Sunday and be saved?

He pulled his uncle's Army foot locker from under his bed and rummaged inside for *The Bible in Story and Pictures*. He opened the cover and read the inscription--- to Richard for twelve consecutive weeks of Sunday school and Church. His cousin had given Jake the Bible when he left for the Air Force. He was killed six weeks into pilot training. Everybody said it was a freak accident. Was it because Jake had his Bible and had no right to it? His mind wandered to the year before Tuck's death. He had begged rides from friends when the family car was gone on Sunday, even hitch-hiked once, trying to make that twelve weeks of Sunday school and church. He stopped after only nine. Was his weakness bringing all this trouble on the family, causing them to lose the flow? He had still not been baptized, and the church had made it clear he was not going to heaven until he was. Maybe, just maybe, he was being punished now.

Each time the thoughts were about to take him over the precipice into despair, Tuck always returned to talk. When Jake saw the small depression in the feather bed, the outline of Tuck's small body, a feeling of peace flowed through him, replacing the fear and anguish.

At supper that night, Rance ate silently, occasionally drumming his fingers on the table. "I think we're going to have to sell the dairy cattle. The water can't hold out more than another few days. Better get out while the gettin's good."

Mattie stared at him with her lips set firmly. "How are we going to feed this family?" she asked.

Rance talked around her question. "I've been thinking about it for a long time. I didn't want to say too much because sometimes a man can talk himself right into failure. I didn't want to give up hope. Now, it's just time to face reality." He looked for understanding in Mattie's expression, but found none. "You've seen this coming just like I have. We have no water for the dairy. We're hauling water for the house." He nodded toward Jake. "I'm not sending this boy into that pool anymore to drown or catch his death of cold."

Jake watched his mother's eyes soften, encouraging Rance to continue with the details he had been working out in his mind. "They've had some rain a hundred miles southeast of here. Hack says that he heard dairy cattle were still worth a little down there. Here, they ain't worth a bucket of warm spit because of the drought. I figure to haul 'em over to a sale barn there. We'll milk 'em before daylight and start hauling right after we milk. With Hack and Seth and the boys' help, we should be able to get 'em all there in time for the sale."

"Have you told the bank about your plans?" Mattie asked.

"Not yet. I'll have to let Frank Durett and the bank know before I take the cows out of the county, but he'll approve. He knows it's our only choice."

"Will there be enough to pay off the note?"

"With any luck, the cows will cover the note. Then we can sell the dairy equipment and maybe have enough money to buy back some stocker cows when it rains."

Stocker cows. No dairy. The news may have been bad, but the thought of gathering all the dairy cows, putting them into a trailer and hauling them a hundred miles away thrilled Jake. Getting beef cattle thrilled him even more. He had a mental picture of himself aboard Scar, roping and dragging calves to the fire to be branded.

Mattie ran her fingers through her black hair. "What do we do for money until it rains?" Jake noticed the first signs of gray showing in his mother's hair.

Rance looked around the table at each of them. "I'll have time to haul more water for other people. I've talked to the county commissioner about driving road equipment for them. Mattie, you know that I've been turning people down right and left for work

171

because I had to milk every day. We'll get by."

"I can go to work now." Mattie dropped her head as tears welled up. Everyone knew that she was thinking of Tuck. A baby was no longer at home for her to tend to.

It was almost bedtime when Rance found Jake. "What are you doing out here in the dark, Son?"

Jake had saddled Scar and was sitting in the saddle, his rope coiled in his hands. Sure that he looked foolish sitting under the moonlight, Jake stumbled his answer. "Nothin'."

Rance walked in front of the horse, picked up the bale of hay, and moved it a few feet. "As long as you're doing nothing, you might as well do it right. That's about the distance and the angle you need to rope from." Rance jiggled the small calf skull Jake had attached to the bale of hay.

"I roped it ninety-six straight times yesterday on the ground, but fifty's the most I ever got from the horse." Jake hoped that ninety-six was close enough to the hundred that Rance had set as the minimum number of consecutive catches of the calf head before he would be allowed to rope from his horse.

Rance smiled. "Well, I guess you're letting that one hundred spook you. Roping's like baseball...a lot of it's up here." Rance pointed to his head. "Course, I don't see how a man can be expected to rope too good in the dark. About time for bed."

"Daddy, I'm thinking that I might rope instead of play baseball. Looks like I'm not gonna be good enough or big enough to play in the big leagues."

"I think it's too early to make that decision, Jake. Maybe you can do both for awhile. When it rains and we buy stocker cattle, maybe we'll fix up a place for Papa to teach you to rope."

Rance started toward the house, then turned. "Jake, you know that roping a running calf that zigs and zags is a lot different than roping that dummy, don't you?"

Jake nodded and stepped off the horse.

Rance walked back to where he was standing. "Let me see that thumb."

Jake held up the completely-healed thumb. Rance took it in his hand. "Remember what it was like to do without this?" Jake

172

nodded.

"I haven't let you rope calves horseback yet because it's a good way to lose a thumb or finger. In this old cracked ground, your horse might fall and kill you. Your time will come soon enough. Now get to bed."

Jake was rustled out of bed at just past midnight on the following Saturday morning. He left his usual milking clothes hanging on the wall nail and pulled on his best work jeans, a cowboy shirt, Levi jacket, school boots, and his felt hat. He strapped on his Christmas spurs. The cattle were still in the bottom pasture at this hour. His job was to saddle Scar and get them up. A real cowboy's job.

Jake walked to the hay barn and put a rope around Scar's neck. Rance had given permission to use the saddle. He watched the full moon over the horse's back as he tightened the front cinch and buckled the girth strap. Holding the saddle horn with his right hand, he grabbed a handful of mane with his left, jumped into the stirrup, and pulled himself up into the seat. He was pleased with himself for hitting the stirrup the first time without a can or stool to stand on. The creaking of leather and the movement of the horse under him was exhilarating as he headed south toward the back pasture. Moonlight was sufficient to guide him, and he let Scar break into an easy short lope as he followed the cow trail that led to the woods in front of Blue Bottom Creek. Smoke flew from Scar's nose as he snorted into the cool morning air.

He found the cattle easily enough. Most were lying down at the edge of the woods, chewing their cuds. He slowed Scar to a walk to avoid startling any into the woods. When he was safely between the cows and the creek, he softly whistled and yipped, letting them make their own way to the barn without too much nudging. Running took pounds off, and they would be sold by the pound today. The cows herded up nicely, and Jake eased them north toward the dairy barn. He counted them in the moonlight just as he did at every milking. Twenty-one. All there. As the cows eased into the milking lot, he felt pleased and proud. Each time he worked cows with a horse, he understood his grandfather's philosophy better. "Work done horseback was somehow nobler than any work done afoot".

"Good job, Bolivar." He heard his grandfather's voice behind him. Jake could see that Buddy's reins were loose against his neck, and Griffin was doing something with both hands. He saw the glow from the end of the cigarette and realized that Papa Griff had been building a roll-your-own. "Now let's go get the dry cattle and calves," Griffin said as he pointed Buddy east toward his house.

"Hold on, boys." They heard Rance's voice and saw his silhouette approaching from the barn. He was making a loop in the end of a rope. Rance slipped the loop over Jake's saddle horn, pulled it tight and handed the coils to Jake. "Now you're tied hard and fast and won't have to dally in case you need to rope one of these calves." Rance paused to look at Griffin and smile before turning back to Jake. "Wouldn't want you to lose a thumb in a dally." Jake's moonlight shadow washed his father's face in darkness, so Jake could not tell if he was being teased or not. When his father pulled the knot tight at the base of his saddle horn, he knew he was serious.

Rance put his hand on Jake's knee. "You stay close to your Papa and don't use this unless he tells you to."

Jake tied the coils to his saddle and fell in just a little behind Griffin as they headed toward the east pasture where the dry cows and calves were grazing. He watched his grandfather sit his horse and tried to emulate every move. Griffin was sitting erectly, but looked as loose as a bag of flour sitting in the saddle. Jake had grown legs long enough to put some weight in the shortened stirrups. Sitting in the saddle was now like riding a rocking chair. As they broke into a long trot, he moved his hips, shifted his weight, and bent his legs ever so slightly to match the easy motion of the horse.

Without a word of instruction to Jake, Griffin rode toward the east side of the fence and pointed one arm toward the southwest. Jake hoped that the arm meant for him to ride down the west side. On opposite sides of the pasture, they each eased south and worked their way behind the grazing cows. Jake was a little nervous working with his cowboy grandfather but still filled with exhilaration. They easily pushed the cattle to the lane and down to the holding pen beside the barn to be loaded. Jake was disappointed that the work had been so easy.

Griffin dropped his reins across Buddy's neck and used his legs to signal the horse to stop before turning to speak to Jake. "Let's save the calves till last. Some of 'em are old enough to wean and could be trouble. We'll wait till everything else is loaded before bringing 'em up."

Gray and Rance were about half through milking, and Seth had already left for the sale barn with the first batch of cows that had been milked. Griffin tied Buddy and walked around the cow lots toward the back porch of the house. In the crisp morning air, Jake could smell wild onion cow breath mixing with the dust, manure, urine, and milk emanating from the lots and the dairy. Griffin, however, smelled Mattie's freshly brewed coffee. Jake stayed mounted and rode the perimeter of all the lots, checking and counting, pretending he was the owner of a large ranch in the middle of a roundup for shipping in the fall. He untied his rope and eyed the cows' necks, but threw at fenceposts instead.

As the last group of cattle left the dairy parlor, Jake rode into the lot to help his father and brother push the remaining freshly milked cattle into the waiting trailers of neighbors who had volunteered to help with the hauling. As his neighbors drove away, Rance stared as he rolled a smoke. "Kinda funny, ain't it. Most of what we own is going down the highway in the dark in rusty trailers pulled by worn-out pickups." Rance seemed to be talking to nobody in particular, so Gray and Jake just looked at each other without replying.

Rance looked at his watch. "Still just a little after four. I don't want to stir up those calves any more than we have to till we're ready to load 'em. Mattie has coffee ready, I imagine." His mood seemed to lift at the mention of Mattie and coffee. "Might even talk her into a sausage and biscuit." Mattie had sausage, eggs, biscuits, and ribbon cane syrup ready. Jake devoured his food, even the eggs fried in bacon grease with crusty whites. Everything seemed to smell better and taste better this morning. Jake watched his mother as she fried more sausage patties. She had a smile for him and Gray when they came in for breakfast, patting both of them gently on the shoulder.

After breakfast, Jake and Griffin remounted and began pushing the calves toward the holding pens. "Keep your eye on that little long-tail heifer, Jake," Griffin called out. "She has her tail and her head in the air and looks like she would run at the drop of a hat."

Jake had already seen the nervous heifer. She constantly pushed her head against the fence, looking for places to escape. Raising her tail to run, she had already made a couple of attempts to leave the herd, but Jake had been ready and pushed her back. The horses had still not broken a sweat, and Jake was more disappointed. Just as they reached the lane leading to the holding pens, the restless heifer spotted a low spot in the hog wire fence and went for it. She cleared the fence without much effort. Jake could probably have not prevented it, but he felt responsible. He looked at his grandfather, ready to receive his scolding.

Griffin was frowning, but offered no criticism. "Just let her go till we get the others in the lot. Then we'll go fetch the little bitch." They pushed the other calves down the lane to the holding pen. Griffin, again without a word, headed into the big pasture the calf had escaped to. Jake had to lope to catch up. The rising sun gave them enough light to see the calf almost halfway to the tree line. Tail in the air and head up, she was trotting in circles, looking for a way to escape. She stared at the approaching horses, then at the herd she had left.

Griffin eased Buddy into a slow walk and spoke without looking at Jake. "We need to get around this little wench before she breaks and runs for the timber. It'll be hell to get her out of there. That south fence won't stop her, and if she makes it to the Blue Bottom, we may not find her till it's a cold day in hell. She might not stop running until she reaches the Sulphur."

They started due south, hoping to circle behind her without causing her to run, but as soon as they started toward her, she ran for the timber. Before Jake could react, Griffin had Buddy running at full speed, trying to cut her off. It looked impossible to Jake, but he followed. He leaned forward in the saddle, dropped his reins to Scar's neck, and let him run. It was always accepted that Buddy was faster, so Jake was pleased when Scar allowed him to keep pace with his grandfather. Just in front of the trees, Buddy pulled in front of the heifer and cut her off. She tried to go around, but Scar was ready and blocked her escape into the woods.

"Let her settle a little; then we'll try to push her over to the east fence line and take her back. She's damned determined to get in those trees. If she won't give up, we'll have to rope her. Take your rope down and shake out a loop just in case." Griffin was building a loop as he spoke. Jake's heart, already racing from the run, was now in his throat. He had trouble getting the saddle string unwound from his rope.

Just as he shook out a loop, the calf started to run back toward the house. Buddy and Griffin left in hot pursuit, trying to keep her away from the weak fence line. Without instructions from Jake, Scar followed, Jake's loop dragging uselessly behind. Scar kept him just behind and to the left of the calf, while Buddy and Griffin stayed parallel on the right. Jake rebuilt his coils in his left hand and shook out another loop with his right, still running at full speed. When he was ready again, he saw Griffin watching. Griffin had his rope ready and could have roped the heifer at any time, but he was clearly waiting for Jake to do it.

"When you're through playing with your rope, throw a loop on this little heifer and let's keep her from running to Oklahoma," Griffin yelled to be heard above the wind.

Jake raised his arm, took two swings, and threw. The loop slapped harmlessly against the neck of the heifer. He felt the tension, felt the blood rush to his face. Glancing at his grandfather, still running full speed, he began to rebuild the coils and loop. Griffin gestured with his elbow high in the air. Jake raised his arm again, this time with his elbow high, and took two swings.

As he turned the loop over for his third swing, Scar and the heifer seemed to slow down. Instead of a dead run, he felt as if he were moving in slow motion. He could feel the momentum coming from the tip of the loop in his right hand and index finger, could see the smoke coming from Scar, the heifer, and from his own nostrils. He could see the loop gliding toward its target completely under his control. He followed through as he delivered the loop cleanly over the calf's head and around its neck. The loop curled back across her

177

back, keeping the calf from getting a foot in the loop. Jake jerked the slack and pitched it forward to tighten the loop around the calf's neck. He allowed it to slide loosely through his hand until he felt a strong jerk against his saddle horn when the calf reached the end of the rope. A sense of calmness and power rushed through his body as he felt the weight of the calf pulling on his saddle horn. He pushed his legs forward in the stirrups to signal his horse to stop. Scar brought his hind legs under his body and pulled back slowly, allowing the calf to be stopped without flipping over.

Jake took his eyes off the calf for the first time and realized that they were only a few yards from the dairy barn. He tried not to grin but failed as he looked at his grandfather. Griffin sat on Buddy in front of the calf. He had already pulled the makings from his pocket to roll a smoke while his horse took a needed blow. Buddy snorted as Griffin looked at Jake with a smile in his eyes and nodded his head. Jake knew that meant "well done."

Looking toward the house, Jake saw Rance leaning against a cattle trailer, arms folded against his chest. When Jake looked at him, he unfolded his arms, put a finger and thumb on the brim of his hat, and tugged slightly. Jake took a deep breath. The Rivers' flow was back.

Chapter 23

From Main street in Enloe, Gray Boy and Jake looked through the front window of the Enloe State Bank at their father. Rance sat in a chair in the bank lobby close to the marble teller cages waiting to see Frank Durett. Jake studied his father. Rance was restless, shifting his weight and drumming his fingers on the arms of the chair. Jake thought he looked worried, vulnerable, and even a little frightened. The check from the sale of the dairy cattle protruded from a bib pocket in his overalls.

Gray picked up a small rock and threw it toward the railroad tracks on the edge of downtown. "It's kinda sad, ain't it? Daddy is carrying everything he has worked for the last five years in his pocket and has to bring it down here and give it to the bank."

Jake shook his head. He had hoped the check might bring a brighter Christmas, possibly a few stocker cows, and some calves to rope. "You mean he won't get to keep any of it?"

Gray spat on the sidewalk. "I doubt it. He drives all the way up here because he thinks Frank Durett is his friend. Hell, Durett wouldn't put a water hose up his butt if his guts were on fire. He's no better than the bankers in Cooper, just farther away." Gray looked through the window again. "Daddy looks sorta pitiful and scared."

Jake looked away, suddenly feeling guilty for intruding on his father's privacy. "I guess the cows didn't bring as much as he hoped. Do you think we're in trouble with the bank?"

Gray put both hands in the front pockets of his Levis. "I don't know. I just know we're in debt, always have been, and always will be. When I move out, I ain't ever gonna be obligated to any damn banker. I'm not gonna beg anybody for anything."

Jake hated it when Gray made things seem hopeless. He tried to shed a brighter light on the situation. "He and Mr. Durett are friends. He won't hold Daddy's feet to the fire."

Gray nodded toward a black, four-door sedan parked in front of the bank. "See that? Bet you anything the people driving that new '56 Chevy are not from Delta County. Nobody here can afford a car like that."

Jake walked closer to the car. "It's got blackwall tires."

"Bet you'd still take it if somebody offered you the keys, wouldn't you?"

They wandered down the street that divided Enloe's business center. Enloe was about the same size as Klondike but seemed more prosperous because of the bank. While most banks in tiny towns like Enloe had failed during the depression, Enloe State Bank had stubbornly held on. The town also boasted a seed processing plant a few doors down from the bank, and Gray and Jake wandered inside to watch the machinery. Jake didn't share Gray's fascination with things mechanical, so he stayed only a few minutes before walking outside to sit on a bench. The sun was listing a little to the south, announcing the onset of winter, and it felt good on Jake's shoulders as he watched people come and go out of the post office.

The smell of hamburgers cooking wafted across the street from the general store, making his mouth water. A short string of Christmas lights hung in a crooked line over the door to the store. Somehow, the smell of hamburgers and the lights lifted his spirits and gave him something to look forward to. It was dinnertime, so he walked back to the bank to see if his father was finished. The lobby was empty and Rance was not in sight. Jake walked closer to the teller cages, hoping to get a glimpse inside Frank Durett's office.

"He's in with Mr. Durett, Jake. Just have a seat. He'll be out soon." The voice from the stern-looking teller sounded like a command to Jake. He obediently eased into the chair just outside Frank Durett's office. Frank's voice drifted through the thin walls and out the door. Jake wondered why they had not closed it.

"Damn this drought. Your cattle didn't bring what they should have, did they?"

"No, they didn't. Where do I stand after you figured all that interest, Frank?" Jake was relieved when his father's voice sounded strong and confident, not pleading.

"The check from the cows will cover the note on them and the interest, but there's less than a hundred bucks left. But, you already knew that, didn't you?"

"Pretty much. Frank, I'm going to need a few hundred to tide me over until I can get some money coming in and maybe sell my dairy equipment. Can we make a short term note due in say, about six months?"

Jake heard Frank's chair squeak and took a deep breath when the banker did not answer quickly. "Did you see those two fellows with suits behind the teller counter?" Jake stood on his tiptoes to see two men in suits working at a desk behind the tellers. Now he knew who was driving the black Chevy.

"Yeah, I saw 'em. Why?"

"The state has cut off any more loans until further notice."

Jake could hear his father shifting in his chair. After a long pause, he finally spoke.

"How come?"

"I loaned lots of money to people that can't pay because of this drought. You probably have friends that haven't survived." Jake wished he had never returned to the lobby. He imagined the pain and humiliation his father must be experiencing. Frank's voice was reduced to a whisper, but Jake could still make out what was being said. "Oh, I think most of 'em will repay the bank someday, but not until we get some rain and at least one good crop in." Jake waited for his father to answer, but a small thumping sound was all that could be heard. He assumed it was Frank stabbing his desk with a pencil eraser or Rance drumming his fingers against his chair. Finally, Frank broke the silence. "It gets worse, Rance. I'm under orders to take checks just like yours and apply all of them to outstanding loans, even loans that are not due yet."

Jake heard and even felt the sound of his father's chair scraping across the floor and against the wall. "So you're telling me that I'm going to leave here without even the small change from that cattle check? Hell, Frank, I won't even be able to buy groceries. I already owe both grocery stores. And what about Christmas?"

"I keep telling these auditors that you can't squeeze blood out of a turnip. I'm sorry, Rance. I hope you know I'd help you if I could."

Jake looked up to see the two suited enemies leave the lobby, heading across Main to take their noon meal at the general store. Frank apparently had seen them, too. Jake heard his father move toward the door and he hustled across the lobby just in time to avoid being caught eavesdropping. Just outside the door, Frank Durett pointed at the check that was still in Rance's overalls. "Take that to one of the tellers and tell them to apply this amount to your loans; withhold the rest in cash." Frank slipped a piece of paper into Rance's hand.

"Thanks, Frank, but if this is going to get you in trouble, I won't do it."

"Thanks to that bottomland cotton crop, you don't have any past due crop notes. It's not right to apply that money to notes not due. Just don't tell anybody. Come back to see me when it rains. We'll loan you some more money." He shook Rance's hand.

Rance did as he was told and motioned for Jake to follow as he left the bank. On the sidewalk, he looked at the eighty-nine dollars and change he had in his hand. He placed the folding money in his overalls, carefully snapping the pocket closed. Jingling the change in his hand, he looked at Jake. "Go find your brother. Let's have us a hamburger."

When Rance killed the truck engine in the driveway, Mattie was hanging clothes on the backyard clothesline. Mattie gave Rance an expectant look. Jake was surprised when Mattie smiled after hearing Rance's retelling of what happened at the bank. "My friends have been trying to get me to go to work at the sewing factory in Commerce for a long time. I think I might like to take a job now."

"I've been hanging around at Red Pickard's place since we sold the dairy cows. He says I can do mechanic work for him," Gray offered.

Jake felt left out. He couldn't think of a single way he could add to the family coffers. Frustrated, he blurted out, "What can I do?"

Rance laughed. "As a matter of fact, you've already been of-fered a job. Hack has been wanting to hire you since last summer. He needs somebody to do odd jobs around his place. You can get off the school bus at Hack's most afternoons, and we'll pick you up before supper. Hack says he can pay you four bits an hour." Rance reached into his overalls and pulled out a dollar bill. "A man at the general store in Enloe told me that the drive-in show in Commerce was open tonight for a special feature and was charging six-bits a carload. Anybody want to go?" Jake was not happy to be working on a dairy farm again, but his heart leapt at the mention of a drive-in movie.

An hour later, they pulled into the Commerce Drive-In. Not wanting to be seen with his family, Gray piled out of the car and disappeared down a row of cars. Mattie sent Jake to the conces-sion stand for drinks. Jake stared at a young couple and their two children entering the small building in front of the big screen as he stood in line. All of them were dressed in their pajamas and slip-pers. The parents wore robes.

"Who's James Dean?" Jake watched as coming attractions ended and the main feature began. *Rebel Without A Cause* flashed across the screen.

In bed that night after the movie, Jake watched the moonlight reflect off the swinging bulb above his bed in the dog trot. Anxiety about everyone working and going off in different directions soon replaced his original excitement. He felt his time to be alone and to visit the Pelts disappearing. His mother would no longer be at home after school. Of course, it did not matter because he would not be there either. He had less than a week's respite from the dairy business, and he was already back in it.

The temperature hovered in the low eighties on Christmas Eve and Christmas Day, so they blamed the weather for the somber mood at Christmas. They wanted to talk about Tuck, but dared not. Jake was glad when it was over. Even school seemed better than the dreariness of home.

Chapter 24

By late spring, Jake was sure that Hack and Rance had agreed on a regimen to his new job that would test his mettle. He had overheard them use phrases like, "Make a man out of him," more than once. He hauled hay in a driving north wind, searched for new calves afoot in the dark bottomland, unloaded the dairy's waste every week and spread it across the pasture by hand. He worked everyday after school and all day Saturday. Jake had been afraid that Hack would ask him to help with the twice-daily milkings, but he had not.

Conditions improved a little when spring arrived. Hack occasionally let him use the tractor to shred, fill holes, or drag the cow lots. Jake liked the responsibility and sense of worth the job gave him. Even on the worst days of winter, it was better than staying at home alone in a cold house. Everybody in the family worked away from home now.

On the first really warm day of spring, Jake found himself digging muck from an old barn that cows used for shelter. Sure that the barn had never been mucked before, he saw it as another test. How many did he have to pass? Steam rose as he pried loose another pitchfork full of manure and molded hay. The steam brought a pungent, repugnant smell to the hot barn hall. Jake pitched it into the wagon. "Damn, this crap has been here longer than I have." He leaned against the wagon and pulled a short list from his pocket. Using the pencil stub Hack had given him, Jake checked off the list. Haul hay to the dry cows; repair fence around beehives; harrow cow lots with tractor; muck hay barn hall. Hack surely knew that the last item on the list would take at least two days. Did he expect him to finish it today? He stuck the pencil and list back into his pocket and picked up the pitchfork.

"Whew. Stinks in here, Jake. What kind of stuff are you stirring up?" Hack grinned as he walked into the hall of the barn. Jake had never heard him use profanity, so he hoped Hack had not been listening when he had cussed to himself.

"I think it's too hot in here to do this today, Jaker. Why don't you take the rest of the day off? Val and I want to leave early on a little trip to her mother's, so you can take Saturday off too. How much do I owe you for this week?"

Jake hesitated. He knew that Hack kept records of his hours. "Counting today, I've put in ten hours."

Hack reached into the pocket of the army fatigues he wore most days. "Let's see, at fifty cents an hour, that'll be five dollars. Here's four bucks more for tomorrow, so your paycheck won't be too short."

Jake stared at the five dollar bill and four ones in his palm. It was a dollar short of what he usually earned, but pretty good for a week where he did not work on Saturday at all. "You don't have to pay me for Saturday, Hack." Jake protested weakly. Hack dismissed him with a gesture and Jake started trotting toward the Klondike highway before he could change his mind. Gray Boy was not due to pick him up for another two hours. No matter. He would cross over to 24 and hitch a ride.

Hack called to him before he left the yard. "Guess I forgot about your ride. I think we can fix that." Hack pointed to a battered bicycle leaning against a clothes line post. "It's a girl's bike, but the tires are pumped up, and it'll get you home."

Jake didn't want to be seen on a girl's bike, so he avoided 24 and headed south down the dirt back roads. Thoughts of the cash in his pocket and the day off tomorrow caused him to pump the pedals hard down the sandy lanes toward home. Part of the roads were as hard as concrete sidewalks, but other spots were so deep in loose sand that Jake had a hard time keeping the bicycle going. As he approached the Hurt farm, he stopped pedaling and stood astride the bike.

The Hurt house was one of the oldest in Delta County, even

older than the Rivers' house, but the Hurts always kept a fresh coat of paint on it. The wooden dairy barn was even painted to match the house. Jake wondered how they kept the barn so white. The house was small and the yard was surrounded by a white picket fence. A small garden between the yard and the dairy was enclosed by its own fence. Chicken wire had been attached to the inside of the fence to keep out varmints. Oak trees surrounded both the house and barn, and peach, pear, and plum trees dotted the yard.

Claire Hurt was working in her spring garden, dropping seeds in a furrow she had made with her hoe. She wore a long gingham dress dotted with pink and blue flower petals. A bonnet protected her face from the sun. Everything about the Hurt place appealed to Jake. It had a sense of order, cleanliness, and warmth. He had always felt a special bond with Claire, but was not sure why. Claire came regularly to read to the children in elementary school and often substituted for other teachers. She was always at school at Easter, Thanksgiving, and Christmas to read stories to the children and explain the meanings of the religious holidays. Jake's mind usually wandered when his teachers spoke, but Mrs. Hurt always held his rapt attention. Her soft voice and demeanor calmed the children and put them in the holiday spirit.

Jake's sense of elation brought an uncharacteristic urge to stop and visit, but he could not overcome his shyness enough to approach Claire. She had not seen him standing in the road. Just as he gave up and started to pedal on, he heard her voice.

"Jake Rivers, don't you dare ride by here without stopping to say hello," she shouted.

Jake was startled and more pleased than he could understand when she not only recognized him, but demanded his presence.

"You park that bicycle right over there and come sit with me on the porch. I've been wanting to visit with you, and it's more than coincidence that you happened by." Claire's smile was warm and inviting. "I baked some cookies this morning. They may have cooled some, but they're still fresh. Would you share some with me?"

"No, thank you, Mrs. Hurt. I was just heading home. Hack, Mr. Gentry, that is, let me off early today." Jake gave his automatic, polite response when someone offered him food or hospitality. He regretted it the minute he heard the words leave his mouth. Why was it polite to lie and say you did not want any when someone offered you fresh cookies? He had never understood why it was necessary to make someone beg you before you accepted hospitality or food.

"Well, I have been needing to talk to you, and the only thing I have in way of payment for your time is fresh cookies." Claire smiled as she leaned on her hoe. "My feelings will be hurt if you don't try some."

Jake smiled and put the kickstand down on the bike. He opened the small gate leading into the yard and stepped on each stone that led to the porch so as not to make tracks in the swept yard. Claire came out of the garden and met him on the porch. She put her arm around his shoulders and guided him to one of the wicker rockers. Even though she had been working out in the sun, her dress smelled of fresh soap, and her hands smelled a mixture of dirt and cookie dough. The smell of water on dry dirt came from her freshly watered garden.

"Now you sit right there while I put up my bonnet and fix us a plate of cookies and a glass of fresh milk. You prefer your milk without cream, don't you?"

Jake was surprised that she knew that. "Oh, anything you got will be fine."

She brought the milk and cookies out on a large platter and set it on the small table between the two wicker chairs. Jake tried to study her without being obvious. He couldn't guess her age, but her face looked as if it had never seen the sun. It always had a slight sheen to it as if she had just applied soft cream. Her auburn hair showed a few streaks of gray like his mother's. She wasn't as pretty as Mattie, but seemed more at peace with herself.

Jake's mouth watered when he saw four chocolate oatmeal cookies on his plate. It seemed as if she had known he was coming and baked his favorite cookie in advance. The white, store-bought napkins beside the cookies made him a little nervous, and he wondered if she expected him to place one in his lap or under his chin. He decided to leave it on the table, just using it to wipe his mouth

188

after each drink of milk.

Jake could barely hear the sounds of the milking machines coming from the dairy barn. "J. B. is already milkin', I guess." J. B. Hurt, Claire's husband, was a tall, lanky, slightly stooped, soft-spoken man. Jake had been told that he had been very handsome as a young man. Doctors had found cancer in his jaw bone several years before and removed almost half of his face, including most of his upper lip, leaving his teeth and gums displayed in a permanent grimace.

Claire nodded her head. "I'm glad we have two deep wells on the place and a big lake. Otherwise, we would be out of the dairy business. Even with that, I don't think we'll make it through another summer like last one." Claire noticed Jake's eyes looking toward his bike. He had heard enough about dry weather. "Jake, how long has Tuck been gone?"

Jake answered quickly. "More'n a year."

"I would like to talk about him. Would you talk about your little brother with me?" The directness of the question startled Jake. He did not want to disturb the calm feeling he was experiencing.

"I guess so."

Claire reached over and covered Jake's hand with her own. The hand felt soft. "Did you know that J. B. and I lost a baby girl the same year you were born?" Jake did know, but shook his head slightly.

"Mattie and I were in the hospital at the same time. We showed each other our new babies. Our little girl was born with a heart problem we didn't know about. She became ill the day before we were to take her home from the hospital." Claire smoothed the folds of her dress. "Your mother and daddy came by our room to see us as they were taking you home. I looked under the baby blanket and saw you cradled in your daddy's arms, all healthy, good skin color, sucking on your fist. We were to take our baby home that same day." Jake watched the tears well up in Claire's eyes. She dabbed them away with a handkerchief pulled from a pocket of her dress. Her smile returned. "She was a beautiful child, fragile like a porcelain doll. Her illness became worse that day, and she died the next."

Jake felt uncomfortable hearing the story. He had heard it from Mattie and Rance before but felt guilty that he had never attached much significance to it until he heard it from Claire's own lips. Her smile grew brighter as she looked into Jake's eyes. "That's why I have always shown a special interest in you. You probably didn't know it, but I always felt that you were part mine, especially since J. B. and I were never blessed with other children." Jake's skin tingled as he heard those words. "That's why I have been talking with Mattie and why I want to talk to you about losing someone dear to you. Will you let me do that?" Jake nodded his head.

"Know what I felt when we lost our baby, Jake? Anger. Oh, I shook my fist at God, raging at His injustice to us. I was envious of your mother and daddy, too. Why did they get to take home a healthy son when they already had two other children?" She paused when she saw the look of apprehension cross Jake's face. "We had no other children, you see, and our little girl was taken away. We were in church every Sunday morning and Sunday night, yet we lost our only child."

Jake felt guilty sitting in the chair that could have been occupied by Claire's little girl, eating the cookies that she should have been enjoying.

"Mattie tells me that you are having more problems dealing with Tuck's death than your brother or sister. Is that true?" Claire asked.

Jake looked down at his feet and thought before answering. "I guess so. Tuck and I shared the same bed, and we played together a lot. He was better than almost anybody about getting me out of a bad mood. It seemed like he was always in a good mood, and it just sorta' rubbed off." Jake's voice trailed off, reducing to little more than a whisper. He wasn't sure what Mrs. Hurt wanted him to say.

"Does it seem unfair to you? Do you feel that God is punishing you?" Claire kept gently probing.

Jake rocked in the wicker chair. "It sure seems unfair. Tuck was as good a person as I ever saw. I never saw him do anything more wrong than wet his pants. He was the center of our family. Seems like we just weren't good enough to keep him, so God took him." He took another bite of cookie and looked away from Claire across the field in front of them. "Everybody said it was God's will, so I guess it was, but I just don't understand why. Why did he have to pay for something I did or the family did?" Jake paused, surprised at himself for speaking so frankly. He put his half-eaten cookie on the plate. "The preacher said that he has gone to a better place, and I guess that's true. 'Cause if there is a heaven, Tuck is sure there. But I just don't understand why God gave him to us if he was going to take him back about the time we got to where we really needed him."

"Do you feel that you're to blame?" she asked.

"Sometimes. We played in the snow just before he got sick."

"I felt that way too . . . for a long time." She took both of Jake's hands into her own. "I stopped loving God and started only fearing Him. I heard about a God to be feared in my church and from my own minister. Then, one day, many years ago, a young evangelist came to visit our community to deliver a sermon under a tent. I went to his camp-meeting looking for answers to my problems with God." Claire laughed softly and lightly pinched Jake on the arm. "You've probably been to one of those revival meetings. You know, Jake, the ones where they try to scare you into heaven." Claire laughed out loud. Her laugh was full of joy and genuine pleasure and was reassuring to Jake.

Jake nodded his head and laughed with her. "Mother and I have been to several of those things since Tuck died."

"Well, this young evangelist was not one of those shouting kinds. His vocal cords seemed to quiver and rattle when he talked, but his voice wafted over the entire tent, vibrating our ears when it touched them. He was sort of a rumpled kind of fellow. His clothes were not pressed properly, and his shoes could have stood a good shine, but his facial expression and his eyes were captivating." Claire paused. Jake's head was down and she had to lean down to see if he was listening before she continued. "I thought he looked a little like Abraham Lincoln."

Jake's head came up at the mention of Abraham Lincoln. He thought of the man who had whispered in his mother's ear. Claire rocked in her wicker chair, her eyes taking on the dreamy look of fond memories. "I invited that young evangelist to our home after the revival meeting. Why Jake, he seemed to know more about me than I knew about myself." She pounded the flat of her hand on the chair's arm for emphasis. "He told me about a different God than the one I had grown up with. He didn't take away my pain after losing little Anna, but he did help me to deal with it. You see, he did not believe that it was God's will that I lose my daughter. God was not punishing me."

Claire put one hand on Jake's shoulder. "I don't believe that God took Tuck away from your family, either."

Jake gave her a questioning look. "So, are you saying that you don't believe there is a God?"

Claire returned both hands to her lap and smiled as she rocked. "Oh, no. My faith in God is stronger than it ever was. I just see Him as kind, gentle, and loving rather than angry and vengeful." She turned to face Jake. "I no longer believe that God is personally directing every one of our lives and everything that happens to us, good or bad." Claire put her hand over her heart. "I believe God resides here." She put her other hand over Jake's heart . . . "And here."

Jake looked west and noticed how low the sun was. Gray Boy or Mattie would be coming for him at Hack's if he didn't get home soon. Claire noticed his concern, stood and took Jake's hand to lead him off the porch. She stopped to take in the soft gray and magenta colors of the sunset before turning again to Jake. She seemed lost in her own thoughts, and Jake was not sure what to do or say. She put her arm around his shoulder as they walked toward the bike. "You are too young to fully understand what I am about to say, but maybe you will remember part of it. I believe He gives us choices about how we conduct our lives and instructions about how we should live our lives, but I don't believe He then takes away those choices by directing everything that happens to us. Does that make any sense at all to you, Jake?"

Jake was confused, but he nodded. He liked the sound of what she was saying. "I think I understand some of it. You're saying that maybe God didn't take Tuck to punish us. Maybe it just happened. If that's true, then why did it happen?"

Claire shook her head. "I can't answer that, and I believe anyone who says they can had better be a true messenger from God. Some things happen, good and bad, because of our actions and choices, good and bad. Other things happen at random because of the fundamental laws of nature." She smiled at the confused expression on Jake's face. "Those are the hardest to understand, but it isn't necessary that we understand. We just have faith that God is doing the best he can and loves each of his creations."

Jake hoped she didn't notice that he was riding a girl's bicycle as he put one foot on a pedal. If she noticed, she didn't say. She put her hand on his shoulder for one last thought. "Jake Ridge Rivers, I don't believe that we have to be grateful that your Tuck and my Anna were taken from us to go to a better place. We have a right to be hurt, even angry, because that was unfair. But life is unfair, and God is there to help us when unfair things happen to us, not to prevent them from happening. We did not deserve the pain that our losses caused, but God stands ready to help us deal with the pain by giving us strength and courage." Claire paused to see if Jake was taking in any of what she was saying. His eyes showed that he was. She squeezed him in a tight hug.

As Jake headed home on his borrowed bicycle, he watched the sun slowly set in front of him. Floating over his head, a Presence cloaked in white, with a kind, smiling face, and hands posed in a supplicating gesture had replaced the frowning, displeased, angry Presence cloaked in gray that Jake had imagined before. Claire Hurt had drawn that presence for him. He felt warm inside, like he had with the Rivers' flow.

Chapter 25

Six weeks after his talk with Claire Hurt, Jake sat beside his mother on the third pew of the morning-sun-aisle of the small church in Klondike, clutching his Bible. He stared at the huge painting of the crucified Jesus that hung behind the preacher. Blood flowed from Jesus' palms. As announcements were made of the need to pray for the ill and infirm, Jake's concentration waned as he watched the spring sun peek through the church windows. He followed the path of the dust particle tunnels created by the sun's rays and envied the people they seemed to point to, wondering if a magical quality attached to the tunnels of light.

As the collection plate was passed, he opened the cover of his Bible for a sneak peek at the inscription. "To Jake Ridge Rivers for six consecutive weeks of Sunday school and church." *The New Testament* was no bigger than his hand and certainly not as nice as the one his cousin had received for twelve weeks of perfect attendance, but it was something. Maybe he would start over when they gave the twelve-week Bibles again. Maybe not.

As the preacher tried to scare the congregation into heaven by threatening them with hell, Jake thought of Tuck. He was in heaven for sure. Jake felt eyes on him and looked up to see Claire Hurt smiling at him from across the aisle. He smiled back at her wink. He had the Bible because of her. Visits to the Hurt's home were now frequent and comfortable for Jake. He had even helped J. B. milk a few times. Claire and J. B. had agreed with his father's assessment of the man speaking from the pulpit today; he was a fool, but he meant well and was doing the very best he knew how. Claire told Jake that he probably wouldn't find all the answers in church, but it was a good place to look. When the invitation began, he met the preacher's gaze without flinching and kept his seat. His time would come, and he would recognize it when it did.

Jake's mind wandered during the invitation. Tuck had been gone over a year, and his life had changed in ways that he could never have imagined. Jake had told his Papa Griff that he wanted things to be the way they were. Griffin had replied, "That's asking too much. Things change." As the sun rose higher, one of the spiraling dust tunnels focused on Jake, and he felt himself floating above the congregation, his mind drifting back to events that seemed so long ago.

When the dairy cattle sold, the family seemed to scatter, almost consciously avoiding being together at the same time. Jake was working for Hack; Gray was working at Red Pickard's garage; Mattie was working at a sewing factory; and Rance still hauled water, drove heavy equipment for the county and did occasional vet work. The drought had taken their dairy, but they were putting food on the table. Nevertheless, Rance and Mattie seemed to quarrel more often about money. Mattie had told Jake that Rance's pride was hurt when she bought groceries with her own money. Jake was not so sure about that.

He had not realized how much Trish's presence in the next room meant to him until she married Pete and moved away. They lived in Houston now. He envied her fresh start. Pete was teaching, and Trish was working as a secretary. They had a red '55 Chevy. Jake was hoping to catch the bus to visit them in Houston during the summer. The drought was over there, and he wanted to see green grass and trees.

Trish's bedroom was Jake's for the taking, but he stayed in the dog trot, afraid that Tuck would not return if he moved to another bed or another room. The first Christmas without Tuck had been frightening for the whole family, but they had made a valiant effort to recapture the spirit of the season.

His mother had regained much of her former strength, but it was a different kind of strength, more independent somehow. She seemed determined to stand with her family, but also apart, unwilling to expose herself to the kind of pain she had experienced when her family was her entire life. She had an outside life of her own now, her own money, and friends at work. Jake had heard her tell Claire that she had been vulnerable, weak, and unprepared when Tuck had died, and she was determined never to be that way again.

Rance seldom stayed out all night on drinking binges, but he did spend more time on Dad Flannigan's porch and in the cane-brakes behind the store where bottles were shared. Jake had discovered that the man he worshiped was vulnerable and had come to accept it. He had even become a reluctant ally of sorts in his father's drinking, exchanging crooked, guilty smiles when Mattie's intolerance for alcohol brought a coldness to their home.

Jake chuckled a little and pulled his shoulders back as he recalled the fights between himself and Gray Boy. After Tuck's death, Jake had become more sensitive to teasing and physically attacked his brother at the slightest provocation. He was not above picking up a baseball bat or other weapon to even the odds. Jake had learned that his brother would not seriously harm him and found the physical punishment he received during a brawl less painful than the mental humiliation Gray Boy was expert at inflicting. He always lost his battles, but earned Gray's respect by never calling for help or telling on his brother. Reluctantly wielding a razor strap, Rance finally recaptured his authority and stopped the fighting between his sons. Truth be told, both boys were glad to call a truce. Rance brooded for two days after the whippings.

Jake was proud when his brother was chosen most handsome and best all-around in high school. A guitar and singing temporarily diverted Gray Boy's thirst for speed and danger but did not quench it. He was saving up to buy Red Pickard's Indian motorcycle.

Chapter 26

"Hey, slugger." Jake turned on the dugout bench toward the sound of his sister's voice. He had not seen Trish for almost two months. Seeing her now made him realize what a big part of his life she had been. Trish was leaning on the cyclone fence, the fingers of one hand threaded through the twisted wire, the other hand behind her back. Jake thought she still looked athletic enough to take the field and beat any of them at baseball. Her clothes looked new.

"Hey, yourself. What are you doing here?"

"Came to see you play, what else? I brought you an early birthday present, too. I probably won't be home when you turn twelve." Trish took the hand from behind her back and tossed something over the fence. Jake caught it before it dropped on his head. He caressed the new Rawlings glove, felt the softness of the leather and then put the glove to his face to inhale the wonderful aroma of new leather. A white baseball sat firmly in the glove's pocket, secured by a wide leather band to help the glove form a better pocket. It was darker than the glove he had long admired in Cardwell's store, but just as beautiful. Jake was speechless.

"Didn't think you'd mind if I broke it in a little. Pete threw me some fast balls to limber it up. I think it's ready if you want to use it the rest of the game tonight."

"I sure will. Thanks, Trish. This is the nicest glove I've ever had." Jake looked at the worn-out glove lying beside him on the bench before turning back to his sister. "You spending the night?"

"Guess so."

"Where's Pete?"

"Oh, you know Pete. He's found some of his buddies to play

poker or dominoes with. He'll be along about bedtime. You're riding home with me, so don't go off with anybody else. Better get your mind back on the game. Y'all have two outs." Trish turned and walked away.

It was the middle of Jake's third and final season of Little League baseball. The Indians had improved their record from the year before, but were out of contention to be 1956 league champs. Nobody had stepped up to replace Linc Little's strong pitching and the good hitting of the older, bigger boys Jake had played with the first year. Jake hated losing. He was playing with more confidence, getting more hits and throwing stronger, but something was missing.

When two of his teammates moved away just as the season began, Coach Daniels pulled Jake and Bo aside. "You two are the oldest players I have now. These younger boys look up to the older players. It's your job to step up and help me turn this team around." Coach Daniels had repeated that message throughout the season. Bo had responded, but Jake had not.

At the Dairy Queen on the way home, Trish treated them to Frito pies and Cokes. She dug into the Frito sack with the plastic spoon as she spoke. "You were kind of hard on that second baseman tonight, weren't you?" Jake sat on the seat beside her, almost tall enough to see over the dashboard now. The game was over, his team defeated again, but the Frito pie was good and sitting in a red '55 Chevy was even better. The year-old car looked new to Jake. He especially loved the red steering wheel.

"I guess. It makes me mad when he misses easy skinners over and over." Jake wanted to end the conversation.

"You never missed one before?"

"You know I have, but he misses most of 'em. He just won't put his glove down and trap the ball. Most of 'em go right through his legs, just like tonight. Cost us two runs and the game."

"That little guy looks up to you, Jake. I could see that. You should be nicer to him."

"Little guy? He's bigger'n me."

"You know what I mean. You're a year older and more experienced - a better athlete than he probably ever will be, no matter

200

how big he gets."

Jake didn't reply, but Trish pressed on. "What's really wrong, Jake? You used to play above your head. Now you play below it."

"Nothin's wrong." Why was she asking all these questions?

Trish shook her head and backed out of the Dairy Queen parking lot. When they reached Cardwell's store, she pulled off 24 and killed the engine. "I think I know what it might be. How many games have Mother and Daddy been to this year?"

Jake held his glove and ball tightly in his lap and shook his head. "I don't know. With the drought and all, baseball doesn't seem all that important, I guess. Gray's been to most of the games, though."

"Guess that's not the same for you, is it?" Trish's voice was soft and gentle.

"They never missed a single basketball or baseball game that you or Gray Boy played in." Jake looked out the side window to avoid facing his sister.

"I know that, Jake. But they were younger then." Trish ran her fingers around the red steering wheel. "The drought had not taken everything they owned back then. They can't seem to get past losing Tuck along with everything else bad that has happened." She reached across to touch Jake on the shoulder, but he pulled away. "Doesn't mean that they don't love you and aren't interested in your sports anymore. They'll get better. Someday, it will rain again. That'll lift their spirits. They'll buy some cows and you can rope calves, too."

Jake kept looking out the side window. He had heard it all before. It was never going to rain, and he was never going to get to rope calves. "I envy you and Pete. You live away from here. Away from the drought. Have y'all got any of those new appliances like that woman talks about on TV?"

Trish laughed. "You mean Betty Furness, you can be sure if it's Westinghouse? Nope. We live in a small rent house, Jake. It's not much nicer than our old house. Tell you what, though, if I lived here, I would never miss a game. You know that, don't you?"

Jake squeezed the glove a little tighter and nodded.

"When I come next time, and I will come again before the season is over, I want to see my little brother being a leader out there. You remember what it was like in your first year? Linc Little and most of the older boys helped you out. Now it's your turn. OK?"

Jake took a deep breath and nodded again.

Chapter 27

Jake saw him get out of a car by the cornfield two days after his talk with Trish. The small boy walked toward the baseball diamond alone. He had Coke-bottle thick eyeglasses and had not grown to his teeth or his ears. Jake watched the car drive away. It was familiar to Jake, but he could not recall where he had seen it before. The boy had a glove in one hand and a new white baseball in the other. His baseball cap, ruined by too much creasing by too-small hands, was pulled so low on his head that the bill sat on his glasses. He didn't hesitate in the road but walked through the small gate in the cyclone fence by the dugout. Jake was standing in the on-deck circle, ready for his turn at batting practice. From a distance of thirty paces, Jake somehow liked this boy.

"Hi, I'm Wilbur Penny. What's your name?" Wilbur stuck out his hand toward Jake. He was smiling eagerly, his already large eyes magnified by the thick lens of his glasses. His chipmunk-like mischievous smile made Jake smile involuntarily. Jake was not accustomed to such bold friendliness, but he awkwardly accepted and shook the small hand. Jake felt his calloused and sun-browned hand contrast with Wilbur's soft and white one.

"Hidy. Jake Rivers is my name."

"I want to play baseball. Can I get on this team?"

"Prob'ly, the season's about over, so I guess it won't matter much." He took Wilbur over to Coach Daniels and introduced him. Joe looked at Wilbur and figured that the other team coaches would not object if he inserted him as back-up to the right field starter. Practice was nearly over when he arrived, so Wilbur had done little when it ended. He followed Jake off the diamond. "How about coming over to my house for a Coke float?" Wilbur asked. Jake stared at his new friend. The boy had known him less than an hour and was already inviting him to his house.

"Naw. I was goin' down to Miller's for a malt before I go home," Jake lied.

"Aw, come on. A float is almost as good, and it won't cost you a cent. We'll grab a couple, and I'll walk with you to 24. Mama bought a gallon of Lilly Ice Cream home from Commerce yesterday." That was enough for Jake. Wilbur made him feel like a big brother again.

Jake studied the small white frame house and the green St. Augustine grass that lay in the yard like a carpet, thinking of his own unpainted house and bare yard. The car that had seemed familiar to him earlier sat under a small tin carport.

"How do you keep this grass green?"

"Landlord has his own well. See it there in the corner?" Wilbur nodded toward a small well and pump house that were partially covered by honeysuckle vines. "The old man demands that Daddy pump water and keep the grass green. Our neighbors don't like it. They say we're wasting water. Daddy thinks so too, but he does what the landlord wants."

Wilbur grabbed Jake's shirt sleeve and pulled him toward the front door. Wilbur's father, a bespectacled older and larger version of Wilbur, sat with his head down at a large desk in the middle of the living room. He didn't seem to notice when the boys walked in. The desk, the floor, and shelves against the walls were piled high with books, folders, and papers. Jake had never seen so many books, even at school. Wilbur led Jake to a separate bookshelf in the corner. "These are mine."

Jake's eyes scanned the four shelves of books. Mark Twain, Zane Grey, and Jack London books jumped to his attention, but his eyes rested on a shelf completely filled with books about baseball, including a baseball encyclopedia. "Wow."

"Dad, this is Jake Rivers. We play baseball together. I invited him home for a Coke float."

The slight man in a rumpled white shirt and loose, narrow black tie greeted Jake absently without looking up. "Hello, Jake. Wilbur, you know where the fridge is; just help yourself. Don't leave a mess for your mother to clean up." Jake studied Wilbur's father, thinking that he had seen him somewhere before, but the man kept his head down and continued working. Wilbur fixed them both floats and left the ice cream and a mess on the kitchen counter. They sat down on the green St. Augustine and leaned against a big sycamore tree to enjoy their floats.

"Dad's working on his master's degree at ET over in Commerce. Mom works there as a secretary," Wilbur said. "What do your folks do?"

Jake hesitated. Nobody had asked that question before. "We used to have a dairy and raise cotton before we ran out of water." Jake couldn't get his mind off the books, especially the one that had Lou Gehrig's name on the spine. The Iron Horse of Baseball was one of his heroes, even if he had been a Yankee. "You're proud of your books, ain't you?" Wilbur nodded, his face indicating that Jake had asked a dumb question. They stepped back inside to put their empty glasses in the sink.

Wilbur's father rose from his desk again, pointing his finger at Jake. "Haven't we met before?"

Jake nodded his head as recognition came. "You're the man who helped us put out the fire. The man who takes pictures."

Mr. Penny smiled and nodded. "Oh, I didn't do much. Like I told your dad, I wouldn't have even noticed if it hadn't been for the mockingbird."

Jake stared at his tennis shoes, afraid to ask the question that was on his mind. "How did the pictures turn out?"

"Well, I caught that bird in flight, but it's kind of blurry. I guess it was just flying too fast. The whole picture is sorta blurred. I kept it because it's still interesting to me. Won't ever be published, though."

Wilbur put his hand on Jake's shoulder. "Want to see it? It's hanging in the hall."

Jake followed him down the darkened hallway, where an eight by ten photo hung in a cheap, black frame. Wilbur flipped the hall light switch. Jake studied the photograph. The white cowbirds were in an almost perfect circle surrounding a squirrel and a rabbit. Sitting between the squirrel and the rabbit was a blurry, transparent

205

image. The mockingbird, wings outstretched, glided just above the blurry image.

Wilbur's father walked into the hall and stared at the photograph. "Don't know how the shot turned out like that. Could be a double exposure, but it doesn't look it. I have never forgotten to roll the film before snapping another picture." He paused and put his hand on Wilbur's shoulder. "Wilbur swears he didn't touch the camera, though he's been known to before." Mr. Penny walked back to his desk and sat down.

Jake continued to study the blurry image, wondering if Wilbur and his father saw what he did or if he was imagining the faint outline of a small boy. He carefully outlined the image with his finger. "You see that?"

Wilbur squinted through his thick glasses. "Do I see what?"

Jake shook his head and looked away. "Nothin', I guess."

Wilbur tugged on his shirt sleeve. "Come on. Let's walk downtown." Jake wanted to study the picture more, to take it off the wall and home to his parents to see if they saw what he did. Instead, he followed Wilbur down the hall.

Jake learned a lot about baseball and Wilbur before reaching the downtown square. "Will your parents be coming to see you play?" Jake figured Wilbur's dad for the studious type, not a baseball player, or even a fan.

"Probably not. They really don't like for me to play. They're afraid I'll get hurt."

The admission made Jake feel even closer to his new friend. "So, why do you play?"

"Same reason you do. I love the game."

"Even if your parents aren't interested?"

"As long as I make straight A's and read a least two books a month, they say they won't keep me from playing baseball." Wilbur winked at Jake. "That means they won't ever stop me."

Chapter 28

The Indians soon learned that Wilbur could not hit, catch, or throw, but he more than made up for his lack of physical skills with enthusiasm and knowledge of the game. He understood squeeze plays, sacrifice flies, when to bunt, when to steal, when to take, and when to swing better than any of his teammates or even Coach Daniels. He used terms that Jake had heard before, but only during big league baseball games over the radio.

More important, Wilbur kept team spirits up, even when he seldom played until the game's outcome had been determined. As players returned to sit beside him on the bench, Wilbur consoled every strike-out victim as enthusiastically as he cheered every home run. He became the catalyst that allowed Jake to become a true leader on his team. Jake stopped complaining about younger players' mistakes and started encouraging and training them. While helping Wilbur learn to hit, catch, and throw, Jake learned about the complexities of baseball from Wilbur. Coach Simpson's description of baseball as a beautiful sport took on added meaning for him. He also tried to adopt Wilbur's approach toward books, no longer concealing his penchant for reading. Wilbur brought a book to every practice and game. Jake took it home to read, then exchanged it for another at a later practice. He began to almost look forward to school starting again.

On the night before the last game of the season, Jake finally got up the nerve to invite Wilbur to spend the night at his house. After practice, Wilbur asked his father's permission. "I guess it'll be all right. I know Mr. Rivers, after all. I'm going to the library in Commerce, so I'll drop you off." When the car stopped in front of the Rivers' driveway, Jake saw his house through Wilbur's eyes and wished he had not invited him. They stood on 24 at the driveway entrance as Wilbur's father drove away. Wilbur held his cleats and a small overnight case that probably belonged to his mother. He stared at the tall house without paint. Jake waited for Wilbur to say something that would spoil their friendship. Wilbur glanced at the house, then pointed toward the dairy barn.

"What's that?"

"That was our dairy barn."

"Y'all have cows?"

"Used to. Remember? We had to sell 'em when we ran out of water."

Wilbur's face showed extreme curiosity. "You got to milk cows?"

Wilbur's enthusiasm made Jake's shame turn into pride. "My brother and me had to milk a lot. I used to have to milk our Jersey by hand."

As they reached the house, Scar whinnied a greeting. Wilbur broke into a trot. "That your horse?"

Wilbur seemed equally impressed by the things that Jake was ashamed of and those that he took for granted. The two-holer outhouse, the washtub, and the kerosene and wood stoves were exciting curiosities for Wilbur. His enthusiasm and constant questions captivated Rance and Mattie. Gray Boy tried to ignore Wilbur, but was soon won over when Wilbur treated him like a hero and wished aloud for his own older brother. He seemed to make them all take pride in themselves as a family and in what they had.

At bedtime, Jake was embarrassed when his mother checked Wilbur's ears and neck after their baths. Wilbur showed no modesty, parading in front of Mattie in his underwear as he pulled his pajamas from his small bag. Jake sat on the footlocker in his underwear as Wilbur stood before him in a pair of pajamas festooned with baseballs, gloves, and bats. Jake suppressed a smile and wondered what his mother had done with Tuck's cowboy and Indian pajamas.

"Which side of the bed is yours?" Wilbur asked.

Jake hesitated as he looked for Tuck's small impression. The feather mattress was smooth. "You take that one." Jake pulled the string on the light as Wilbur crawled into bed.

Wilbur lay with his hands behind his back. "How many home runs have you hit, Jake?"

The question surprised him. "None."

"Me, neither. I've never even had a hit. What makes that light swing?"

Jake repeated the stories he and Tuck had shared about what was swinging the bulb that hung from the fourteen-foot ceiling by a six-foot cord. When Jake found it almost as easy to talk to Wilbur as it had been to talk to Tuck, he told Wilbur about his first experience with the flow. "I knew where the ball was going to be before it was hit. I threw longer and harder to first than anytime before or since." Jake's confession was followed by an uncomfortable period of silence. In the darkness, he wondered if Wilbur was laughing at the story. "You believe me?"

"Sure, I've heard that Mickey Mantle and Lou Gehrig both went to special places in their minds when they walked into the batters' box. When that happens, you know it's goin' out of the park."

"You kiddin' me?"

"Nope. I've been there myself once. Only I was reading a book."

Trish drove in the driveway as Jake was leading Wilbur around the cow lots on Scar the next day. Wilbur whistled when Trish stepped out of the red '55 Chevy. Jake's face flushed with pride. "She's got a 283 engine in her."

Wilbur looked down at Jake from Scar's back. "You mean the car? I was whistling at your sister."

Trish walked over and shook Wilbur's hand. "I'm Trish, Jake's sister. You must be Wilbur. Wilbur pushed his eyeglasses back and smiled. "Jake says you can play baseball better than most boys."

Trish grinned and grabbed the nape of Jake's neck. "Better than my brothers, anyway. If this one would just listen to me, I'd have him hitting about four hundred instead of three. He tells me you know more about baseball than just about anybody."

Wilbur took Trish's compliment as a man dying of thirst accepts a drink of water, but Jake protested. "I'm hittin' three-twenty-three."

They all turned toward the rumbling noise and saw Gray Boy turning in from 24. He roared down the driveway, put one leg down and brought the Indian cycle to a sliding stop in front of the red Chevy. He had not told his father, but Jake knew that Gray had bought the cycle from Red. Without as much as a nod, Gray opened the Chevy's hood. From the dark under the hood, he called to his sister. "School teachers around here can't afford wheels like this. You or Pete working two jobs?"

Trish took a step toward Gray. "Hello to you too, little brother. As a matter of fact, Pete is working two jobs to pay for that red machine. That's why he isn't with me."

Gray Boy shut the hood. "If this was mine, I wouldn't let any woman drive it this far away from me."

"Well, it ain't yours and you're not Pete." Trish jerked her thumb toward Wilbur and Jake. "Tonight's the last game for Jake. Last game he'll play in Little League. We need a pitcher to practice a little."

Gray Boy shook his head as if the offer did not warrant a reply. He started away from them just as Rance and Mattie drove up in the truck. Rance backed the truck up to the back porch. Gray knew the procedure. As the truck stopped, he uncoiled the hose from the water tank and dropped the end down the cistern. Rance stepped out and opened the valve. Delivering water to his own house usually made Rance irritable. Gray listened for the first splash in the cistern, then turned and headed toward the cow lot.

Using rocks and dried cow patties found in the parched, cracked, former cow lot, the four of them set up a home plate and three bases. With Trish pitching and Gray catching, Wilbur took his turn at bat. He missed the first two pitches and turned to Gray. "Show me what I'm doing wrong." Jake's face showed astonishment and a little jealousy as Gray put his hands on Wilbur's shoulders and adjusted his stance by gently pushing his legs apart with his foot. He took the bat and illustrated a level swing, then held Wilbur's hands and illustrated a complete follow through. Wilbur whooped with each crack of the bat as he hit four out of five pitches that Trish threw. Gray laughed and showed him how to crouch when he needed to draw a walk.

Jake stepped to the flat rock that served as home plate for his turn. Anxious to show his friend how it was done, Jake jumped on the first three pitches, hitting ground balls that sent Gray Boy and Wilbur to the edges of the lot to shag. He was ready for praise as Trish approached him and took the bat. "Are you big enough to take advice from your sister, yet?" Jake felt the familiar resentment and fear of criticism rise in his chest and travel to his head. He would not take advice from Gray Boy and was reluctant to listen to his sister, especially in front of his new friend. He ducked his head and felt the blood rush to his face. Ashamed of the way he felt, but unable to control his feelings of hurt and anger, he took a deep breath when he heard his father's voice.

Rance walked toward them. "She's right, Jake. Always has been. You're lunging at the ball. That cuts down on your power. Take another swing and we'll all watch."

Thoroughly humiliated, Jake took another swing, aiming for the fences, and missed. Rance nodded. "See? You're jumping too early. Where do you think a hitter's power comes from, Jake?"

Jake was ready to answer "arms and shoulders" when Wilbur interrupted. "His legs, hips and butt."

They all turned to stare at Wilbur. For the first time since they had met, Jake found Wilbur's voice irritating.

Trish broke the silence. "That's right, Jake. You're moving too quick. Wait until the last second, then step into it slightly and swivel those legs, hips, and butt into it. Let's try it again."

Nervous with everyone watching, Jake took a good cut and hit a line drive into Gray's bare hands. He was pleased when Gray dropped the ball to rub the sting from his hands.

Rance stepped closer to Jake. "Better, son, but your head and your butt are still moving a little too soon. Concentrate on keeping them still until the last possible minute." Rance turned to Trish. "Throw him some real heat, Trish."

Each boy hit ten more pitches before it was time to go in and change into their uniforms. Jake still moved his butt too quickly. As they started toward the house, Gray put his body between Jake and

211

Wilbur and pushed Jake back a few feet. Surprised, Jake dropped his glove and drew back his fist. Gray held his palm up in front of Jake's fist. "Take it easy. I just want to put my two cents in. Daddy won't agree with me, and don't say I said to, but I think it's time to stop choking up every time you hit." Jake had no time to reply before he was pushed in Wilbur's direction.

Dressed in their white uniforms with red trim, Jake and Wilbur stepped on the back porch. Rance and Mattie sat in wood chairs under the Chinaberry tree and voiced their approval and wishes for good luck as Trish herded them into the red Chevy for the ride to the ball park. Jake stared at his parents through the car window and waved as they pulled away. Arriving at the ballpark, Jake looked for school friends or teammates, hoping at least one or two would see him in the Chevy. None were in sight. As they left the car, dust settled on the freshly waxed red paint, dulling the shine.

Cars arriving on the windless night bathed the sky above the baseball diamond with a cloud of dust. Grass had long since withered and died in the outfield, making the outfield fences seem farther away and the entire field bigger. Base path lines wiggled occasionally where the lime spreader had stumbled across a crack in the hard-pan earth, causing the lime to spread unevenly. These grim reminders of the drought dulled the suspense and excitement that had been present in the days of the first momentous season of Little League baseball in Delta County.

The Indians had to win this final game to come in third. They had not beaten the Giants all year, and things were not expected to change tonight. The stands were half-full, fans talking more to each other than watching the game. Most were parents, there only to see their children play. From shortstop, Jake imagined the ghosts of Linc Little and Charlie Wagner above him, frowning on another lackluster season.

The familiar rumble of the Indian idling up to the left field fence brought him back to the present. He looked over his shoulder to acknowledge his brother. Gray always parked the Indian by the left field fence and leaned against the seat to watch Jake play. Almost always, he was joined by one or more young girls, vying for an invitation to sit on the back half of the Indian's seat. Jake knew that Gray came to pick up girls, but he could have done that lots of other places. He searched the stands and sidelines, but could not find his sister. As his eyes passed the bench in the dugout, Wilbur waved.

The game was scoreless through six and a half, with no great plays, hits, or pitching to interrupt the monotony. In the top of the seventh, the Giants scored two on a walk, an error, and a passed ball. Jake stood helplessly at shortstop, hands on his knees, ready for the ball that never came. He had flied out to centerfield and walked once. Answering the beckoning crook of Coach Daniels' index finger, Wilbur jumped from the bench to play right field at the top of the eighth. The Giants went three up and three down with no hits. Neither Jake nor Wilbur fielded a ball. At the bottom of the eighth, the Indian second baseman who could never stop a ground ball, hit one over the right field fence. Giants 2, Indians 1. The Indians held the Giants scoreless in the top of the ninth.

Wilbur was in the on-deck circle as the second batter struck out in the bottom of the ninth. He turned to look at Jake. Both shook their heads. With two out and Wilbur Penny at bat, it appeared to be all over. Crowd noise increased as fans started to rise from their seats, gather the cushions they were sitting on, and say goodbye to their friends. In the commotion of leaving, nobody noticed the slight rumbling noise. Lundy Clark, Jr. announced, "Batting ninth in the batting order and now playing right field, Wilbur Penny is at the plate." The loudspeaker made a crackling sound on its own as a streak of lightning shot through the sky over the withered stalks of corn. Lundy Clark spoke again. "Folks, with two out, this could well be our final batter for the 1956 season." Wilbur stepped back from the batters' box and stared at the announcer.

Still batting lead-off, Jake was in the on-deck circle and tried to coach Wilbur again on choking up and watching the ball from the time it leaves the pitcher's hand, but Wilbur's enthusiastic grin made Jake laugh.

"Just get down in your crouch position like Gray and Trish showed us. You won't have hardly any strike zone. Maybe he'll walk you." Jake had to pause and laugh again as Wilbur's face showed only enthusiasm, not fear. "Just get up there and get on,

213

Penny. I'm up next, and I want another chance to bat. Maybe I'll bring you in, and we'll win this game."

Wilbur crouched to shorten the strike zone, and the first pitch from Robert Don Hooten was a ball. Wilbur looked back at Jake and grinned. Robert Don threw the next one in the dirt, trying to get low enough to hit the strike zone. Wilbur looked toward the third base line at his coach. Joe Daniels gave the take signal, but suddenly changed his mind and touched his finger to his tongue, the signal for hit away. Jake was surprised when he saw the signal, but figured Joe Daniels wanted Wilbur to get a piece of at least one pitch before the season ended.

Robert Don showed his frustration on the mound. He gave up extra base hits to the better batters, but he almost never walked anyone. His pitches were predictable - low, fast, and over the plate. Robert Don visibly slowed his third pitch and delivered a perfect strike. To both their surprise, Wilbur hit a high blooper toward second base.

The center fielder moved lazily forward, thinking the second baseman would catch it. The second baseman backpedaled, but not fast enough. Jake watched in amazement as the pop fly seemed to float down. "It's gonna drop in for a Texas Leaguer; Wilbur, run it out!" Wilbur needed no instruction. He was already two steps from first base when the ball dropped between the two fielders. Wilbur clapped and jumped up and down so hard on the bag that his batting helmet fell back on his neck. He now represented the tying run, and Jake, the winning run.

Jake wanted to hear the announcement of that statistic from Lundy Clark. When it did not come, he looked toward the announcer's table. Lundy had unplugged the microphone and was gathering up the score sheets to protect them from the wind. Jake had barely noticed the wind pick up speed or the roll of thunder as Wilbur was making his surprise hit. He had practiced ignoring the tease of dry thunderstorms for over two years. Lightning just meant danger from fire, not rain. If you did not expect rain, you would not be disappointed.

Thunder rumbled , and lightning was again visible behind the corn field. Familiar dust devils were already kicking up in the infield from the swirling wind as the clouds rolled. Fans started to look skyward as they headed for their cars, discussing the weather and paying little attention to the game. Jake felt the exhilaration from the cooler air as he took his practice swings. He felt support from his friend on first base. Spectators' eyes were on the skies, not on him.

Jake felt the hair on the back of his neck stand up. There must be electricity in the air. He reached down to pick up a handful of dry dust. Rubbing the dirt between his hands to dry them, he dropped the end of the bat to the ground. The dust floated away from the bat as he slowly moved his hands down to the bat's knob. Feeling the full weight and leverage of the bat, he bounced the tip on the plate as he stepped up. He knew.

Robert Don delivered the first pitch the way he usually did, low and fast. Jake concentrated on keeping his head and butt still as he watched the ball catch the inside corner for a called strike. He stepped out of the box. "Put it outta' here, Jake. Time to swing for the fences." Jake looked in the direction of the voice. His father was standing in the aisle in front of the stands, leaning over the cyclone fence. He smiled at Jake and clapped his hands. Jake studied the smile. Was it crooked? No, it was the old smile. Rance raised his right arm, and Jake saw Mattie move under it, holding Rance's hand across her shoulder. She smiled and waved at Jake with her free hand. Trish moved from behind the bleachers to stand on the other side of Rance. In tomboy fashion, she stood in a crouch position with both hands on her knees, her eyes shifting from Jake to the pitcher.

As Jake stepped back into the box, drops of rain made splotches the size of quarters on home plate. Jake gave it little thought. It never rained, just teased. Robert Don threw another low pitch on the inside corner. Strike two. Jake stepped out of the box again. Thunder rumbled and the wind picked up behind Jake as Robert Don picked up the resin bag, moved it around in his throwing hand, and tossed it behind him. Ahead of Jake in the count, Robert Don took his familiar stretch wind-up and delivered his best pitch, fast and down-the-middle. Jake waited on the pitch, holding his head and butt still, knees slightly bent, until the last split second.

It was easy, the pitch seemed to be coming in slow motion, the ball was bigger and brighter than he had ever seen it. At the last split second, he picked up his front foot and stepped into the pitch, feeling the leverage of the full bat length as his body twisted to put his butt, hips, and legs into the swing.

With a resounding crack, the ball left the bat on a plane a little higher than the one that Robert Don had thrown. With the wind's help, the line drive sailed just over the shortstop's glove, gaining height, headed toward Gray and the Indian. Thunder rolled again as Jake ran at top speed toward first. He kept his eyes on the first base coach, a high school boy filling in for tonight's game, to see if he should take second. The boy was looking toward the ball, not at Jake, and was giving no signal. Jake tried to find the ball as he turned the corner and touched the edge of the wet first base bag. As he headed toward second, he knew he could easily overtake Wilbur, who was running at his top speed around second.

The first base coach finally yelled into the wind. "She's outta' here, kid. You can stroll if you want to." Jake slowed and found the ball in the rain. It was still on the rise as it went above Gray's head and several feet beyond. He slowed to a trot, then a slow jog, trying to stretch his moment of exultation.

As Jake touched second, rain was coming down too fast for the thirsty, hard earth to absorb it. Jake tried to appear humble as he looked down at the ground. He watched tiny rivulets form and dribble into the cracks in the baseball diamond. Wilbur was already touching home, tying the game and scoring his first-ever run. It had always irritated Jake when home-run hitters took so long going around the bases, but he understood now. Halfway to third base, he felt the rain pouring down his neck, soaking his uniform, making it heavy, but he chose to continue his slow pace. He walked across home plate, scoring the winning run and ending the game.

Home runs always brought the entire team to home plate for handshakes and back pats. Jake's teammates were not waiting. They had been collected by coaches and parents and rushed to shelter. Only Wilbur waited for him. Rain slid down the small boy's glasses as he waited patiently, his broad smile showing off the teeth he had not grown to.

aaa aaaaa.

As Jake touched home plate and the umpire declared the game over, Wilbur took Jake's hand, shook it firmly, and then slapped Jake on the back and put his arm around his shoulders. Jake looked toward the bleachers, but no fans remained. Few had even seen his first home run. He looked down the alley where Rance, Mattie, and Trish had stood in the rain. Rance still stood in the same spot, rain pouring off the brim of his hat. He firmly touched the brim with his thumb and finger and nodded toward his son. The familiar honk from the truck sounded Trish and Mattie's congratulations. Jake waved and smiled.

He turned to look toward left field. Gray Boy was soaked, but he stood in the bed of someone's pickup, one arm raised as he looked toward Jake. A round white object was in his raised hand. Jake knew that the baseball from his first home run would be on his pillow tonight.

Jake picked up his home run bat and pointed it at his brother, feeling something happening in those few seconds as he stared at Gray Boy, his hero and his nemesis. His brother represented everything he wanted to be and everything he did not, but for the moment, Jake accepted this wave of good feeling, of being loved. This was truly the Rivers' Flow. Memories sped through his brain. Looking toward the shriveled corn stalks bending from the wind, he saw Tuck clapping on his father's shoulders, felt the rush of adrenalin when he caught his first calf from a horse. He wasn't sure what the thoughts and visions meant, and he could never find the words to describe his feelings at this moment, even to himself. He knew it was a silent but definite message that would never be put into words, another passage that changed his relationship with his brother and his parents forever.

Jake knew that if Gray Boy had been standing beside him, they would not have exchanged words or hugs. Across the length of the baseball field, however, they silently communicated. Jake watched as Gray jumped down from the pickup, pushed back the kick-stand on the Indian, straddled the cycle, and hit the kick-start. The Indian rumbled to life and eased off in the rain. Jake watched until the Indian's engine roared, and mud and water slung from the tires, taking Gray Boy into the wet darkness.

www.ingramcontent.com/pod-product-compliance
Lightning Source LLC
Chambersburg PA
CBHW012205030726
47494CB00022B/2308